ANDY SOUTTER was born and ra... currently lives. He ...mance artist and musicia.., ..as contributed essays and stories to a diverse range of periodicals and anthologies, and is the author of two books of cultural commentary: The *Drive-Thru Museum* (1993) and *Australiaville* (1996).

DN Angels

Andy Soutter

THE DO-NOT
PRESS

First Published in Great Britain in 1999 by
The Do-Not Press
PO Box 4215
London SE23 2QD

A paperback original.

ISBN 1 899344 46 2

British Library Cataloguing in Publication Data. A catalogue
record for this book is available from the British Library.

b d f h g e c a

Printed and bound in Great Britain by Caledonian International.

FOR HELEN

'We are not of today, or of yesterday.
We are of an immense age.'
Carl Jung, 1961

'The fundamental things apply.'
Dooley Wilson, 1942

ONE

1. TAKE ME TO
THE RIVER

THE PIANO lay in ruins before him, its wreckage mingled with glistening shards of shattered mirror.

So much for the first bar of his musical debut.

He fumbled amongst the debris, retrieved the score and read on. Next came a line of text:

Listen to my works, ye mighty, and despair.

And at this moment he felt the floor begin to creak and shift beneath him.

Hurriedly he gathered up the voluminous, whisky-stained folio, and he had just enough time to escape the room before the joists gave way with a shriek and collapsed as the windows caved in and vomited glass. He raced down the stairway as it flexed and complained, and along the hallway through a hailstorm of falling plaster, holding the thick manuscript over his head for protection.

He got out just in time. Breathless, he stood on the gravel drive and watched as the house imploded: the walls falling inwards, the roof collapsing with a roar, and a dustcloud bursting outwards to briefly shroud the scene before settling to reveal the flattened remains of slate, tile, brick and timber.

The house was now nothing but a couple of acres of rubble surrounded by a stand of tall yews. The scene resembled a graveside gathering, the trees sombre and mournful.

Mikoyan's words came back to him like an oration: *It is just building. These things are temporary affairs. Why play Sisyphus?*

Unburdened now, he turned away and set off down the hill. He wondered what Ms van Helsing would make of the score. He blushed at the thought of her. Ha – still crazy after all these extraordinary years. Well, he thought, I don't know how I got into this body of mine, but there's obviously only one way out. And it beats dying.

Below, the river lay like a fat green snake.

❤

How had he got into all of this? A long, empty road one summer evening. And a black car approaching. And him with his thumb out. Had it all been that corny? The smoked glass Porsche, interior stinking of whisky, a goat skull on the back seat, a copy of *L'Inferno* on the front shelf... and Wilson, flaming beard, dressed all in black, with the gold medallion on his chest which read *Try It*.

Flying Dutchmen... or women...

Wandering shoemakers...

Joseph of Arimathea...

They spat at Jesus, or something, and were condemned to wander the earth for ever.

Condemned?

...the car taking off with the brute force of a 747, the stereo blasting out a choral anthem, and the Scot Wilson shouting across to him 'These old Krauts had the right idea – howta *totally fragment* the known universe in one easy lesson... I mean you've got atomic wipeouts, you've got nova bursts, you've got black holes... and *then* you've got Karajan and the Berlin fuckin' Phil, right? I mean, *really!*'

Him making some comment about Wilson's shirt – it did have a touch of the Lionel Blair. And Wilson saying 'Hey, button yours up, will you? That crucifix is bothering me.'

Why? – 'It's an instrument of torture, that's why. And you'll only end up strangling yourself with it.'

Picking up two Danish hitchhikers who crammed their creamy limbs into the back... and the Porsche finally dropping

12

him off before speeding north towards the moor; him walking down deep lanes to a village flooded with cars. Three girls sitting under the granite cross of a war memorial while their father changed a wheel on the caravan.

He tried the pub, but there was no work at the inn... so then a walk down a farm track, steeper and steeper, a mile, two miles, and into forest: a dusky mist, the smell of pine and wild garlic, rotten logs reeking with honey fungus; and the sudden river: wide, rising tide, vertiginous wooded banks, and crows flocking from the treetops in a tumble of black confetti and raucous echoes.

Then a tumbledown gate and a dilapidated redbrick boathouse. Overgrown garden and saplings obscuring the windows. Inside, dust on old furnishings; seventies paperbacks, faded and mildewed; mousedroppings; a grimy telephone, black bakelite and rusting chrome, long dead; a maritime chart; a screwed-up pair of purple satin knickers; a tattered and faded Persian carpet; a fireplace where spiders crawled across grey ashes and the remains of a log; on the mantelpiece a yellowed shopping list, the scribbled biro now faint – *oats, peanut butter, longlife milk...* and then the horny feeling he always got when alone in places like this, like a disused railway station, or an old cricket pavilion in winter: stale air and ghostly fingers between his legs.

He found a tin with no label which turned out to contain spaghetti rings. And he found the remains of a fat, multicoloured candle, put it on the kitchen table, and ate by its light. He was suddenly exhausted. Outside the window a stone stairway led down to the river; the water was already lapping at the top step. As darkness fell the distant chorus of crows dwindled to silence, and he nodded off to sleep. In his dreams he saw the Scots musician, who had now grown a pair of horns and was conducting the three girls from the war memorial, whose eyes had grown deathly pale and who sang an infinitely sad and beautiful song.

When he woke up it was still dark. His neck ached. Upstairs in a small room he discovered a horsehair mattress on the floor and a swathe of old red velvet curtain that would do as a blanket.

He lay down under it with the crumpled knickers under his cheek. Faint moonlight illuminated the bare room. The drone of a small outboard came and went. The heat from his face warmed and softened the satin, which, as he drifted to sleep, began to release traces of scent: musk, rose, and a faint anal odour, sweet and nutty.

It was the slow thump of a dredger's engine that woke him to the thin light of dawn. And then the startling fact of a woman with a mass of crimson hair kneeling before him in a long cotton nightshift.

'Don't go,' she was saying, entreating him, 'Don't go.'

And then the first flash of sunlight blinding him for a second. And then the woman – nowhere to be seen. He got up, listened, looked around, peered outside, but there was no trace of her.

The local ghost no doubt. But what a ghost. What a turn-on.

Don't go? Don't go where? Stay here? What for?

He stayed. That night he met the woman again, some while before first light. She embraced him, she called him her angel and she persuaded him to score her back with his nails and draw blood. She said her name was Kate and she had a story about coming from the moor at Fastbuckleigh. It was hard to follow. Her accent was weird and thick as cream cake. She talked about people called Love and Fish. Some kind of commune she was involved with. She was no ghost, she was some mad hippy girl with her head full of magic mushrooms: ''Tis so beautiful here... fain would I tarry...' wandering around the briar roses in the garden at daybreak. Then wandering off. What a tease. Left him jerking off alone. Story of his life. Still, he waited around all day on the offchance she'd return. And during this time he learned from the PA of a passing tourist boat – a bunting-covered craft called the *Heart's Content* – that he had holed up in a four-hundred-year-old summerhouse with Victorian additions which had been let go to ruin over the past fifteen years since the landowner's wife had died there...

This girl was probably too young to be a wife. Anyway, ghost or not, he had the hots for her. In fact the idea of making out with a ghost was more exciting.

14

Evening came. He watched crows defend their nests against a marauding buzzard – periodic dogfights in the sky as it made its predatory way downstream. The tide came in, and with it the smell of the sea and a stream of small boats heading upriver before dark. In the kitchen a bottled-gas stove was operative so he cooked up some beans and ate them sitting at the window watching the stars come out. He fell asleep there, clutching the crumpled knickers and willing the crazy girl to return.

He was woken by a clattering and splashing outside. He saw a torchbeam flash and a figure emerge from the river and stride towards the door. Then a knock, and the door opened. It was a woman wearing a yellow plastic anorak and jeans. Her hair was bedraggled and she was barefoot. She spoke in an offhand manner.

'Awfully sorry to bother you, but it's so boring. I've gone aground over there on the point. I saw your light and I thought someone might help me get off the sand before the tide drops any further. May I…?'

She took a seat, threw back her hood and ran her hands through her matted hair. 'Gosh, I'm exhausted,' she said, 'I missed the tide, you see. I knew it was a risk, but there you are.'

'Why not wait for it to come up again?'

'Oh…' she seemed to grope for an explanation – 'I don't want that creep of a Harbourmaster to come poking around. Anyway, it's a yacht. It's quite big actually. But we could try and tug her off.'

She looked at him more closely. 'Do you sail?' she said. 'I'm looking for someone to crew for me. I'm going to the Mediterranean. Do you speak French?'

He told her he knew some Italian. 'Oh yes,' she drawled, 'I suppose that's *the* language, really.'

'What?' he said.

Now she was staring at what he still held in one hand.

'So *that's* what happened to my knickers,' she said.

'Yours?'

'There used to be so many parties here,' she said. 'All the time. Austen let the place out to all sorts of really interesting people. Fire eaters, Indian musicians, poets… wonderfully

15

mad. I've had some super times here. It was paradise in those days – fairy lights in the garden, music, starlight, barbecues, all sorts of amazing people to meet… a relatively harmless collection of venereal diseases… and then Steffi died, and the buzz went out of Austen, and a whole scene went, really.' She paused and her eyes wandered, a little glazed, round the room. 'And there were *so many intoxicants,*' she said breathlessly, 'Honestly, I don't know how we managed them all.'

'Back in the good old seventies.'

'There was so much happening then,' she said, regaining her nonchalance, 'People don't realise. Anyway, who are you? Are you a student? What are you doing here?'

He often asked himself the same question. 'I'm dossing,' he said. 'Looking for work.'

'Yes, I've a good feeling about this,' she said, 'good things have always happened to me here. Do you want to work for me?'

She named an attractive and irresistible sum of money.

'Good,' she said. 'Well then, let's steel ourselves for the task ahead,' and she produced a silver phial which contained a white powder. 'Care for some sherbet?' she said.

Refreshed by this they rowed vigorously out to the point, where they found the sloop high on a sandbank. They boarded it, resigned to waiting on the tide.

His name was Theo Riddle, he told her. And he told her about failing to get a grant to study art, and working three pain-in-the-arse months as a trainee hairdresser as well as all sorts of shit before that, before quitting in disgust and hitting the road. She told him her name was Phyllida Green and she was taking some items to a sale in the south of France. 'When I was younger I was going to be a painter,' she said. 'But then I realised there was a lot more money in art – ha-ha.'

❤

The yacht refloated itself on the morning tide and they motored it downriver. A couple of miles further and the engine died. Out of fuel. 'Shit,' said the woman, 'I didn't… oh, shit.'

And then came the whine of the harbourmaster's dory, a black wedge in the distance.

'Listen,' she said, 'as far as he's concerned I'm borrowing this boat from Tony, my ex, right? We're just going to be footling around the coast for a while.'

Curioser and more curious.

'Just be ready for this guy,' she said. 'Big Job, everyone calls him. He's a little strange and obsessive. They say he worships a grandfather clock. The story is that just after he was conceived his parents set off from Norway to emigrate to America, but the ship went down in the Channel. They survived by hanging on to the clock and drifting ashore with it near Kingsmouth. They say he prays to that clock. And he only drinks water – salt water that is; eats nothing but fish and dry bread; lives in a tiny cottage with the barest of necessities.'

'He's crazy, in other words.'

'But he knows every single craft on this river, and he's the law. And he's a stickler. In other words he's a pain in the arse, so be careful.'

The dory pulled alongside. 'Hello there, Mr Andersen,' she said sweetly. The Norwegian, big and black-bearded, boarded the *Ubique*, saluted stiffly and asked politely for Tony. She explained.

'Ah,' said Job Andersen. Phyllida gave him a wonderful smile, which fixed itself rigid when she saw him pull out his vodaphone. 'I shall call him and check up. You understand it is my duty.'

'I'm afraid he's in America at the moment.'

'Nevertheless I will check.' He dialled and waited. There was no answer. He peered through the cabin hatchway. Then he stood staring at them for a moment. Then he said 'I wish you a joyous holiday. But it is sinful to stop at this point. Please be moving very soon.' And he saluted and left.

Phyllida Green reached for her cigarettes. 'My God,' she said, 'I nearly died while that phone was ringing.'

Theo began to wonder how compromising this boat would turn out to be.

'Let's just say Tony doesn't know I'm using it,' she said. 'I've got a crate of paintings I can make a killing with in Antibes, and this is the ideal way to go.'

17

While he rowed across to the nearby creek with an empty petrol can he formed the opinion that the Green woman was corrupt and that he trusted her by the slimmest of margins. But he liked her nerve. Or was it that he fancied her? Not really. So she stole someone's boat. There were worse things to steal off people. Food, dignity, and all that stuff. And hearts. But no-one died from a stolen boat. What was that she'd said? 'I'll teach you navigation. Anybody can navigate. It's mostly instinct anyway.' Oh really?

He steered his way up the inlet, past yachts at their moorings, past where three bent masts poked out from a sunken wreck. Rusted hulks and unpainted hulls were laid up along the waterfront. He came to the ramp of a small boatyard, beached the dinghy and walked in. Strains of Mozart – the one that Safeway always played – issued from the darkness within, from somewhere inside a tall plywood hull propped up on stilts where someone was playing a clarinet. He called out, and the music stopped. A curly-headed man stuck his head out from a hatch, narrowed his red-rimmed eyes and scrutinised him for a second. Then he smiled. 'What can I do for you?' he said in a voice that was bluer than a Tory party banner. Diesel? Yes, he had a can somewhere. He clambered down – he was wearing nothing but an undersize maroon silk dressing gown and a pair of flipflops – and shuffled across the shed to retrieve a jerrycan. How old was he? 35? 45? Extremely sinewy. Knobbly knees.

'What's your boat?'

The *Ubique*.

'Really?'

Here's the diesel. Here's the money. And now here's a wreck of a van drawing up in the yard, a woman in overalls getting out, and an excited black Staffordshire racing into the shed, skid-stopping at his feet, yapping its throat out, a large quivering turd.

'BUSTER! BUSTER! SHADDUP BUSTER!' the woman screeched as she ran in after it, grabbed its collar and looked up at him: 'You must be a foreigner. He never barks at English people.'

18

An American voice. 'But I'm English, aren't I?'

'Uh – uh,' she said, shaking her head. 'Can't be. Leastways not pure.'

And then Trueblue pipes up: 'Buster can smell foreign blood at least fourteen generations back. We tested him on the Honourable Rodney – lives around here, runs the Attention-Seeking Party up in Fastbuckleigh, you've probably seen him on TV at elections – and Buster sniffed out a three-hundred-year-old connection to Chinese royalty.'

'Had Horseface in hospital for a week,' says the woman.

'So you'd better come clean,' says the man.

'All right – my mother's from Italy.'

Cue ugly growl from ugly dog.

'There you are,' says the man, self-satisfied. 'Impure, mulatto, half-caste, crossbreed. You're a variegate, you see. Buster knows a mongrel when he sees one. No offence.'

'That's alright,' he says, 'it keeps me from all those inbred diseases. And what about you?' he asks the woman. 'You being American.'

'English stock,' she says.

The man lights a cigarette. Taped to the breezeblock wall behind him is a billboard-sized Martini poster – a blonde and a glass. The woman here has straight light-brown hair in an over-grown pageboy and oldfashioned hornrimmed glasses – fifties French intellectual look, like she was writing a novel every day at the *Deux Magots*.

'Paul!' she shouts. 'Put your damn cigarette out. You want to blow us all up?' And then the diatribe, delivered so cooly it sounded like she did it every day: 'You're obnoxious. You're a toilet area. And about as dynamic as a glacier. This boat should have been ready six months ago and we should be long gone by now. And you're not even much fun in bed anymore. And you stink, Paul White, you never damn well wash and you run around with your crosseyed calculations and you choose to forget what's really going on even if it does occasionally crawl across the threshold of your consciousness. I bet you've been smoking dope all morning like the slob you are and I bet you're going to try and use that useless cheap stuff for the bulkheads

19

and I bet you didn't call Stoyles like you were supposed to and I bet you're now going to start with some series of explanations which will be as incredible as they are implausible starting with "It's not that simple, Ruth," and rapidly jetting us to the land of bullshit and fairies.'

And he counters with his best schoolmaster: 'Ruth, listen. It's not as simple as that.'

'How far back does the imbecility go in your family?'

'And insanity in yours?'

'Cheap,' she says. 'That's *so* cheap.'

'Comes free of charge.'

'God you're desperate.'

This was getting interesting and he might have learned more if the pair of them, paying him no attention at all, had not taken their dispute up a ladder and into the boat, with their genetically sensitive dog in loud pursuit.

'Just because your name rhymes with *truth* you needn't—'

'And yours with *right*, and *shite*, and *blight*…'

As he left he heard the clarinet begin, Ruth shout, and the instrument suddenly stop again.

♥

Departing from the *Ubique*, Andersen hadn't gone very far before he caught sight of something very peculiar. It was the distant dark silhouette of the *Wilja*, and on the deck of the barge a bizarrely shaped object, backlit by the early sun and slowly changing shape, like some kind of animated cactus. But as Andersen drew nearer he finally saw that the apparition was actually a person. A woman, in fact. Doing some kind of inexplicable movement. It looked a little ritualistic. Or was she just watering those blood-red geraniums which lined the deck?

He drew alongside the black hull. The woman seemed to pay him no attention. She was dressed in thin cotton pants and a T-shirt, and she was turning gradually on the spot, shifting slowly from one dreamlike pose to another. Here eyes were focused on the distance, like a sleepwalker. Through the flimsy backlit cotton Andersen could clearly see her limbs. This annoyed him even more. He cut his engine.

She smiled down at him.

'What are you doing?' he called up.

'I am a needle at the bottom of the ocean,' she said.

'I beg your pardon?'

'It is called T'ai Chi,' she explained.

'What?'

'It's a kind of dance. It's good for you.'

Andersen's face remained expressionless. He just said: 'You will stop your dancing, please.'

She looked confused. She wiped a strand of hair from her face. She took a couple of steps nearer to him and then squatted on her heels. 'I'm sorry? What did you say?'

'You cannot dance on this river.'

Andersen stood upright in his craft, his hairy features only a few feet away from the young woman's blue eyes and bobbed hair. These blue eyes then began to sparkle, and she laughed. She thought the harbourmaster was having a little joke. But her laugh enraged Andersen. He took hold of a rope. 'Take this, please, I am boarding you.'

At Andersen's request, the woman collected the boat's papers and her own passport.

'But I am legally parked here, no? My friend it is her mooring.'

Andersen said nothing. He sifted through the papers. She had come across on the barge from Amsterdam a couple of weeks ago. She was Bibi van Helsing from Delft. To Andersen, Delft meant blue china. He didn't like china. It didn't survive at sea. And to Andersen the youth of Holland seemed to be living in a state of legalised disorder. He liked this even less. He overlooked the fact that he was standing in a lounge cabin which had been designed and furnished along obsessively orderly lines, and was modest, spare, and spotlessly clean. He held on to Bibi van Helsing's papers and announced that he was going to search her boat thoroughly for 'prohibited cargo.' He didn't say exactly what. He suspected everything.

So he had everything out, everything up. He went through every locker and every container of every size. He had her remove the contents of each drawer, wardrobe, biscuit tin and

21

spice jar. It was a while before he'd had enough. As one last act, he checked the back of a picture. Then he looked more closely at the print. It showed a naked woman dancing upon stormy waves. The picture made Job feel strange and awkward. He didn't understand why.

'What is this?' he inquired.

'It is the goddess dancing among chaos. A Greek story.'

Andersen shook his head solemnly. 'Chaos, chaos. Chaos is not good.'

'But it is the story of Creation.'

'Dancing women and chaos are not good,' said Andersen definitively. Then he returned Bibi van Helsing's papers and picked his way through the debris he had caused. She followed him out and watched him reboard his dory.

'I shall be keeping an eye at you,' he said before swinging round and churning off.

Bibi van Helsing stood watching him go, a curious smile on her face. She didn't feel bad about what had just happened. She felt just as good now as she had done when the Harbourmaster first appeared. In fact she felt good and healthy all the time. Which is why she tended to look upon other people – normal people – as invalids. The very fact of normality – i.e. that you feel good sometimes and not so good at other times – was completely foreign to her. Bibi van Helsing never felt bad. About anything. Sometimes she could be unreasonable about this. You might be treated like a psychological cripple because you were worried about the weather, or what to cook tonight. Mention of a slight headache could unwittingly cause a serious diversionary conversation that more often than not caused a worse headache. She could be a little over the top. But with Andersen, she probably had a case. And so the healthiest woman in the world went happily below again to clear up the devastation of Job and wonder about the Harbourmaster's collection of personal demons. She thought it might have something to do with a high-sodium diet.

In the tight little town that lay upriver, in his bedsit above a pub,

Windeatt was also up early that morning. Once he had dressed he ate a small packet of peanuts washed down with a cup of weak tea from a used bag. Then he took his army surplus back-pack and filled it with a number of items which he retrieved from under the mattress. There was a watch, some framed prints and a silver-plated salt-cellar among other things. Then he slung the bag on his back, donned a crash helmet, and went out to the street where his moped was parked against a wall.

Windeatt was officially out of work, but he had a trade of sorts. He had discovered it a year earlier while tramping round the countryside looking for farming or gardening jobs. Standing in a farmhouse hallway while the wife went off to fetch her husband, he had spotted a gold ring lying on the hall table and promptly pocketed it. Once the woman returned to say there was no work for him he took his leave in his usual servile manner, and sold the ring the same day to a grockle for a few quid. Pleased with this, he began to repeat the procedure, pilfering from wherever he was left alone for more than a second.

But he was often the obvious suspect, so he was always being chatted up by the law. It was more through luck than skill that he had never yet been caught in possession. This constant attention never bothered him, however. He told his lies and he survived precariously. It was what he was used to. He had been in the Navy, and then in prison for deserting it. This beat both.

He started up his moped at the twentieth kick, then puttered away down the hill and out of town. The oversize crash helmet gave him the appearance of a great top-heavy insect with stunted limbs buzzing along the lanes.

When he arrived at Gimpton Creek he found Mr White and Ruth sitting on oilcans with mugs of tea. The dog Buster sniffed at Windeatt's old trainers and nuzzled against his calves. White looked up at him and gave a curt: 'Hello.'

'Morning,' said Windeatt cheerfully, and then altered his features so that he might look as stern as they did. This seemed the right way to behave. There was a moment's silence. Then he said, 'Something wrong?'

'No,' said White, almost smiling, 'Nothing. What do you want, Windy?'

'Oh, just something you might want to take a look at,' he said, indicating his backpack.

'You creep,' said Ruth. 'Why don't you just creep off? I don't want you peddling your soiled little objects around here.'

Windeatt winced. White stood up. 'Come inside then,' he said.

Windeatt looked back at Ruth. 'I'm sorry Mrs White but you never said nothing or nothing.'

'Get lost, creep.'

'I'm sorry, Mrs White.'

'And *don't* call me that.'

White led him into the cabin of the half-built yacht. He was using it as a combined business- and drawing office. There were a couple of desks, and papers and drawings strewn everywhere, spilling out of drawers and shelves, stacked in rolls, pinned up on boards. There were charts, books (Chay Blythe, Francis Chichester), coffeecups, ashtrays, biscuit packets, electric kettle, brass binnacle compass and a hundred other kinds of clutter. Windeatt's immediate reflex was to clock the small, valuable objects – such as a clarinet in its case, a walkman, and a bulging wallet which lay on the desk.

'This is the last time you come here like that, right?' said White through his teeth. 'I've already told you to call me first. It's too dangerous. And Ruth goes crazy.'

'I'm sorry Mr White but there's no time you see,' Windeatt pleaded, 'I need a quick sale else they'll take back my moped. Behind on payments, see.'

'What have you got?' White said briskly.

Windeatt produced a series of four coloured prints. Cartoons showing the different stages of an eighteenth-century card game. The players were dogs all dressed in human finery, all velvet and lace. White examined them closely. Beautifully done. Worth quite a bit. Very, very English. Americans couldn't get enough of this kind of thing.

He looked up at Windeatt. 'They're not bad. Nick them from a pub, did you?'

'No Mr White, I got them off a gippo.'

White gave a short, cynical snort.

'All right, what do you want for them?'

Windeatt locked his eyes onto White's, and as he spoke his hands fumbled discreetly on the desktop behind his back: 'I *know* they got to be worth five hundred…'

White gave another contemptuous snort and kept his eyes on Windeatt's. He wasn't going to be outstared by this little runt.

'But seeing as it's you,' Windeatt continued, 'and a quick sale's in order, I'll take two-fifty, and that's a bargain.' His hands located the walkman and closed around it. 'Well?'

As White laughed into his face for the third time, Windeatt gently slipped the walkman into his pocket.

'I'll give you twenty-five,' said White.

'Tell you what, I'll take fifty. And I'll throw in some information you might want to know.'

'Tell me,' said White, frowning.

'The *Ubique*'s out on the river, isn't it.'

'I know that already,' said White. 'Here's thirty.' He picked up his wallet and handed three tens to Windeatt.

'Thanks Mr White.'

'Come on.' White ushered him from the boat. Ruth was waiting at the bottom of the ladder. When Windeatt had descended she said, 'OK Windy, give back the walkman.'

'What are you talking about?' said Windeatt, astonished, innocent.

'I can see it right there.' She reached out and pulled it from his pocket.

'But that's mine,' he whined.

'Crawl away, Windy,' she said. White led him outside. 'Remember, call me next time,' he said. 'Get that straight.'

Windeatt put on his insect helmet and started up his bike. Then he suddenly fished about in his trouser pocket. He pulled out a brooch, a fly-in-amber set in old silver. He handed it to White. 'This is for Mrs White's collection,' he said, and then rode off. Windeatt liked Ruth, because she paid him plenty of attention.

Shortly after this, White unharnessed his dinghy. 'I'm going over to pay harbour dues,' he told Ruth.

'That'll be the day,' she said.

He guided the dinghy down the creek. He looked an odd animal. He wore flipflops, grimy white bellbottom jeans, and a tweed sportsjacket two sizes too small which emphasised his wiry wrists and sinuous neck. The shirt he wore was a blue-striped business number which he'd picked up from a local jumble sale still in its Jermyn Street cellophane. He had worn this outfit every day of the week for nearly a year. The only change from routine was the occasional display of an old school tie (*old* being the operative word – it was in tatters) which he wore whenever he watched occasions of state or test matches on TV. His image was part of a conscious philosophy. White aspired to the title *Essence of Gentleman (English)*: you stayed twenty years behind style and you wore the gear till it fell off you or the fashion came round again. You were eccentric but cultured. You knew the world's wines (and cocktails) and could play the Mozart clarinet quintet straight off. You knew a little Latin but you also knew that intellectuals were wankers and that the essence of a gent was ahead of them all. And your cred was supposed to work as well on the street as up at the Grange, because you reckoned you could fit in everywhere and could play the classless act to perfection, dropping aitches and calling people Ralph instead of *Raiphe* whenever necessary.

White was the son of an immigrant cabinet-maker. He'd been to a small, private school. It was here he cultivated the key element in his scheme of things – love of his country. It went a little further than the wholesome, this patriotism. It had some very quirky ingredients, and was deliberately kept half-baked in case the whole thing should explode in his face. And his face – unshaven, blue eyes, a mass of matted curly hair – had once moved Ruth to describe him as Marc Bolan from Hell.

It was the start of a blazing hot day. The river lay glistening and golden before him. It bulged out in a vast, mile-wide reach at this point. One or two smaller boats were already under way in the channels which threaded their routes around the Flat Owers, the steaming, bird-speckled expanses of mudflats. The air was fresh and invigorating. The clusters of yachts with their gleaming steel masts and fluttering pennants looked pretty.

The tractors harvesting the distant hillsides looked peaceful. The sky above was an infinite dome, blue as butane. White found all this very moving indeed. It crowned his activities.

(White also collected postcards of British royalty. Depending on who he was talking to, he would either pretend that it was a joke, or pretend that it was serious. And this was about the essence of him.)

They ran the *Ubique* between the mudflats and moored off Dickham. Phyllida took the tender ashore to fetch provisions. He watched her land amongst holidaymakers and thatched cottages. A moment later White drew alongside.

'Tony aboard?' he inquired.

White was given the same bullshit as the Harbourmaster and invited to wait for her. He took up the offer and gave himself a tour of the yacht and admired nearly everything about it. 'Lovely craft,' he enthused. 'Pity about the engine. I fixed it once for Tony. Those Swedish jobs are OK, but they just don't have the right sound, they whine, you know. Now, a good *Perkins* is like an Elgar serenade. That's what an engine should be, a serenade,' he said with satisfaction. 'Art is everywhere, you see, yes. *Ars Ubique Est*, as they say.'

'I don't think it's reached that outfit of yours yet. Everything else in the wash, or what?'

White merely smiled and tapped his nose knowingly as he took his leave. '*Ars Ubique Est*,' he repeated. 'Tell Phyllida I'd like a word, won't you?'

'You told him you were a friend of mine?' she said as she passed up boxes of groceries from the dinghy. 'God, you might have said relative. I'll be taken for a cradle snatcher. Did he go below? I hope you kept an eye on him. Right, I'm off to find him.' And she swung the tender round again and took off.

Bored, he decided to swim over and take a look at the village. Stripped to his shorts, he was soon wading ashore in front of the inn, knee-deep in mud. Then he went into the bar and ordered a coke. The landlord, a beefy, cold-eyed man, didn't stand on ceremony. 'You're filthy. Get out of my bar.' So he went out and sat in the sunshine on the quay wall. He could see the three prisoner sisters picking gingerly at pub lunches while their parents tucked in. Naval cadets sat around in grey jumpsuits, boots and backpacks. Next to him on the wall was a girl with bobbed, straw-coloured hair wearing a halter top and shorts.

She smiled at him. 'Hi,' she said. 'You're a good swimmer.'

'Thanks.'

'It's real muddy, isn't it?'

'Yeah, I–'

'Mud's real good for you. It's the glass you got to watch out for. They should be cleaning it up. Won't they serve you? I'll get you a drink.' And she thrust out her hand. 'Bibi van Helsing.'

'Theo.'

'What would you like?'

'Coke.'

'Coke is bad for you.'

'Mud, then.'

She bought him a Coke.

'The landlord here has a real problem,' she said. 'He is not well. He hates me because I don't drink alcohol. He is always wanting to buy me vodka. I tell him "No thanks, but I'd love a mineral water," but he will not buy me mineral water. He says if I'm gonna be like that I can buy my own. Problem.'

'I'll buy these.'

'I'd sooner you put something into his diet,' she said. 'He's uptight and constipated. And he beats his children. I think he has some shady operations also because he has a Mercedes and the kids have ponies and he is only the manager of the pub. Come, I take you for a walk. We pick herbs.'

'How romantic.'

He followed her off the quay, studying the way she swung her hips.

'I am from Holland,' she told him as she plucked mint from a meadow. 'I am making a tour. It is beautiful here, but the people have a lot of problems. Will you hold these please?' She loaded him up with mint. 'Come. There are chives in the next field.' And there were. 'Look, there is my barge.' She pointed

28

out the *Wilja*, moored in a bay.

'I wouldn't mind getting into business,' he said, 'but it looks like you've got to be bent to make any decent money.'

'I am in business,' she replied. 'I do very well. And I am perfectly honest, sir.' She drew a halo above her head, batted her eyelids and mock-curtsied.

'So what do you do?'

'I am a healer,' she said lightly. 'Have a chive.'

'No thanks.'

'Why, because they make you fart? But it is good for you. I fart.'

'Congratulations. What – is that like a faith healer or something?'

'In a way. It is a different kind of medicine. I use flower cures and scent therapies and such things. Come along one day and I will treat you.'

'There's nothing wrong with me,' he said.

'Ah,' she smiled, 'there is always something.'

'Name it,' he said, a shade too quickly.

'Oh, that's easy.'

'What?'

'You need to lose your virginity,' said Bibi gaily.

'How would you know that?'

'It's part of my business.'

'Sounds like funny business to me. How old are you, anyway?'

'Nineteen. So what? I have helped many boys. And girls. You make an appointment, you come along, and you go away feeling *much* better.'

'Healer, eh? Ain't there another word for it?'

'That is part of your problem. You get angry to hide your insecurities. Like the landlord back there.'

'Know it all, don't you?'

'I like you,' she said, chewing on a chive. 'You have a beautiful body. You have nothing to be ashamed of.'

'Who said I was ashamed of anything? Lay off, will you?'

'OK. I must fix dinner,' she said, 'but come over sometime.'

Back at the pub the crowd had thinned out. The prisoner

sisters were gone. In the doorway of the inn he noticed the land-lord giving his little girl a cuff round the head. He swum back to the *Ubique* at a fast crawl, and was a little breathless as he climbed aboard. Nothing as frustrating as a fast crawl, he thought.

2. OUT OF HIS HEAD

BY NOW it is late afternoon. The air is hot and still. The tide is high, the flats all submerged. Close to where the *Ubique* is moored, in the deep channel, a cormorant takes a tumble dive.

Theo lies on deck in the sun. His limbs are as pale as a fish's belly. His Bermudas have dried out on him. The small gold crucifix glitters around his neck. Beneath their dark brows his eyes are closed, but he is awake, just. He is thinking about White. Then a passing runabout buzzes by and rocks the boat with its wash. The movement and the sound knock away the image of White and replace it with a succession of rapid fragments: a glass, a foot, a word, a bird, a laugh like the flashing countdown of signs and digits before a film begins.

He's in a club with his mother. She hands him a crisp which he keeps under his tongue. Then she skips off to the dancefloor. Now his father sidles up to him and says 'Keep your hands off my girl, right? Or I'll break every bone in your body.'

He doesn't want any trouble. 'I'll do a deal,' he says, 'Timeshare, OK?'

His father is unimpressed. 'You've already had more than your share,' he says, 'Now leave my wife alone, you dirty virgin.' And then he bursts into tears and falls grief-stricken to the floor.

Sirens wail above the techno thump and three nurses rush in to pick up his stricken father. As they carry him away one of them hands Theo an appointment card. He glances at it, pockets it, and decides to visit Phyllida Green first.

She is pleased to see him. She gives him money, undresses to her black lace knickers and leads him to her boudoir. But as he draws close to her he sees that the knickers are in fact made of fine wrought iron, worked into elegant patterns of metallic tracery. He realises now that he will have to consult a priest.

So he sits down in the confessional and presses his face to the ornate metal grille. The priest tells him he's not watching enough TV, reading enough books or learning enough languages. He thanks the priest and leaves for his appointment at the clinic.

He's shown into the operating room, where Bibi van Helsing stands waiting in her surgeon's outfit. 'Hello Theo,' she says as she slips on a pair of latex gloves. 'OK so now we can check out all this confusion.' She turns to her assistants. 'Strap him down, please.'

The burly assistants grab his arms. he feels a little apprehensive. He looks at Bibi. 'I hope you haven't done this before,' he says.

'No,' she says.

'Good,' he says, 'because there are some doctors like you who have operated on hundreds of men. They've examined them all over, they know them inside out. It's a scandal. There's too many slags in the medical profession. I want a virgin surgeon.'

His limbs are duly clamped to the operating table. Bibi stands over him. 'When I said "No",' she says, 'I meant not with *you*. Lights!'

He is further pinned down by the white-hot glare of ranks of thousand-watt lamps.

'Wait!' he says, 'this isn't fair! All my mates had surgeons who were straight out of medical school.'

'Your friends lied to you,' says Bibi van Helsing. 'Half of them are still waiting for their appointment. The rest were treated by myself. Camera!'

32

He can't move a muscle, and he's naked but for his shorts. This is turning serious.

'Stop!' he says, 'You're much too young to be doing this!'

'I am four million and nineteen years old, thank you. That's quite old enough. Action!'

A vicious buzzing splits the air. He looks up in horror to see a circular saw descending slowly upon him, directly above his head.

'Are the tapes rolling?' says Bibi, 'Good, keep that blade coming.'

The shining, whining steel is now only an inch from his skull and closing. He feels the wind it creates tickling his eyebrows. Then it touches him, right between the eyes, and begins to slice through skin and then bone. But it doesn't hurt too much, and besides, there's a pleasant distraction coming from the sensations beneath his shorts. His skull is now split from front to back, a crimson, vulva-like slit.

'Put some coffee on, please,' Bibi orders her assistants. 'She's coming through.'

As she speaks, two soiled, gloved hands appear from the cranial volvulus and take a grip on the roots of Theo's hair before slowly hauling their owner into view: dressed from top to toe in camouflage battledress, this person now wriggles clear of the hairy, bloody purse, jumps to the floor, sighs, then leans against the operating table, panting a little. He can see that it's a young woman as she removes the green balaclava and shakes out her tresses. Then she takes a deep breath.

'Wow!' she says, 'jeez! G'day!'

'Hi Diana,' says Bibi van Helsing, 'what's new?'

Whoever Diana may be, she has freckles and comes from the rough end of Ramsey Street. 'Shit is that coffee I smell?' she says. 'Hey, I could really use some of that. And is there any food around? I'm that bushed I could eat the *crutch* off a *rag doll*. Let me get rid of some of this gear.'

She unloads herself of her armoury of weapons which includes a long, curved silver dagger, a crossbow and an Uzi. Then she grabs the coffee handed to her and knocks back the brew in one, smiling at the little group around the operating table.

33

'Well?' Bibi says.

'Boy, have I got news for you?' Diana says.

All eyes are on her.

'Is it safe to talk? OK, for a start,' she begins excitedly, 'Alexander the Great was an alky. Yeah, a total groghead. Couldn't even undo his shoelaces. Used to cut them off with his sword. And he was always falling off his horse. It's true. We were there on the Persian campaign. And you know before that we were in Egypt? Escaping with Moses' militia? We sussed out the Red Sea scam then. You know how, like, it's supposed to have parted, like giant walls of waves either side of us and all that? It didn't. Nothing like it. Heap of crap. It was the dry season, see, it was just marshes. We walked it. Mind you it's only like that for a couple of weeks, but somehow old Mose knows just when. And then *wham* – the rains come and catch Fez Face behind without his boats. How about that? Hey, give us some more coffee, will you? This isn't doing the trick. Tastes a bit off to me.'

'Its decaff,' says Bibi.

'It's *what*?' says Diana.

'It's good for you,' says Bibi.

'Hey, wait a minute,' says Diana, 'you guys aren't vegetarians are you? I remember the first veggie I ever met – guy's name was Cain and he had a *wicked* temper… oh, thanks…' She takes the fresh cup and knocks it back. 'Yeah, and here's one you don't know yet either – you know the Turin Shroud? Fake! Sham. Dud. A total hoodwink. Because I was living in Turin in 1257 and the person who made it lived on my block. Sure she did. Nice lady, very talented, but she need money badly so she took a less-than-honest commission.'

'Everyone knows that,' says Bibi, 'they carbon-dated it. It was on TV.'

'Straight up? I guess I'm not watching enough TV,' says Diana, then she looks at Theo. 'G'day,' she says. 'Hey, you know you have your great-great-great-great-great-grand-mother's eyes?'

Unshackled now, he sits up. 'OK then,' he says, 'If you're so smart, what's the best preconditioner for non-greasy hair?'

She knew.

'All right then – My kid sister's favourite colour?'

'Blue.'

'Could have been a guess.'

'It used to be a revolting shade of mauve,' she says with a sly smile. Then she collapses into a chair and begins tugging her boots off. 'Sorry if my tootsies hum, guys, but they've come a long way.'

A meal has been served in the post-op suite. He watches her lay into it ravenously. She looks about his own age. He thinks he'd better get down to basics.

'What were you doing in my head?'

She looks up from her plate and takes a gulp of wine.

'I wasn't just in your *head*,' she says, 'but sometimes that's the easiest way through. Wine? No? Please yourself.' She gives an indifferent toss of her head, and her earrings quiver and flash.

'Like the earrings.'

'Oh yeah?' she says, 'Look at this –' They are made of many tiny pendants suspended like chandeliers. She carefully detaches one of these and shows it to him. It's a slim, silver phial. She unscrews the cap and holds it under his nose.

'Have a sniff.'

The scent which wafts forth is both sweet and savory – and kind of seductive. 'Nice… yeah.'

'Tell you who gave me this – one of Solomon's wives.'

'King Solomon?'

'It wasn't Jack Solomon.'

'So how old are you?'

'Four billion and sixteen. But as far as my looks are concerned it's the sixteen that matters.' She screws the top back on the phial and replaces it. She's a looker all right.

'So, you're an immortal, right?'

'Jeez, I wish I fuckin' was. On the other hand I might get bored. But I *might* be immortal. I mean, I've never died yet. Plenty of my friends have, though.' She wipes her mouth and takes another sip of wine. 'Look at it this way – I'm immortal till they get me.'

'They?'

'You think it's easy, surviving like I have? Why do you think I've got all this gear?' – she indicates her paramilitary paraphernalia – 'I'll tell you – because in this world everyone wants your butt. It's dog-eat-dog, Theo, and you'd better remember that, for both our sakes.'

'*Both* our sakes?'

'We're in this together, boy,' she says, and then suddenly changes her tune. She snuggles up to him, takes his arm and puts it around herself. 'Will you take care of me?' she whispers sweetly and seductively. 'Will you protect me?' she says, pouting her ruby red lips. It's too provocative. He's overwhelmed, and makes to kiss her.

Instantly she withdraws. 'Not like that, you drongo.' She slaps the backs of her palms onto her knees. 'I'm talking about a deal. You scratch my back, I'll scratch yours. I can let you have a lot of very useful information.'

'For example?'

'This, for a start: I don't like the sound of this trip you're planning. You've got zero experience at sea, and Phyllida isn't a good enough sailor to see you through, because crossing the channel in a boat like that is like trying to drive a dinky toy across the M1. And as for the rest – forget it. I'd give us a thousand-to-one chance of making it alive.'

This is not what he wants to hear.

'No way, Diana, I'm making this trip.'

She sighs. 'All right, here's the deal,' she says. 'Scotch this little suicide venture, and I'll do two things for you. I'll make you rich, and I'll tell you the secrets of love.'

This sounded attractive. But – 'How do I know that?'

'I've been around a long time. Facts are money. And as for love, I knew the person who wrote the book.'

'Maybe.'

'Listen,' she says, earnestly, 'You ever hear that phrase *Lucky to be alive*? Of course you have. But *you*, you don't know how lucky you really are. Boy, you're so lucky it's frightening.'

When Phyllida returned, found him sprawled out on deck and

prodded him awake, he looked up and didn't remember that she wore wrought-iron lingerie, that his father was a jealous man, or that he'd sprouted a strange woman from the top of his head. All he had at that moment was a vague feeling of unease combined with a nebulous image of Bibi van Helsing and a circular saw. And even this was now fading fast.

His captain seemed excited, a little flushed. She told him that their departure might be delayed a day or two. She'd been talking business with White. He was coming to dinner tonight. He had some paintings for sale.

She said he could do what he liked for the rest of the day, so he rowed across to Dickham to see what was happening. As he tied up on the jetty he saw the eldest prisoner sister standing watching him, scuffing her suede sneakers. Her siblings were some way off feeding geese. She wore a lifejacket over her hooded top. She nodded casually at him and he nodded back.

'Nice yacht,' she said.

'Yeah. What's yours?'

'I wish,' she said, looking contemptuously at her lifejacket. 'I'm supposed to wear this stupid thing just to *look* at water.'

'No, it's cool, that orange.'

'Yeah?' She resumed her poker face and stared at her sneakers. 'Got any draw?'

'Sorry.'

'Any clubs round here?' she asked.

'I don't know.'

'Do us a favour?' she said, digging in the side pockets of her baggy pants. 'Get us some fags from the pub?'

'OK.' She handed him some cash.

'And a Two Dogs and a miniature Cointreau.'

'Right.'

'I'll wait here. My jailers are back there.'

When he got back the girl – such a wide, soft, preoccupied face which she hid with her hair – had hidden herself behind a rack of hire dinghies. She lit them cigarettes. A big wash sloshed against the jetty.

'So where are you going on that thing?' She gave a nod toward the *Ubique*.

'South of France. You been?'

'Sounds a bummer of a place,' she said, 'crawling with the gruesomely gilded.'

'You a poet or something?' he said.

'Yeah,' she said, 'I'm going to be a good one.'

'Who are your favourites?'

She knocked back the Two Dogs. 'Byron and Sappho.'

'They sound like hairdressers.'

'Fill high the cup with Samian wine,' she quoted and passed him the bottle. Then cocked her head at the source of a distant calling voice. 'That's my jackbooted daddy. Do you know Sylvia Plath? Heavy...' She brushed her hair from her face and smiled. 'I'm going to Thailand next year no matter what. He can't do a thing about it. I'll breathe odes all over him. He can kiss my poetic arse. See you.' And she got up and ambled back into captivity.

Then Ruth hoved to in a dinghy. 'I'm getting some vino for tonight' she said. 'Want a drink?'

Ruth drunk lager without lime and ate peanuts as she told him at length about what a bastard her man was. She met White a year ago when she was down here leading an outward-bound course for kids. He was building this yacht, so she joined up with him. They were planning to go island-hopping in the Caribbean, but now they were running out of time and money, and it was all White's fault. He lived in a fantasy world, she complained, and lazed his days away dreaming of easy money – cleaning up on some big deal or other – while she was left to do all the graft.

'I'm thinking of quitting and taking off again,' she said. 'I can't stand it down here any longer. It's meant to be the wide-open spaces, but it's just a dumb suburb. Nothing but gossip and incest.' She crunched violently on a nut and then looked him in the eye. 'How long have you and what's-her-name been together?'

He told her the situation, then asked her how she made her money.

'I sell fossils to tourists.'

'Money in that, is there?'

'Sure. All you do is pick them up off the beach, polish them up and there you are. But it's so galling to sell something that's half-a-billion years old to some airhead to use as a doorstep.' She took a rock from her pocket and showed him. Embedded in the stone was a crystallised spiral.

'Baby ammonite,' she said. 'Take a look. Could be your ancestor. I dig up grandma, clean her up and sell her as a paper-weight.'

As he turned the fossil over in his hands, he felt weird. He began to sway a little.

'Hey, are you OK?' said Ruth. She leaned across and shook him. 'Someone put something in your Pepsi?'

'I think I must be hungry,' he said.

Unfortunately for him, Phyllida's dinner was a case of garlic-with-everything. The heavily herbed dishes steamed on his plate like hostile, malodorous monsters. He picked his way through them like a soldier through a minefield while the others talked about the importance of the correct type of cheesegrater and the best corkscrew for Loire Valley wine. White ended everything he said with, 'Of course, you can't get them here.' Phyllida always knew a place in Piccadilly where you could. And Ruth would chip in with the price.

Ruth was no longer sniping at White. Everyone talked a kind of polite nonsense. Something was going on. They were holding back. They sipped their wine, and whenever there was a silence they would smile extra-hard and maybe add a little murmur. Phyllida served a fruit salad and asked White about his boat and his plans. White said he wanted to go abroad for a good while. England was going to the dogs. The kind of government made no difference – there was always too much interference.

'I always thought an Englishman's home was his castle,' he said, 'and now I can't even put in a new bog door without some council mongoloid telling me it's the wrong colour. Laws, rules, regulations… we didn't make ourselves great by following the rule book. We went out and built an empire without cringing to some great global planning department. Ha! – wonderful pears, Phyllida.'

39

'Thank you. You're so right, of course.'

Then Ruth broke cover. 'You're just a child, Paul. You want everything your own way. You want to run around breaking rules all your life. You're living in never-never land.' She paused for a mouthful. 'Too much cinnamon on these pears, Phyllida.'

'But there's far too much bureaucracy,' said Phyllida.

'*I* live in never-never land!' said White with indignation. 'Would you mind telling us where *you* live, then?'

'With you, worse luck,' said Ruth.

'I'm sorry,' White apologised to Phyllida in a lowered voice. 'She gets like this.'

'Go on, Paul,' said Ruth. 'Why not tell her the whole story? Tell everybody how you found me at a party where I was committing suicide in the bathroom and how you found me there and took me to hospital and had me stomach-pumped and how you stuck by me and had me psychiatrised and pumped full of shit and how you've been trying to run my life ever since.'

There was a silence, and nobody was smiling.

'This is not what we're here for,' said White, and raised a questioning eyebrow at Phyllida.

'Come outside for a moment,' she said to him, getting up. White followed her from the saloon.

'He always runs away like that,' said Ruth. Her eyes were shining. 'OK,' she said, 'so while Drake and Her Majesty get it together on deck, why don't we dance?' She turned up the stereo, began to sway her hips, and locked his hands in hers. As they danced he recognised a familiar smell on her, but he couldn't place it. It was both sweet and sour.

'Hey,' she said, 'let's go hang-gliding tomorrow! Don't worry about Paul, he doesn't own me. He tells people I'm crazy so he can play guardian. He says I'm mad to care about the things I do. He's so damn arrogant.'

The two others reappeared. White went to his bag and produced a small oil painting in a gilt frame. In the foreground a young woman with her back to the viewer was playing a virginal. Beyond the dim-lit room she sat in could be seen

40

another, then stretching beyond that another, and beyond this at perspective's end – you had to look closely – was a distant chamber flooded with bright sunlight, and through its window a view of a town on a river.

'Now, this is definitely a Dutch master,' said White, 'and—' here he lowered his voice – '*I* think it's a Vermeer.'

'Is it signed?' said Phyllida.

'I haven't found the signature yet. He always hid it somewhere.'

Phyllida examined the picture. 'Just look at that technique,' enthused White, 'the tilework, the perspective, the mastery of tonality.'

'It's rather pretty isn't it?' she said. 'What do you think, Theo?'

As he looked at the painting he came over queazy. A pressure on his stomach was forcing him to take deep breaths. Ruth, who was making a great show of disinterest from across the saloon, glanced over at him.

'Theo is impressed,' she said. 'What do you think, Theo? Worth a million?'

That's when he found himself saying, in a strange kind of squeal, '*Quis scrivit librum amoris?*'

'Come again?' said the startled Phyllida.

'He's just showing off in Latin,' said White. '*Who wrote the book of love?* Virgil, I think. Or was it Pliny the Younger?'

'Crap, Paul,' said Ruth, 'It's a pop song.'

'In Latin?' said Phyllida.

'It's probably just—' he was going to say the rich food and the rocking of the boat, but neither would earn him cred with his employer so he substituted 'that chequered floor in the picture… touch of vertigo.'

'Can we get back to the business in hand?' White said.

Phyllida looked at the painting again. 'I'd be interested,' she said. 'Can you show me some more?'

'I'll get in touch with my source,' said White.

White and Ruth took their leave. As they did so, White took him aside. 'Listen, old boy,' he said confidentially, 'I shouldn't get involved with Ruth if I were you, there's a good chap. She's sick, you see. Unstable. I know her very well, I promise you. She's not interested in you, it's just her way of getting some sort of revenge on me. So – steer clear, eh? And there won't be any trouble.'

'Revenge for what?'

'Things she imagines. She's insanely jealous of Phyllida, for a start.'

White paused and looked out across the water. 'It's beautiful here, isn't it?' he said, indicating the glistening mudflats. 'Know why they're called the Flat Owers? Because when some laddie from the OS came tramping around here a century ago and asked old Fred the Ferryman what their name was, Fred tells him they're called the Flat Oars, for obvious reasons, but our laddie couldn't penetrate the accent, you see?' It's what you get when the classes can't communicate. Silly misunderstandings. We don't want any of those, do we?'

At the end of that evening he climbed into his berth, knackered, and drew the curtain. Phyllida was still up and he could hear her rustling about. All these women... but they had always been like that – a certain self-assurance. They all seemed to know something he didn't. That's why he liked wearing their clothes sometimes, or to sleep as he had at that boathouse with his cheek on a pair of old knickers. It made him feel closer to the secret. The clothes signalled things to him. Things he couldn't even put into recognisable feelings, let alone words. It was more than just the horn. And then the flickering countdown again.

She was sitting in a café over the road from the clinic, wearing a trenchcoat and reading *Soldier of Fortune* magazine.

'What are you having?' she said.

'Something English. Omelette and chips.'

'I was trying to get through to you back there,' Diana said, 'but trust my luck to have it come out in garbled Latin. I'm still not pushing the right buttons.'

When the waiter brought his omelette it was with rice. 'Take it,' Diana said, 'one of your great-great-great grandfathers was Chinese. Hey and did you know that your great-great

Grandmother was African? Yeah, first woman to escape from a slave ship. What do you reckon on that?'

'Great. Great-great. Anything you don't know about me?'

'It's my job. I'm your genetic history. I'm telling you, there's a chance that a kid of yours could be a little black bubba. And there's also a smaller chance of it being Eskimo. Want to know how come?'

'You're meant to be telling me about love and money,' he said.

'It works best through stories,' she said.

'Forget stories. Just give me the basics.'

She looked thoughtful. 'Love and money's hard to put in a nutshell. I tell you what though – I can give you the meaning of life, will that do?'

'I guess it could come in handy.'

'OK, it's simple: the meaning of life is to live to tell the tale. Got it?'

She stirred her coffee. The foam spiralled slowly around in the cup.

'See, you're not only lucky, you're also very old. And I'm your *age*. And I look like this because who wants to speak to a diagram? It's like you're the disk and I'm the stuff. The rich text. See, I've had a zillion lives, I go way back beyond that old Rift Valley. I've been on every continent and I've been in and out of every race there is a hundred times over. I've got stories that go back to the fuckin' *Trilobites*,' she said heatedly, 'Jeez and I wish you'd listen. You've got to wake up a bit. We're at the business end of history here. Tomorrow's not guaranteed, you know. Look at me – why do you think I've got my back to the wall? There's carnivores out there, matey, anytime now someone could poke a nozzle through the pane and try to blow us all away. Happens every day. Could be Luigi & Co., could be the military, could be some solitary Rambohead, could be our friend Mr White. We've got to be careful of him. He'll snuff you out before you can say "reproduction".'

'Reproduction?'

'Ah yeah, that's another meaning of life. If you don't believe me, check out Shakespeare's sonnets.'

'Don't tell me. He was a relative of mine.'

'I taught him all he knew,' Diana said.

♥

Job's day was beginning badly. He'd just paid a visit to the police forensics man at Kingsmouth armed with the suspicious phial he had taken from the *Wilja*.

'Contact lens fluid,' the scientist told him. 'I use the same type. What did you think it was?'

Job hesitated. He had no idea. 'Wrong' was the only word for what he had captured.

'You know I thought it might have been illegal spirits,' he blurted out, 'like vodka or rum, or some kind of explosive?'

The forensics man smiled and said nothing. Job could see his own asinine words hanging foolishly in the air between them. He quickly apologised, excused himself and left.

Now he had another problem: how to return the fluid – which he must – without looking a complete fool? He was pondering this quandry as he returned to his cottage upriver, but he had no sooner closed the front door behind him when he realised that something was even more wrong. He stood still and listened. There was no sound. No steady tick from the grandfather clock. But he'd only recently wound it… he hurried to inspect the heirloom, and it took only a glance to see what was wrong. The big brass pendulum bob was gone. The long rod hung still, naked, stupid.

What? How? Why? It didn't take Job long to find out. He'd been burgled. Every drawer and cupboard in the house was thrown open, contents scattered. Andersen was stung to the root of his heart. He stood amongst the chaos of his few humble possessions in a mute rage. It was the silence, the utter quiet which lay upon his defiled home – this was the worst insult. And then the maddening sounds of undisciplined nature which crept in on the ambience – a wasp, a distant sheep's bleat, a pleasure boat's megaphone – whispering all around him, unorchestrated, untamed by any baton.

Nothing else had been taken. Nothing else at all was missing. Nothing but the beating heart of the only thing he owned which was worth a valuer's time – his ancient, lifesaving, long-case clock. Its silence was a living death. Without its regular beat the march of time collapsed into an unpredictable, turbulent stampede. Job felt a heavy voltage of fear slam across his chest. But he knew what he must do.

He spent the rest of the day making good. He didn't just put his belongings in order. He laundered, cleaned, dusted and disinfected everything. He fumigated every wardrobe, he scrubbed down every shelf, table and chest of drawers. Everything perishable he junked till his trashbags were crammed with fruit, fish, vegetables, half-spent tubes of toothpaste and pieces of soap. He washed the ceilings, scrubbed down every wall and floor, took out his two humble carpets and gave them a thorough and savage beating. He cleaned every windowpane inside and out. He washed down every door. Then he took a hose and mounted a ladder to spray the roof and exterior walls; and after that he sluiced down the garden path and the front gate. Then he sprayed his vegetable garden and turned the earth over in an hour of strenuous forking. Then he mowed the lawn and burned the clippings; then he sheared the hedge and burned the trimmings.

Finally, towards evening, he took a large irregular hunk of granite from his rock-garden, still damp from the hose, carried it indoors, and with the aid of a rope he contrived to lash it to the pendulum rod of the grandfather clock.

Tick... Tock...

Order was restored. Job knelt and prayed for seven minutes and seven seconds. Then he went out to where his dory was moored at the creekside. He cleaned the boat until it shone, and the legend HARBOURMASTER stood out proudly against the sleek, pristine hull. Then he went off to clean up the river.

Tick... Tock... Tick... but the rhythm was imperceptibly uneven, and time was being nudged out of order.

Clearly, Andersen had cracked, and the person responsible for the blow had already sold the lump of brass before lunch, to a scrappie who operated from a field behind Gimpton Creek. Two quid is what Windeatt got for it. He'd had an hour to kill

45

that morning before signing on so he puttered around the lanes on spec and came across Job's abode. Disappointed to find nothing of stealable value on those austere premises he had finally come to the clock. He actually considered hauling it out and somehow transporting it away on his moped, but in the end settled for its pendulum weight as a consolation prize. Having signed on, flogged the brass and cashed the giro, he was now eating a ploughman's in the Ferry Inn at Dickham, reading a story in the *Mirror* about the SAS. All around him stood men in cravats and yachting caps, women in Guernsey sweaters and deck shoes, clutching Camparis and G&Ts: explosions of laughter, cigar smoke and Chanel. White made his way through this crowd to join him, giving a scornful snort as Windeatt turned the page to a double-spread underwear feature.

'Still hooked on that rag?' he smiled. 'You won't learn anything from that, Windy. Now–' and he leaned forward and fixed Windeatt's tight-squashed features with an authoritative stare – 'If you took the *Western Times* you might learn a thing or two.'

'Sorry Mr White. Force of habit.'

White produced a copy of an archaic-looking weekly. 'Where are we? Ah: hatched, matched and dispatched.' He passed the paper across to Windeatt, pointing out a notice in the deaths column. The entry read:

> MIKOYAN. On July 4th at Gimpton Ferrers, peace-
> fully, Nouritza Anastasia Nicolaya Mikoyan, aged 96.
> Beloved wife of C D Mikoyan Esq. of Gimpton Ferrers.
> Funeral July 7th, 4pm, St Gregory's, Gimpton.

Windeatt read it and belched. 'So what?' he said.

'You don't know about old Mikoyan, do you?'

'Never heard of him.'

'Ha!' said White, his eyes gleaming. 'Well, he's a mysterious fellow. No-one knows much about him. Keeps himself to himself. Big old house on the hill. They reckon he's *extremely* old. Drinks nothing but fermented mare's milk. The story is that he came over here from Europe fifty years ago, loaded with art – millions of pounds worth – and he's been here ever since. That house is his private museum.'

'It's like Nazi gold,' Windeatt said excitedly, 'Like them Krauts who bunked off to South America.'

'Smart fellow, Windy,' said White seriously. 'He just could be a Nazi. Of course the last place you'd look for him is here. And he's sitting up there on top of a pile of stolen masterpieces.' White was warming to his theme. He took a sip from his glass and went on: 'Ask yourself this: where are all the missing treasures? The van Goghs and Leonardos? And *where* is all the lost *British* art? The Constables, Turners, Hogarths? Think about it, Windy. That's our heritage he's got up there.'

Windeatt's face twitched as he thought about it.

Then White said, 'Windy, are you a patriot?'

Windeatt felt a surge of pure faith. Like White, he loved adventure stories with lots of swastikas in them. The suave officer and his batman cooly seeing off hordes of advancing, *Britischer Pig-Dog*-shouting Jerries. Windeatt felt like Little John, Gunga Din and Maggot Malone rolled into one. He promptly rolled up his sleeve to reveal a Union Jack tattooed on his skinny white forearm.

'For life, Mr White,' he said grandly.

'Really?' said White. 'Because *I* seem to remember hearing that you deserted the senior service.'

Windeatt was appalled that his secret was out. 'I never did, Mr White,' he said hastily, 'I'd never do that. Not me. No. I failed a medical.' His voice grew self-pitying. 'I wanted to serve. To serve my Queen. But they didn't want me, Mr White. Saddest day of my life.' He pouted and picked up his beerglass, looking all set to cry into it. Surprised, he found himself genuinely touched by the performance he was giving. It had been the words *They didn't want me* – a truth spoken in falsehood, the story of his life. White's eyes drilled into him.

'Can I trust you?' said the suave officer.

'Yessir,' said the faithful native.

White saw himself as the Wolf of Kabul, as depicted in the *Wizard* comic of his boyhood: the lone British officer operating behind enemy lines in 19th century Afghanistan, with only the help of his native servant Chung – whose sole weapon was an old cricket bat.

'Can you drive?' said the Wolf of Kabul to Chung.

'Yessir,' lied the faithful native.

♥

It was at this moment that Bibi van Helsing approached their table and asked if the small patch of bench next to White was taken. Disarmed at once by her smile, the gallant Wolf of Kabul stood up to let her squeeze through while Chung, disarmed by the rest of her, stared and shifted in his seat. Then White reclaimed his attention and pointed to the newspaper.

But Bibi would not be ignored.

'It's so crowded in here,' she said, beaming at the pair of them. There was a brief, English pause.

'Yes,' smiled White. There was another little silence. Bibi was still beaming.

'There's more room outside,' offered White.

'But I must be inside,' said Bibi, 'I've been in the sun all morning.'

Then she said, 'Oh – I see you have a newspaper. I hope you have seen my advertisement?'

'I beg your pardon?' White said.

'I am a therapist. It is public relations,' she explained. Then she held out her hand. 'Bibi van Helsing.'

'Paul,' said White, with a brief handshake.

'Windeatt,' said Windeatt, giving her a little wave.

White assumed his knowing look. 'Therapist, eh? What kind?'

'It is natural therapy. Have you tried it? Would you like to?'

'Not much point really,' said White. 'Never felt better in my life.'

'Nothing wrong with me,' said Windeatt.

'Why don't you try Ruth,' White suggested. 'She likes that sort of thing.' Then another thought occurred to him. 'Wait a minute. You're a practising therapist?'

She nodded happily.

'Are you qualified in England?'

'What do you mean?'

'Well,' he huffed, 'there are laws about these things you

48

know. You're a foreigner, aren't you? Yes, you see technically you're an alien. You can't just go where you please doing what you want. And anyway, you're a bit young, aren't you?'

'Oh, you're never too young to learn,' said Bibi. 'And besides you know, this 'foreigners' and 'aliens' business... you English are strange. The Pound sign is standing for an Italian word, your Sterling is named after some expatriate Dutch people like me, the name of your country and your language is German, the tune of your national anthem is German and even your royal family is German.'

White was both impressed and irritated by her. Nineteen and two degrees. Bitch. 'It's not that simple,' he said.

'Who is Ruth?' she said.

'My girlfriend. As I say, she seems to need that kind of thing sometimes. Does her good in a way.' Then White turned conspiratorial. 'To tell you the truth,' he confided, 'she's a bit unstable, our Ruth. No self-discipline. Stays up till dawn a lot – that sort of thing. I do all I can of course, but... she's mad about ammonites at the moment. Totally fixated.' He smiled and shook his head condescendingly.

'She's nice, Ruth is,' offered Windeatt, '–got a tongue on her, though.'

'Oh?' said Bibi with a smile. 'Perhaps I should cut it out.'

The two men looked fazed.

'Only joking,' said Bibi.

White was seized by a brief coughing fit.

'That's a nasty cough you have there,' said Bibi, 'I can cure it if you like.'

'No, no. Just a bit of dust in the throat. Nothing wrong with me.'

'Are you sure? I give discount for the first session.'

White was getting needled. 'Listen,' he said, 'if you think I'm so ill I'd like to hear about it. Come on, tell me everything that's wrong with me.'

'And me,' challenged Windeatt.

'Actually I would say there are quite a number of things,' she said.

'Come on then,' said White, 'let's have a diagnosis.'

'Well,' said Bibi, eyes shining and freckles aglow, 'it's interesting that you both have the same problems even though you might look so different, and you Paul are obviously a little older...'

White folded his arms and sat up straight. He didn't like being compared with his hunched-up factotum. 'For instance?' he demanded.

'Let's see,' said Bibi. 'OK. You're not sleeping too well. You both get headaches. You both smoke a lot and worry about it. You don't remember your dreams but they give you uncomfortable feelings. You get stomach-aches. You catch colds, and once a year you get the flu. Also you feel guilty about masturbation. You worry about money and your position in life. You don't get on with your parents. You eat too much salt, sugar and saturated fats. You speak from your throat instead of your diaphragm, your posture is uncentred, you have crystals in your feet, miasms concerning your childhood, and you have a lot of tension, especially round the neck and shoulders. And you, Windeatt, have flat feet.'

Windeatt was uncomfortably impressed.

'Ha!' said White goodnaturedly to conceal his embarrassment. 'They're hardly terminal illnesses.'

'And I also think,' Bibi went on, 'that you are afraid of cancer, old age and AIDS. Also you both suffer from hay-fever. I have a herbal remedy that works always.'

'What, for the whole lot?' said Windeatt.

White and Windeatt politely declined Bibi's introductory offer. However, White told her where she could find Ruth.

'Mad as a hatter,' said White when she had left. 'She and Ruth should get on.'

'She ain't got two degrees,' said Windeatt scornfully.

'Probably not,' said White, 'Anyway, foreign degrees are worthless, it's well known.'

'Got a nice arse, though,' said Windeatt.

White smiled indulgently and then drew Windeatt's attention back to the newspaper. 'See the date of the funeral? Today. See the time? This afternoon. Now, What does that suggest to you?'

3. SQUID, GALOSHES, MOONLIGHT

THAT MORNING Theo went down to Kingsmouth to pick up supplies from the chandlery. Ruth was at her stall in the market place, deep in conversation with Bibi van Helsing. It looked very serious. He thought twice about stopping, but Ruth spotted him. 'How are your voices?' she said.

The stall was surrounded by curious tourists. Ruth was doing good business for someone who was meant to be crazy. Bibi made him nervous. It wasn't just that her wardrobe consisted of the thinnest cottons ever produced. He was glad when she excused herself and left.

'Yeah, I'm leaving Paul,' Ruth announced. 'Bibi and I've just been talking it through. Helped me get things into perspective. I must have been crazy to hang around that schmuck for so long.'

'Why did you try to top yourself?' he said.

'I'm not crazy, he'd just prefer it that way. I got drunk, got an incredible headache, took a bunch of paracetamol and passed out. That's perfectly normal, for Christ's sake. Paul just had to play the rescuer. I guess I played along. Everyone gets lonely, don't they? I hate myself for it, but I'm not crazy, I'm just smarter than him, and he knows it, and he hates that.'

Two Japanese were at the stall. The woman was taking an intense interest in an ammonite the size of a car wheel that Ruth had sliced and polished till the crystals dazzled. The man had a small notebook out and was busy making drawings of the smaller fossils she had made into paperweights and earrings. There was something odd about these two, but he couldn't put his finger on it.

'You ever speak in tongues, Ruth?'

'Wish I did. Things might make more sense. You're lucky, you're charismatic, you know, like those tribes. The spirit enters them, talks through them, cleans them up. Maybe it's one of your past lives speaking through you.'

'What exactly happened? I don't remember much.'

'You went a bit spacey and started talking in Latin.'

'Bollocks, I don't know any Latin.'

She pointed at his head. 'Somebody in there does.'

'You're not serious.'

'You're just sensitive, that's all.'

'I hate being called sensitive.'

'It's OK,' she said, 'we allow you to be a little macho too.'

The Japanese woman announced that she would buy the giant ammonite. Ruth produced her card machine. The man was still drawing fossils when his companion finally held the wrapped stone in her frail arms.

'It is guaranteed, no?' she said.

'That is a chunk of pure planet you're holding,' Ruth assured her. 'I'll guarantee that till the beginning of the next ice age. I can't be responsible for subsequent major geological or climatic upheavals.' And she turned to the man. 'Get some good drawings?' she said cooly, annoyed he wasn't buying.

'Yes, thank you,' he said, 'I am illustrator. It is for my work. I am very interested in fossils. Also in mi-cro-organ-isms.'

'Oh yeah?' said Ruth, 'And what about the whales that feed on these microorganisms of yours? Your people are busy wiping them off the planet.'

The man gave a short bow and doffed his pork-pie hat.

'I apologise for my people,' he said.

'That's OK,' Ruth said sharply.

When they left Ruth turned to him and said with satisfaction, 'That's *it!* That gives me enough for a new set of wheels. I'm going to find me one right now, and then I'm going far away from here.'

'I've worked out what's so strange about those two Japs.'

'What?'

'One, they bought a *large* object. Two, no cameras.'

He left her dismantling her stall, and set off back upriver with the gear he'd bought. A mile or so clear of Kingsmouth, where the river banks steepened and the forest closed in, he noticed a small creek and a cottage at the water's edge. He could just make out a figure in the garden who seemed to be hosing down the roof. When he had returned and unloaded, Phyllida had some more work for him:

'Paul has bought some paintings and things that he and I might negotiate over. He needs someone to help him pick them up from the seller, but he can't be there himself. The vendor's man will come and pick you up, OK?'

Then the noise of an approaching outboard caught their attention. It was the Harbourmaster. He circled the *Ubique* slowly, examining it closely before drawing alongside and boarding. He saluted Phyllida.

'I must inform you,' he said stiffly, 'Of certain marks of grease and dirt that cling at your hull.'

'I beg your pardon?' said Phyllida.

'Your stern also has these marks,' said Andersen severely. 'I must ask you to clean this boat immediately.'

Phyllida looked bemused. Andersen promptly began to hiccup. This was due to the inordinate and hurried amounts of water he had drunk during his sanitary efforts at the cottage. 'I shall be back to inspect,' he gasped between bouts, and hurriedly left, still racked by the convulsions.

❤

Like Robin on his first solo outing in the Batmobile, Windeatt streaked downhill to the quay. He screeched to a halt a foot from the water's edge, revving loudly, and stuck his head out the van's window.

'You Theo? Hop in then.'

Reversing across the quayside Windeatt then managed to ram an old red telephone box; there was a crump and a splintering of glass.

'Bloody engine. Got to get it fixed,' he said, pulling away immediately and whining up the hill. The van smelt of oil, timber and roll-ups. At its helm, Windeatt was trying to assume an air of calm authority which matched badly with the reckless way he forced the rustbucket through the lanes. After he had narrowly missed an oncoming tractor and ended them up in a hedge, and was busily trying to extricate the van, he fumbled with the gears and said casually 'Yes, I work for Mr Mik – Mik – Mikky – Mikkan. We'll be loading the stuff up and delivering it to your Mr White's place, right?' He finally found the right gear, freed the vehicle from the hedge and roared off towards Gimpton.

The house stood alone on a wooded hilltop. It was built of deep red brick, with steep slate roofs. Carved snakes entwined its tall chimneys. Dark swatches of Cypress and Yew rustled against turret rooms and leaded windows. Paint was flaking from the eaves and gables; the masonry was crumbling and many of the windows were cracked. The mansion bore an air of melancholy neglect. A startled blackbird skeetered across the drive, where moss was busy taking over from gravel. Windeatt jerked to a halt outside the front door and cut the engine. Somewhere at the back of the building a dog was barking.

'I'm going in round the back,' Windeatt announced. 'Wait here and I'll be along.' So he waited under the porch. The heavy doorknocker was a dragon of dulled brass, The brickwork was verdigri'd. Despite the heat of the day it was cool and damp here. The unseen dog ceased to bark and there was silence. He ran his fingers along the cold scales of the dragon's neck. After some five minutes the door creaked open and Windeatt beckoned him inside. 'Right, let's do it,' he said briskly.

The house was dimly lit and hung over with faint traces of perfumes, sweet and sour, like the morning after in some exotic restaurant. In the panelled entrance hall all manner of ancient objects were displayed – oriental masks, African spears, horse-hide shields, ancient maps ornamented with unicorns and mermaids – and there were paintings, too, most of them so grimy that it was barely possible to make out the picture.

'Quite a gaff.'

'Everything from the hall,' said Windeatt, 'Pack 'em up in these dust sheets.' So he set about the task while Windeatt went to and fro elsewhere carrying out paintings, vases and silverware. It occurred to him that there was a lot of money involved in this transaction. White must be depending on reselling this gear immediately if he was as skint as Ruth had claimed. So why wasn't he here? This was looking distinctively dodgy. But he gave it the benefit of the doubt. Windeatt, who had never stopped looking at his watch, did so again. 'We're pretty much through,' he said, 'but there's one more thing for you: the end of that corridor, up two flights, first left there's a small room. All the pictures from there.'

It was a little study which smelt of cigars. The walls were lined with books and pictures, the mahogany desk piled high with a chaos of papers. The paintings were small ones, interiors as gloomy as that in which they now hung in, and dimly-lit portraits of figures in backdated dress. He went to the window and parted the drapes. The room overlooked an overgrown lawn: bindweed curled round the stone pedestal of a small cupid. Then he saw the dog, an old, lanky Borzoi which was spreadeagled and still. Was it asleep – or had he been set up?

He collected the pictures and made for the front hall, but somewhere he took a wrong turn and found himself looking down from a first-floor window at the front drive, where Windeatt was busily loading the van. He was about to turn away and descend again when he saw a black car approaching, and he saw Windeatt's reaction, which was to jump as though stung, drop the articles he was holding, slam the doors, throw himself into the van, start it up and hurtle off past the approaching vehicle, taking off its wing mirror in passing. The black car did not turn to pursue him.

He began to look desperately for a way out of here, but it was a maze of musty corridors, locked doors and sealed windows. Then with a further rush of panic he realised he'd left his jacket

55

with all his dough and i.d. in the front hall. He felt a sudden cold sweat trickle down the backs of his legs, spun round, and found himself confronted by an old man, short and rotund, who wore a black suit and who held a brass-topped cane.

'Since you are unable to find your way out, I suggest that you make yourself at home,' said the man, ushering him through a doorway. He opened his mouth to make excuses but the man waved it shut and followed him into a lowlit room where rugs covered the floor and objects of copper and brass glinted from low tables. The man pointed him to a seat by the window, sat down opposite and lit a cigar. Shafts of light streamed through the blue fog and profiled his hooked nose and little upturned military moustache. Nearby a small table was set with a coffeepot on a burner. His host gestured to this and politely asked, in a voice that seemed to come from somewhere beyond the Black Sea, if he would care for some coffee. Then he leaned forward on his cane, gave a faint bow and said, 'My name is Mikoyan. You are called Theo I believe. One lump or two?'

There was a nervous rattling as he stirred five lumps into a tiny cup of thick black brew. Mikoyan's bulbous, dark-ringed eyes watched him closely while the trace of a smile glimmered below his pointy moustache.

'So,' he said, 'You have come to rob me. I saw your associate as he left. May I ask which of you is responsible for death of my dog?'

He explained that he'd been set up, he'd been stupid. And stupidly, he heard himself saying 'I'm innocent.'

Mikoyan leaned back and puffed lightly at his cigar. 'No,' he said, 'You lost your innocence years ago, day you first said to yourself "Who am I?" '

Philosophy. This was all he needed.

'Besides,' said Mikoyan, 'at your age – at any age – it is crime to be innocent.'

'Come again?'

'You may well frown,' said his host, 'but consider me. In space of one hour I have buried my wife, seen my dog poisoned, and been relieved of good number of material possessions.

Which of us should be more troubled? But no matter. What makes me smile is that I have left my house unlocked for forty years, and this is first time I have been robbed, and on such day. I wonder what it means. And of course I also have you over barrel, as they say – trapped, as it were, inside deepest, most malodorous galoshes of Mullah Nassir-U-Din.'

He opened his mouth to say 'Who?', but the old man waved it shut again. 'Spare me your whinings,' he said, 'you have nothing to tell me. I am one hundred forty years old, I have heard it all. Your story is not relevant. I would have no trouble securing your conviction. But fact is that this does not interest me. Instead I have task which I wish you to carry out for me. Something I myself should have done long time ago, but did not, and have suffered for it. Look at me,' he said with a sudden severity, 'I am mess. Just like you. Although perhaps a little wiser. And luckier, it seems. This house of mine may be rotting, but it does not yet resemble creek of muck that you are currently up.' He chuckled.

'What do you want?'

'Simple act of religious observance,' said Mikoyan. 'I will explain. It concerns one of my ancestors. Her history has been passed down through my family for hundreds of years. Most of what I know I was told by my grandfather as he lay dying in Paris in days of Commune.

'My ancestor met her death long time ago, long way from here, in murderous circumstances. She was buried without head. This is great insult, and has afflicted my family ever since. I myself have had to suffer curse of immobility for forty years. Every time I go out of doors bad luck and sickness troubles me. I had puncture on way to funeral, even. And times when I have been forced to travel further away have been dangerous and full of enemy.' He paused as a small cat, which had been exercising its claws on the rug at his feet, jumped into his lap. Stroking the animal, he went on: 'My family is very old. It has outlived more empires than you could name. We are first known of in Khazakstan, east of Caspian, six thousand years ago. We have been travelling ever since. This is reason we survived. Civilisations have come and gone while we Mikoyans have jogged on: sea has turned to land, swamps turned to fields, fields to forest and forest to desert. We have survived wars, floods, famine, and genocide. Ha!' Mikoyan laughed. 'But I am here today. Good afternoon, young sir!' And he gave a little bow. 'Is not weather beautiful? God has smiled on me today. I will have another cup of coffee to celebrate.'

And he did.

'What do you want me to do?'

'Something my family has been unwilling or unable to do for hundreds of years,' replied the man. 'Now, my brothers and sisters are all dead or lost, and I myself am in unfit condition for such undertaking. Please, you must take head, find grave, and reunite with body. Then its soul will no longer suffer and I shall be able to travel in peace. I think you will be able to do this, even though your present exploit has landed you deep in aforementioned galoshes.'

Whatever a galosh was, he had the drift of Mikoyan's bizarre idiom. But then the man said, 'Unfortunately your associate has made his escape with head, so you must first find it and bring it back to me. Then we will have dinner, and then you will go.'

♥

He walked down the hill to Gimpton Creek. When he came to White's yard he found Ruth busy loading up her van. It was dusk and swallows flitted about the yard. Ruth looked at him blankly and said, 'Paul's looking for you.' She heaved a large box full of rocks into the back of the vehicle. Inside already was a toolbox and a backpack.

'Going away then?'

'Sure am.'

'Smart van.'

'Yeah. Snip. Can't wait to put some miles between me and that jumped-up pile of pipedreams Paul, his boat, his schemes and all who sail with him. You really piss me off too. You're as dumb as the rest of them.'

She banged down the heavy wooden box and slid it inside with a shriek of nails on steel.

'You're such a turkey,' she said, 'What are you waiting for?

Get on over to Phyllida's boat and join in the squalor.' She climbed in and started the engine.

'Hang on,' he said.

'What?' she said coldly.

'Where are you going?'

'Anywhere there's tourists. Why?'

'Was there a little runt of a guy unloading stuff here?'

'Yeah. Paul took a bunch of it over to Phyllida. Probably took a condom, too.'

'Was there a head in a jar?'

'A what?'

He told her what had happened.

'It figures,' she said. 'Let's see what we can do.'

In the boatshed she rummaged about under the hull while the dog Buster barked and snarled at him from the end of its tether. Ruth emerged with a large, cork-stoppered belljar. Floating within, in some kind of translucent fluid, was a human head. Its eyes were open, its mouth very slightly so. It sported a shock of black curly hair and a green bandanna. It had been severed sharply at the neck. He stared at it, fascinated, and smiled. 'Nice headscarf.'

'These too,' Ruth said. She had an armload of pictures. 'Come on, let's go before I shoot that dog and torch the place.'

Mikoyan entertained them in his dining room. The roof was open to the sky. Pigeons were roosting on the decaying rafters. Dinner was a plateful of squid in batter. It was like eating rubber worms. A lump of guano fell from above and landed on Ruth's plate with a splat. She observed it calmly for a moment and then looked at their host. 'Nice place you've got here Mr Mikoyan, you ought to take more care of it.'

Mikoyan wiped his mouth with a napkin. 'It is just building,' he said. 'These things are temporary affairs. They come and go. What do I care? Why should I repair? In fifty, hundred or thousand years time someone else will only let it go to ruin, or drive tank through it, or blow it up.'

The moon rose and spread its pewter hue over the candlelit room. Mikoyan served coffee. He lit a cigar and stared thoughtfully at the head in the jar. 'Sometimes she seems to plead,' he said, 'and sometimes to accuse.'

Then he swivelled his pod-like eyes on Theo.

'I give you three months in which to return this to its rightful place. Please do not betray my trust.'

'Hey,' Ruth addressed the old man abruptly, 'let me get this straight. You're not interested in recovering your property? It's just sitting out there on the water under your nose.'

Mikoyan shrugged. 'It is insured,' he said simply. 'You see, I always prefer more abstract forms of wealth. Figures in a bank account... knowledge... experience... love...'

There was a silence.

'So where's the grave?' Ruth said.

Mikoyan drew on his cigar and exhaled slowly. The smoke enfurled the jar like an affectionate fog. 'You are clearly enterprising people,' he said, 'I am sure you will succeed.'

'But where's the rest of her buried?' he asked.

'Oh, I don't know that,' said Mikoyan.

Ruth threw her hands up in despair. 'Oh that's great. Thank you very much.'

'But–' said Mikoyan, 'my grandfather once told me story about someone who does...

'Three hundred years ago,' he explained, 'My family lived in what is now part of London. Shortly after time of Great Fire they let room to young woman who had come originally to sell them painting. This woman had no friends or family, yet strangely enough she was scholar. Always she was reading and writing. She eventually left to enter convent. But before she went she told one of my uncles of gypsy's head which had spoken to her in tavern and told her of where and how it had met its fate. This uncle attached no importance to story and remembered no details except for description of head itself, which she had in her possession and showed to him. By time he mentioned incident to rest of family, young woman had disappeared. But others in my family immediately recognised description of head she had shown to my uncle. Head was member of family, killed long ago. They must reclaim and give it rightful burial with rest of body. They searched and they searched, and it was in this part of country that head was retrieved. But they still did not know where grave was. They prayed to head to speak to them. They made altar for it and heaped flowers around it and burned incense. But none of this worked. They also tried to find scholar woman, and visited every convent in Europe, but they could not find her. Eventually they gave up and resigned themselves to head's silence, and to dreadful luck which has plagued we Mikoyans to this day. We have been despised, spat upon and humiliated, imprisoned and tortured. Our children born with deformities. I myself was lucky to escape concentration camp where I lost most of my relatives…'

Mikoyan's voice trailed off and he gave a wistful smile. 'Deep galoshes,' he sighed. 'Yes, deep, deep, bottomless galoshes.'

Then he went on. 'It is scholar woman who holds key. I am sure that somewhere, her diaries will have survived her, and that they must contain account of her encounter with my unfortunate ancestor. We know woman's first name: Katie. And there is one more thing,' he said, showing them a small oil painting in an old gilt frame. 'This is picture of her. This is painting she sold my forebears.'

In the picture, a striking young woman with dark eyes and smouldering red hair stood holding a broadsword. Prone at her feet lay a bearded man. The panelled and draped room was low-lit, the figures rendered in subtle chiaroscuro. Behind the woman, a door was open and beyond it a chequered-tiled hallway led to another distant chamber, and beyond that another, this furthest room appearing to be flooded with daylight.

'We do not know who painted it,' said Mikoyan, 'there is no signature. It is possibly Dutch – style is similar. Technique is very accomplished.'

'And this is all we've got to go on?' said Ruth.

'I can tell you nothing more,' said Mikoyan. 'I myself have done too little, and probably too late.'

A flurry of leaves descended from the sky and settled across the remains of the meal, the cork-stoppered, wax-sealed jar, and the painting.

'And now if you will excuse me I wish to go to bed,' said Mikoyan. He rose from his seat and snuffed out the candles. 'I advise you to go to London and discover who painted this Katie. He may have left records of his models.'

'That's obvious,' said Ruth.

'I am glad you can spot obvious,' said Mikoyan. 'But obvious is like deer in forest. You can see it, but can you catch it?'

'What if I can't do this for you?' Theo said.

Mikoyan smiled. 'Then you will live your life at bottom of Wellington's boot.'

He saw them to the van.

'One thing,' he said as they moved off. 'Take old man's advice – loosen your jeans, eat more yoghurt, and study Nietzsche. It will help.'

TWO

4. THERE'LL ALWAYS BE AN ENGLAND

'WHAT DO we call it, then?'

He sat with the jar on his knees as they drove along an empty two-lane highway, high in the hills. A string of silver cats' eyes snaked out in front of them.

'It's a *she*, Theo, show some respect.'

'Marie as in Antoinette?'

'Don't be so crass.'

'Jayne as in Mansfield?'

'Shut the fuck up.'

'You think it really does talk?'

'Weirder things happen.'

'But they can't be proved. They're imaginary.'

'OK,' said Ruth. 'Imagine I'm sounding the horn.'

'All right.'

'There you are – you just heard it. If you imagined that that head told you where the rest of her was buried, wouldn't you act on it?'

'I might.'

'Shit,' she said suddenly. The engine had cut out and they were drifting to a halt. She got out, poked around under the bonnet and tried in vain to restart it.

'Know anything about automobiles Theo?'

'Nope. I could imagine it was fixed if you like.'

'What the hell. It can wait till morning. We might as well sleep here.'

He lay under a blanket listening to her snoring from her sleeping bag. As he was nodding off he caught sight of Diana squatting at his feet and rummaging in the box of fossils. She looked up at him.

'Hi,' she said, 'just seeing if there was anybody I knew in here. And listen – I've got some news for you. That woman in the picture? I know her name. But I worked something out, right? It's no good you just listening to me because you won't remember anything when you wake, so what you've got to do is write it down so you'll see it when you wake. Simple, hey? I could kick myself. You know what, for thousands of years I've been trying to get through to a conscious mind. Tried just about everything, but I never spotted the obvious. It's so simple it's crazy, but it just might work, as a friend of mine said when she invented the wheel. See, most people's heads are a complete dingo's dinner, Spaghetti Junction with no directions, and yours is no exception. It was like playing five-dimensional chess with Albert Einstein just to get you coming out with odd little fragments that nobody understands. Hey – did you know I nearly *was* Einstein? I knew his dad, see, and – anyway I'll explain it later. So anyway, I reckoned, what about an idea that's sort of breathtakingly simple? Got a pencil and paper? Copy this–'

♥

The next morning they went looking for a garage. They hadn't gone far when they came to a flatbed truck and trailer parked in a layby. The trailer was a spotless, gleaming, chrome-plated, net-curtained fantasy; the truck was piled high with old fridges and its side was adorned with the word LEVI scribbled in pink felt-tip. Back up in the woods they saw a man driving a knife into the trunk of an oak, carving something. He had a dark, concentrated brow, a blue jaw and a substantial gut. When he saw them approaching he stopped and looked at them curiously.

'Knock-knock,' he said, poker-faced.

'What?' said Ruth.

'Who's there?' Theo said.

'Khan,' said the man.

'Khan who?'

'Khan help you,' he said with a little smile. 'What do you want?'

'I'm looking for a mechanic,' said Ruth.

'Dunno.'

'How about the nearest callbox?' she said.

'Oo… erm… dunno,' he said, fiddling with his knife.

'I guess you don't know about engines either?'

'No, sorry. What, broke down have you?'

'Back up the hill there.'

'Shame.' He looked genuinely sorry. He was giving off a strong smell of bacon which mingled with the fresh scent of the woods the way a truck mingles with a hedgehog. 'Sorry, can't help you.'

But as they were walking away he said 'Wait a mo',' and beckoned them back. Behind him LEVI blazed out from the treetrunk. Several other trunks had also been treated.

'You got any of that wacky baccy?' he inquired gently, blue eyes twinkling.

Ruth shook her head.

'Oh. What you got then? Whizz? CDs? Rolex? Fake'll do. No? Too bad.'

He had now found a biro and was writing LEVI on his wrist.

'It's like this, see,' he said, 'I know motors but I don't work for free, and today like I can't assept money being as it's my little boy's birthday. He's called Levi.' He grinned. 'LEEE-VI,' he chanted, like it was a football team, 'LEEE-VI, LEEE-VI.'

'That's nice,' Theo said. 'How old is he?'

'About two hours. I just come back from the hospital.'

'Congratulations,' Ruth said. 'I've got some fossils.'

'Yeah, fossils, fossils'll do. Where you parked?'

His name was Billy. He reckoned he was a 'True Rom.'

'Some of your mates went by a while ago,' he said. 'Clapped-out old double-decker they had, it could hardly move.' He was fiddling about under the bonnet.

'Mates?'

'Ain't you with them? I thought you was with the comboy, you know. They go up Stonehenge this time of year, get themselves arrested. Stupid bastards. They got no idea how to deal with people, them hippies.'

He eventually got the engine going. 'See, that's all you needed,' he said, pointing, 'a little screw.' He smirked at Theo.

Ruth said, 'Very funny.'

'See, we ain't like them comboy scroungers,' he went on, 'That's all they do, 'kin sponge. We're the real travellers. We work for a living. You want to know a fact? We run the entire scrap metal industry of this country. You'd be surprised at how much is made of scrap. Think about it. Without us, country'd go to rack and ruin. Yeah. Grind to a halt it would. Imagine it. Whole country at a standstill. Chaos. Anarchy.'

'Yeah,' said Ruth, 'and all because you didn't shift a few old washing machines.'

'What fossils you got then?' Billy said, peering into the van. Then he drew back. ' 'kin Hell, what have you got there?' he said, pointing to the stoppered jar.

'Severed head of Marie Antoinette,' Theo told him.

'Straight up?' Billy sat down at the back of the van and rolled a cigarette, his blue jaw glistening with sweat as he radiated fumes of prime Danish. 'Looks like she could do with a fag herself,' he said. ''Ere, you got a nice little money-spinner there, little tent-show, right? Anyway, what about these fossils of yours?'

Ruth pointed to the box.

'Great,' he said, 'but it's a bit heavy to carry.'

'No way, not the whole box,' Ruth said, 'You know how much work there is in those?'

He eventually took a fist-sized ammonite. He said he'd paint it up and use it as a doorstop. ' 'Ere – joke,' he said as he left, 'How do you get a gypsy girl pregnant?'

They didn't know.

'You don't know?' he said. 'And you thought gypsies were stupid.' He grinned at them and walked away, crooning 'Lee-vi,' and writing his son's name on the fossil.

They drove on, and he watched the road signs flash by. The trouble with being on the road was that it reminded of his father, who worked for a company that made these things. With every 'No Through Road', 'No Right Turn', 'No Entry' and 'No Parking' he heard his old man dealing out prohibitions or stunning him with the technical details of a road sign. Such a waste of all that cool reflective material they use.

As they drove up onto the high Wiltshire plain, rolling pastures and military camps spread out in the wide valleys below, he observed Ruth more closely. He had long clocked the essentials – she wore old jeans and workclothes with labels he'd never heard of, plimsolls for crying out loud, and no makeup – and had looked no further. Well now, he thought, she may be scruffy, but she's quite smart. And that looks like a nice pair of bubs under there. Weird to get a thrill from someone who had a hairy mole on her cheek and calloused hands. He wondered what attractions she held for White. Around her neck was a plain silver chain which vibrated with the flesh it encircled. The skin was tanned and plumpish. He pictured her and White in bed. He thought about sex and he thought about families. Who invented the family? Nobody could tell you, least of all Jesus, Mary and Joseph. Mass was a soap with the same story every week. He didn't tune in anymore.

'You religious?' he asked Ruth.

'Kind of,' she said. 'Sometimes I feel a little Buddhist, sometimes I feel a little pagan. Sometimes I feel like Joan of godamm Arc.'

'What do you mean?'

She slammed the stick into third and they sped up a long, steep incline past the roar of crawling trucks. She had to shout above the noise:

'You don't understand what it's like to be a woman.'

Oh God, he thought, she's one of those.

'What about sex?' he shouted.

'What about it?'

He shrugged.

'I'll tell you about sex,' she shouted. 'Isaac Newton, OK? Out in his garden one autumn afternoon? What if instead of sitting there with his notebooks and stuff, he was messing with the drawstrings of some big-bosomed cutie? He would have missed the apple falling, that's what, and science would have missed the boat. And can you imagine Einstein saying, "Gosh I'm sorry I don't have time to figure out relativity right now, I got a date with a terrific piece of tush this afternoon." Or Amelia Erhart saying, "Godammit, I don't feel like flying round the world today, I think I'll go make out with Radclyffe Hall instead." Or Cory Aquino saying, "Ah, to hell with building a new Philippines, I'll give Benazir Bhutto a call and we'll have a candlelit supper and then maybe watch TV in bed." Or Bill Clinton – no, bad example, better make that Hillary… anyway, see, all these folks – the guys making things happen – wouldn't be so rare if the rest of us got our act together.'

'Bollocks. They're all at it.'

'Yeah I guess so. Which accounts for Planet Shit Creek here.'

At the hill's summit she pulled into a layby with a phone box. 'I'm going to call someone I know who knows about pictures,' she said. 'You got something to write on?'

He handed her a chocolate wrapper.

'Is this your writing on it?' she said.

There were a few lines of odd rune-like lettering. No it wasn't his writing, but it was his biro.

'You got a secret language too, huh? It's not Russian, not Arabic. Maybe Thai? Maybe Aztec?'

'Maybe someone at the chocolate factory.'

'Who has your biro and is also an Inca priestess in her spare time. No. You wrote it in your sleep. You are a very weird person.'

'Think there's any money in it?' he said.

'Put it this way,' she said, 'you either win or you lose. There's no in between.'

❤

The village of Great Worth was holding its annual fête. Its streets were lined with stalls and festooned with bunting. Merrymakers had spilled out from the Worthy Arms and were gathered round a team of Morris Men; elsewhere the Bishop was attracting a throng of admirers at the home-made chutney stall, and the local actress was surrounded by an equally large following at the tombola. On the village green the annual cricket match against Little Worth was making its steady progress, and nearby the village infants were bouncing around on a giant castellated inflatable like coloured ping-pong balls. Frocks and frills and summer hats, blazers and shirtsleeves and sandals and lemonade – and the Worth Brass Band striking up with *There'll always be an England*.

'Time to make some money,' said Ruth.

They set up the fossil stall at the edge of the green and soon began to attract interest. This included that of the bishop, who was at a nearby refreshment stand with the vicar and his wife.

'Who are those scruffs?' he inquired of the vicar as he sipped his tea.

'I'm sure I don't know, your Grace,' the vicar replied.

'They're hippies,' the bishop said definitively.

The vicar pulled a long face and nodded sadly while his wife, a small, thin, jittery woman, looked fearfully at the serious expressions worn by the bishop and her husband. In her jacket pocket her hand gripped a small paperweight bearing the imprint of a mesozoic fern. She had just bought it from Ruth as a present for her husband. 'Oh dear,' she said plaintively, and tried to change the subject to that of Mrs Sparkford's treacle tarts.

Ruth went to freshen up and left him running the stall. After he'd sold a fifth pair of turretella earrings (sprayed metallic blue – teenage shit, Ruth called them, but they sell) he realised this was all very good for her, but he was getting low on cash himself. He remembered what Billy had said. Why not? So he set up the head in the back of the van and draped a blanket across the back doors for a curtain. He propped up an improvised sign: THE SEVERED HEAD, gave it a bit of barking – 'A thousand years old and perfectly preserved… from the depths of time her eyes stare into yours… the mysteries of the Orient revealed… Dare you meet its gaze? A pound to find out…' and drummed up a fair bit of custom. There were shrieks and giggles as he let them part the curtain to view the baleful sight.

71

Most people thought it was wax. Some tried to reach in and touch the jar. He threatened them with a curse if they did.

Then the local actress – a kindly-looking grey-haired woman who was always starring on TV as a kindly-looking grey-haired woman – was persuaded to take a peek. She took one look at the head, let out a gurgle of disgust, turned away and went to find the bishop.

'This is disgraceful,' said the bishop to the actress. 'Disgraceful,' he said to the vicar. The vicar nodded sadly again.

'Where is the constable?' demanded the bishop.

'Oh dear,' said the vicar's wife.

Ruth returned to find the Great Worth constable having a quiet word with Theo while the local retired colonel huffed around urging his immediate arrest. Taking the cop's advice to depart, they took down the stall and loaded the van.

'You must be out of your mind,' she hissed at him.

'Easiest dosh I ever earned,' he said.

'You're a total dork, Theo. You have the common sense of a gastropod.'

'And a quick twenty quid. And you've sold stuff too, so cool down, Ruthie.'

'Don't call me *Ruthie*,' she said as she made to turn the ignition key.

Then the constable put his head to the window.

'This your vehicle then is it Miss?' he inquired.

'Yes it is, officer,' said Ruth.

The constable cocked an eyebrow. 'American, are we?'

'Yes, *I* am.'

'I see.' He gave her a cold, searching look, took a step back, looked at the van, stepped forward again and said, 'May I see your passport and your driving licence please, Miss?'

'It's *Mzzz*,' said Ruth, 'and no you may not.'

And so saying she started the engine, crunched it into gear lurched it onto the road and *Mzzzd* off through the village, leaving a curious crowd and the constable talking into his radio.

'Ruth, you're out of your brain.'

'I didn't have any choice.'

Beyond the village she turned off the main road and headed

up into the hills. The sky was darkening and a storm was blowing up.

'I've got no licence. My visa ran out about a year ago, plus I've no work permit,' she said. 'I'd have been deported on the spot.'

'Instead you've got every noddy car for miles looking for you.'

'It'll be OK. We'll get this thing resprayed.'

'What do you mean *we*?' he said.

Heavy rain now lashed across the windscreen. She craned her neck to peer through the rhythm of the wipers. 'You're quitting are you? Suit yourself. You're a total invertebrate anyway.'

'You're not exactly a normal species yourself.'

'Normal! It's normal people who've turned the entire globe planet into one giant toxic trash heap! I have no desire to be normal!' she shouted.

'There's no chance of that!' he shouted back.

'Shut up Theo, you've obviously got nothing constructive to say,' she said, with sudden calm.

Equally calmly, he said: 'That's the law up ahead.'

A white van was parked in the distance. Ruth slid to a halt, turned round and drove back to where a smaller road turned off. They went off up this steep lane.

'They didn't see us,' he said.

'It's *us* now is it?' she said.

The countryside turned empty, wet and windswept. Rolling downs and static, soaking sheep. After some miles of this, Theo noticed a small group of ancient motor coaches parked in a field, a wisp of smoke rising behind the hedgerow. He told her to pull in.

'Why?'

'Keep us out of sight for a while. And maybe they can help with the van.'

The small field they turned into had been churned to a quagmire. Outside one of the old buses a small group in bedraggled greys and blacks and army surplus blankets was sitting around a paltry fire which was slowly losing its battle against the drizzling rain. Ruth and Theo picked their way towards them through the mud. 'Here we go,' he said, 'Trench Zombies from World War One.'

'Keep your voice down,' she said. 'Hi,' she smiled at a young woman who was breastfeeding her baby.

'Hi,' said the woman.

A little girl ran up to them and squealed aggressively, 'What do *you* want?'

'I need my van resprayed. Fast,' Ruth said to the woman.

'Nice weather for it,' she replied.

'Try Harris,' said the boy next to her. 'In the Bedford.' Harris had a thick droopy moustache, round shoulders and bandy legs. He resembled a small bear. He welcomed them to his bus and bade them sit down. The vehicle had been stripped and refurbished as one long living room. The entire length of one wall was occupied by bookshelves. The floor was carpeted in greengrocers' grass. Harris, who was wearing cricket pads, made them tea and rolled himself a cigarette. Hung in the windows behind him were oil paintings of country cricket matches: sightscreens, church spires, blue skies. One also stood unfinished on a nearby easel. Harris' voice was deep and nasal.

'So,' he said, settling down, 'come from Great Worth have you?'

'Yes we have,' Ruth said, 'In difficult circumstances. I need a respray.'

Harris smiled. 'I should say you need a respray. I should say you need bloody fumigating, coming from there. Not exactly Glastonbury, is it? More Heal's Yard than Neal's Yard, eh?'

'Sons of bitches wouldn't let us trade.'

'Well, I'm a painter, as you can see,' said Harris, 'and I've got a spraygun, and I've got some cans in the belly box that should do the trick. Only thing is, firstly it's pissing with rain–'

'We could fix up a shelter.'

'And the other thing is, you just might be attracting Billy Law up here.'

He gave them a good long look. Then he rose and stretched his arms.

'I shall have to consult the Book of Wisden,' he announced, and lumbered over to a section of shelves lined from top to bottom with yellow volume after yellow volume. Harris closed his eyes and picked one out.

'Right. I open it at random, plant my finger on the page, and read – "…and the famous victory in the second test at Port-of-Spain was largely due to May's decision to bat first despite the lowering clouds which hung over the ground when the match began…"'

And he closed the book and returned it to the shelf. 'I think the oracle has spoken clearly enough. Yeah, I'll rig up some plastic. Never lies, Wisden. Spirit of cricket speaking. Spirit of Albion.'

'Lovely day for a game,' Theo said, pointing at Harris' padded legs.

'Always got to be ready for a match,' he replied. Then he beckoned them to the window. 'See out there?' And he pointed over the hedges to the far horizon, where a cluster of dark shapes was visible on the skyline.

'Stonehenge,' Harris said, and paused to let the weight of the word settle down. 'That's why we're here. It's like Jerusalem, see? Everybody's fighting over Jerusalem, Christians, Jews and Muslims. And that over there is our very own Jerusalem, right in the middle of our very own green-and-pleasant. Everybody wants it. The Druids want it. The astrologers want it. The archaeologists want it. English poncy Heritage wants it. The police want it. It's surrounded by razor wire, dogs and road-blocks. Every year there's pitch battles. And what are they fighting for? You may well ask.'

Harris puffed sagely at his cigarette.

'A load of old rocks from South Wales,' he pronounced. 'And yet there's power on that spot, else why all the fuss? They reckon it's a cosmic calendar, a sacrificial compound, an ancient temple, a source of spiritual healing, a nice little earner… you name it, everybody's got a theory. It's ridiculous, I'd say.'

'It's too bad,' said Ruth.

'Yes,' said Harris, 'Because nobody's admitting to what it really is, right? Because Stonehenge is the remains of the world's first cricket pavilion.'

75

'Naturally,' said Theo.

'Incontrovertible,' said Harris, 'Look at the stones – shaped like wickets, aren't they? It's so glaringly obvious you don't notice at first.'

Outside they fixed up a plastic awning under the trees and Harris primed his paint gun. 'That field on this side of the stones,' he explained, 'was the pitch. There's a marker stone on this side. On Midsummer Day at dawn the sun rises over that stone and shines directly down the wicket. That's when and where the primal test match was held. Oldest English ritual, cricket. Soul of the nation.'

'Get real,' Theo responded as he masked the van's windows.

'I'll tell you this,' said Harris, pointing the spraygun at the vehicle. 'The game was last played at Stonehenge a long time ago when England was a free country, and until we play there again, this land is going to the shithouse dogs.' He said this decisively, and squeezed the trigger.

'For Chrissakes, Harris,' Ruth said, 'you're painting my van bright pink.'

'Only colour available I'm afraid.'

'That's real discreet, that is. Why don't you paint COME AND GET ME COPPERS on the back?'

'Cost you extra,' said Harris.

He was slow and methodic. It was nearly dark by the time he'd finished.

'The beauty of this pink,' he observed, 'is that it's so obvious, that it isn't obvious. Like the Stonehenge pavilion. Like the Purloined Letter.'

'Harris, we're both broke,' said Ruth. 'I'm going to have to pay you in ammonites.'

Harris looked thoughtful. 'Cretaceous?' he said.

'No. Fifty pound's worth of Jurassic green.'

'That'll do nicely,' said Harris. 'And I'll throw in fresh numberplates for free.'

He invited them to stay for dinner. Sitting round the fire that night, Theo produced the chocolate wrapper and asked if anyone knew about runes or whatever the marks were. The woman who had earlier been feeding her baby, who claimed she was a witch and had a serpent tattooed on her cleavage, eagerly examined the piece of paper. 'Definitely some kind of matriarchal script,' she pronounced.

Harris then considered the calligraphy. 'It's a primitive cricket scoring system,' he said. 'Where did you find it?'

'I think I wrote it. In my sleep.'

'He speaks in tongues, too,' Ruth said. This brought a smattering of murmurs, a hoot of laughter and a low whistle.

Harris said 'I think I speak for all of us when I say that we're honoured to have you here, old son. Your visit could well be construed as an utterance from the oracle that is Albion. You and your palaeontological partner are definitely visitors of good omen. You are the Umpires of the New Age. Have some elderflower wine.' He passed the bottle. 'As you know,' he went on, 'tonight is Midsummer's Eve. At dawn, we shall be trotting over to that ancient pasture to partake of the annual cricket ritual on the very ground where it was first performed so long ago when men were men, women were women, and you could still be LBW for padding up outside off-stump. Would you care to umpire for us?'

'They won't let you get near the place,' Ruth said.

'We'll see about that,' said the witch.

'Be a sticky wicket, but we'll get a few overs in,' said Harris. 'Leather–'

'—the stag,' said the witch.

'–meets willow–'

'–the goddess–'

'–in the glorious dawn. And the Druids will brew up for us in the pavilion.'

♥

It was after midnight when they bedded down in the van. He had biro and paper at the ready this time.

'You don't seem too keen on this cricket lark,' he said. 'I thought you'd be interested, being as they're old rocks.'

'The only thing that's fossilized about Stonehenge is what it stands for. It's bullshit,' she said. 'They ought to demolish the whole tamale and drive a freeway through it.'

'Yeah?'

'Yeah. Who needs it? It was commissioned and operated by the masters of neolithic agribusiness, using sweated labour and forced breeding. Agribiz never changes. It brings disease and disfigurement wherever it shows up. And those guys back then make Monsanto look like angels.'

'Yeah, I thought you'd have a theory,' he said. Then he said, 'Where exactly are you from, Ruth?'

'Upstate Massachusetts,' she replied. 'My folks are academics.'

'Why don't you want to go home?'

'I'm having too much fun elsewhere. I'm going to Australia next.'

'Why's that?'

'They've got the oldest rocks in the world,' she said.

'How spiffing.'

'You don't know the first thing about rocks,' she said dismissively. 'See, rocks are like jewellery boxes. Like libraries. Billion-year-long movies. Zoos. Arboretums. Comic strips. And after I got bored just climbing them I found out that they're like great big burgers with all these amazing and beautiful fillings... ammonites, belemnites, echinoids, bryozoans... and you dig them up, and you look for ones with the best crystallisation, and keep 'em raw or you mess about with them a little, and folks buy them.'

She fondled a long, blue, torpedo-like polished stone.

'I don't sell them all. Not the real beauties. I keep those. Kind of an investment. I got some real rarities. You know what I really want to do? Discover a new fossil. A new species. It would be named after me. Groovy, huh? Maybe one of those dragon-tailed trilobites – *Paradoxides Ruthae*, pre-pre-Cambrian, older than anything found before. Hey, I'd be famous. I'd change the course of scientific thinking! But maybe just a new starfish, else one of those incredible sea-lilies...'

She turned the blue bullet in her fingers as she mused.

'I dream about fossils,' she said. 'I dream I'm on the sea bed, and it's crowded with people all moving about, and they're all made of crystal, and they have rubies and emeralds for eyes, and their mouths are made of coral, and there are huge shellfish and ferns waving about, and yellow polyps, and electric blue jellyfish, and hoplites and hamites and pavlovias and turrilites and nautili... and then this indescribably beautiful creature which I can only *feel* the presence of. I just *know* it's there but I can never see it or touch it. It's so frustrating.'

She sighed and looked at him. 'What do you dream about, boy? Hey there, are you awake?'

He was well asleep. She moved closer to him and studied his face intently.

It was still dark when he was ruthlessly shaken from his slumbers. She had him by the shoulders and was calling his name.

'Look, you just wrote something. What were you dreaming?'

'I can't remember.'

'You started to mumble – I couldn't figure it out – and then you wrote this.'

The pen was still in his fingers. She grabbed the paper and scrutinised it closely. 'Drew, more like,' she said. 'Bunch of symbols of some sort. Mean anything to you?'

He looked at the markings. There was a spiral, a rectangle with one jagged edge, and a group of stick-people.

'I've been watching you since you fell asleep about an hour back,' she said. 'The interesting thing is you went through REM, which is when your eyes twitch and the really bizarre dreams happen, but you were out of it when this happened. Hey, this is amazing. A totally new sleep event!'

'Maybe they'll name it after you.'

'I'm not kidding. This could be a breakthrough. We know nothing about sleep, nothing. We don't even know *why* we sleep. Something we spend a third of our lives at and we don't even know what it's for, why we're doing it or what's happening when we're doing it. Deep oceans, deep space, deep sleep. We're pig ignorant of all three.' She grabbed the paper back. 'And deep time,' she added. 'All we have to do is figure out this cryptogram.' Then she looked over at the head-in-the-jar. 'Maybe it's something to do with her? Maybe the head is communicating with you.'

'Don't creep me out.'

'Maybe she doesn't like the way you've abused her.'

'Abused her? What?'

'You've got to admit that what you did today was pretty outrageous. Personally, I'd call it pimping. Pure exploitation. *Late rape.*'

He sat up at this. 'It's dead, for crying out loud. What's the difference between it and one of your precious stones?'

'She's a person, you jerk, and she's *un*dead. How would you like that to happen to you?'

'It's for her own good,' he reasoned. 'I'm supposed to bury her, and I've got to survive.'

'She's probably telling you to stop treating her like a whore.'

He looked at the head. It was becoming suffused with a lurid, pulsating ultramarine light.

'Is it just me,' he said, 'or is that thing glowing now?'

'What? Wow! Hey, no, – look out there.'

A van was pulling up at the field gate. It had a flashing blue lamp on the roof. It spilled out a score of helmeted figures who immediately raced towards the nearest vehicles and began smashing in the windows with their batons. There were screams from within. Harris appeared from his bus and despite his bat, pads and helmet was instantly knocked to the ground in a flailing of batons. From another coach a woman was shouting 'There are children in here!' and the invaders were screaming back abuse. Dogs barked, children wailed and objects shattered as Billy Law went about wrecking the interiors of the mobile homes. A boy came at them wielding Harris' dropped bat but cricket lost out to baseball, willow to aluminium, and he went down with a cracked and bleeding skull.

Ruth was already clambering into the driver's seat and starting up the van.

'The gate's blocked,' he said. 'Back up – there's a track through those trees.'

She reversed crazily through the trees, slithering and sliding along the track until they lurched out onto a road. 'Which way?' she said.

'We could always ask a policeman,' he said.

5. FAX OF LIFE

THE BRIGHT pink van rolled along the leafy avenues of Holland Park – here an embassy, there a prep school – and pulled up outside a large private house.

'This is Nounou's place. She runs a gallery. The bitch makes a fortune,' Ruth said.

A maid let them in. In the kitchen they found a dark-haired woman with sepia skin sitting at the table in a silk dressing gown. Nounou was busy painting her toenails.

'Paul's turned to slime,' Ruth told her immediately, as though she was already in mid-conversation, 'and as far as I'm concerned he's history.'

'So you said.'

'And Theo here is weird.'

'You want me to mount a freak show?' said her friend.

'And he has the head I told you about. Show her the head, Theo.'

He placed the jar on the table. A Burmese cat, as haughty as its owner, paced across to examine it cooly and briefly before jumping onto Nounou's shoulder and nuzzling her ear as if reporting back. Nounou and her cat both agreed that the head was 'rather beautiful.'

Then he brought out the painting Mikoyan had given him. Their host examined it for a minute or two before pronouncing on it. 'At first,' she declared, 'I thought it must be modern, a phoney, somebody's idea of an academic joke. You see for style

81

and technique it looks like seventeenth-century Dutch genre – good Protestant burghers and their possessions – but the subject is completely wrong. Too Catholic. They didn't like religious paintings, in fact they went around destroying them. They were buying pictures of little girls at the harpsichord, or portraits of bankers, or studies of spotlessly-kept backyards and tidy interiors. Very domestic. Very cool, like Vermeer, de Hooch... But this is rather bloody business messing up the drawing room, isn't it? Bloody and biblical. Judith and Holofernes: she's a spy in the camp. She gives him the come-on and then slices off his head. Any prospective buyer would have taken one look at it and left the studio fast. They liked cosier stuff. This is like trying to sell a box of chocolates with a picture of the death of God on the lid. But the thing is...' she examined the painting more closely '...I don't think this *is* modern. It's a genuine period joke. I can't see a signature, but it may be hidden somewhere. You think it was done in London? What did you say the model's name is? Katie? Some of the models of the time are known, but I never heard of any Katie.'

'Too bad,' Ruth said. 'But listen, I want to try something with this gizmo. Little experiment with Theo here.'

She produced a tape machine, set it on the table and pressed record. Then she took from her pocket a cut and polished ammonite and handed it to him.

'OK,' she told him, 'Just look at this real close. Look at the crystal structure. Concentrate hard. See how the crystals are different colours as you follow the spiral round.'

He went with it. He heard Nounou say, 'It's an extraordinary figure, isn't it?' And something rattled on the table. 'Like this corkscrew,' she said, '...the bottom of that slipware bowl... Aboriginal acrylics... labyrinths... tornados...'

'Pasta shapes,' Ruth said.

'...Corn Dollys... DNA...'

He observed the ammonite segment by segment. Each crystalline chamber suggested a tiny glass womb containing a minuscule silicon foetus; each of these wombs was imperceptibly smaller than the previous one. You could see the complete regression in the shape of the slimming spiral, but each step of

82

the way was impossible to perceive as such. He opened his mouth to express this, but what came out was gibberish. He felt his mouth taking on shapes, his throat vibrating to frequencies over which he had no control. He sat there listening to himself talking bollocks.

'See?' said Ruth triumphantly. 'He's psychic. You can set him off.'

'But that's not Latin,' Nounou pointed out.

They let him gabble on a while longer before slapping him out of it. Nounou asked him how long he'd had this knack. She made it sound like a skill.

'I never heard any language like that before,' Ruth said, 'Lets see what happens when we play it back at half-speed.'

Slowed down, the sound of his voice seemed more normal. The syllables were clear and precise. But they made no sense.

'It sounds almost like Russian, but it isn't,' Nounou said.

'Maybe it's a language that doesn't exist anymore,' Ruth suggested. 'I mean if we're talking regression, we don't know how far back he's going, do we?'

But Nounou quickly help them figure out the cryptogram. 'Another spiral,' she said. 'A Catherine wheel. What did you say the model's name was? Katie? There you are. You wrote her name in your sleep. Catherine something-something. Saw and stick-people. So we look in the phone book for names beginning with Saw.'

Sawford?... Sawston?... Saw*kin*. The stick-people were kin.

'There you are,' said Nounou, 'Katie Sawkin, late of London Town. And – let me get this right – this head of yours spoke to her three hundred years ago and told her where its body was buried?'

'According to the old geezer,' he said.

'Do you believe him?'

'Theo's a Catholic,' said Ruth. 'If wine is blood and mothers are virgins and some mysoginistic, withered old gangster in the Vatican is infallible, then a severed head can talk. Right, Thee?'

He hated the way she called him that.

'Where do I start looking for this diary of hers?' he said.

'Libraries, for a start,' Nounou told him.

It sounded like a lot of tedious spadework. 'You want to give me a hand?' he asked Ruth.

'I've got problems of my own,' she said. 'And I've got a question to ask you.'

'What?'

'Will you marry me?'

'What?'

'Will you *marry* me?'

'Bit sudden, isn't it?'

'My visa's expired, right? Only way I can stay is to marry an Englishman. God help me.'

He smiled. 'If you don't like the English–'

'Stop messing around, Thee, this is serious,' she said sharply. 'And anyway the best thing about this country is that it's full of foreigners.'

'Don't call me "Thee".'

'Listen, dickhead, are you going to marry me or not?'

'Well… It's not that I don't like you–'

'That's got nothing to do with it, you turkey.'

'It just feels a bit immoral, that's all.'

'Theo, I'll be deported. Isn't that immoral? Don't you think it's things like national boundaries that have got the world into all this mess? Don't you believe in freedom of travel? Or maybe to you I'm just a white wog, huh?'

'It's me that gets called a wop.'

Frustratedly she turned to her friend. 'See what I mean? A good little Catholic boy. Goddammit, Theo, how can you swallow all that shit? In this day and age?'

'What do *you* believe in, Ruth?'

'I know what I don't buy,' she said, 'and that's some paranoid grandad sitting on a cloud dishing out deranged and destructive mumbo-jumbo. How can you swallow such a construction?

He told her there was more to it than that.

'Too right,' she said, 'A whole heap more baloney than I could shake a stick at.' She shook her head in bewilderment. 'The way the church muscles in on marriage like it invented it,' she said, 'Some nerve. Hey, Nounou, you know what I heard the other day? These English teach religion in their schools.

84

How's that for brainwashing? Anyway – you know anyone I could marry? I'd pay.'

Morose and bitter, she was repeatedly kicking a table leg. Nounou put an arm around her shoulder. And then a red-bearded man appeared in the doorway. He wore a black silk dressing gown.

'Lassie,' he grinned at Ruth, 'I could be *very* eligible. How much are you offering?'

It was Try-It. He still wore the medallion. What the fuck was he doing here? Slipping and sliding in Nounou's silken sheets, if the disdainful dealer's 'hello darling' was anything to go by.

Theo looked at Ruth again. He'd had enough of this yank psycho-dyke from Hell. He'd do the rest of the job on his own.

♥

Five minutes later he was gliding down the tube escalator with the head and the painting in a Safeway bag.

There was something uncomfortable, too, about the train. It was crowded, but that wasn't it. Soon he realised he was the only man in the carriage. Nothing but women here: old women, little girls, but mostly young women. Sitting and standing and swaying. Some talking, some reading, some staring ahead with zombie-eyes. The carriage was a-glitter with their adornments, and swum in a haze of Charlie, Miss Girl, Tweed, Checkmate, EarthMagic and Bodyshop, Chanel and Affaire. It was unbearable. Opium, Nuits D'Or, Gotcha, Patchouli and Frankincense all crowded in on his pained olfactorium. Females – tossing their heads, pursing their lips. Wriggling out and wriggling in in skirts and tights and Kinelle jeans at every station. He began to count these stations: nine stops and not a single male got in the carriage. At the tenth a bluerinsed woman tottered in with a Yorkshire Terrier in her arms. He thought he had a chance here. He tried to get a good view of the quivering red creature but in the end he had to ask the owner what sex it was. It was a bitch. Wasn't it just.

Women. At Liverpool Street mainline he had to walk to the far end of the train to find a coach without a female in it. Then he rumbled home. He wanted some men around him, some deeper voices, squarer shoulders, Adam's Apples. Walking home from the station he saw Fat Ronnie drive past in his all-white cabriolet. No good at all. The trouble was, he reflected, blokes never know how to dress. They doll themselves up like overgrown babies and zoom around in glorified prams. On the other hand, what do *I* do? Babble like a sprog. In speeded-up Mesopotamian or whatever.

And now here was a bloke, here in Shepherd's Close. His own father, tall and blonde, heaving a ten-foot-wide satellite dish into position on the front – you couldn't call it a lawn. It was a manhole cover with a grass border. The man was puffing about on his knees with a spanner, red-faced and swearing to himself beneath the saucer of black gauze. He didn't notice his son arrive. Theo stood admiring the dish with its needle antenna. It looked like some alien flower, soaking up methane storms on planet Neptune.

'Love the dish, Dad.'

His father looked up. 'Oh, it's you. Give us a hand with this.'

'It don't let much light in the lounge though, does it?'

'Watch your mouth, you.'

Theo ran his fingers along the black mesh. 'No, but it's beautiful, I love it. Pointing up at all that. What do you think's out there, Dad?'

'I'll tell you what's out there. Fifty channels, that's what's out there. Stop taking the piss and hold this, will you?'

'Fifty channels. And I thought it was the infinite glittering cosmos. What's for lunch?'

'You'll get no lunch round here till you pay your way. *Capisce?* So what happened to your great enterprise then? Run out of ideas already?'

'What's up with him?' he asked his mother indoors.

She smiled shyly and cupped her face with rubber-gloved hands. 'I told him I'm pregnant,' she said. Her hands promptly gave birth to an enormous grin, and she threw her arms around him.

'Blimey, at your age? Nice one,' he said. 'Go easy, will you?'

'He says it's the last thing he wants. Stroppy old fool. And you know what? You know what he asks me to do?' Her face was straight again. 'You know,' she said with a glance at her belly, 'You know: the–'

'What, an–?' he said.

'I could not believe it! I – could – not – believe it. But *caro mio*, aren't you happy?'

'Deliriously, Mum.'

'And he will kick you out quick if you don't get a job, you know this?'

'I haven't come back, I'm just picking up some stuff. Going to sell some clothes.'

'You're in trouble. I can tell. You're in trouble.'

'No, really. Everything's fine.'

Over lunch they wound up his old man by speaking Italian. *Capisce* was the only word his father knew.

Then he packed up all the togs he could get into two suitcases, and put the jar in a backpack. He took the train to town, left his baggage in a locker, and went over to King's Cross and found a bed in a hostel – one of fifty old hospital beds laid out in a dusty hall that had once been a gymnasium and still had wallbars. A kid from Belfast who had the neighbouring bed and who had a small puppy with its mouth taped up (NO DOGS was pinned to the wall) advised him to flog his clothes at Camden Market.

That night in the small hours the dormitory was quiet except for the rhythmic workings of fifty pairs of lungs, some in worse shape than others. Freight trucks rolled by down below in the street, and there were distant clanks and hoots from the railway yards. He felt himself being prodded. He sat up in bed. Diana was sitting there. She looked at him and shook her head in despair.

'Jeez this place smells like a massage parlour on the Khosan Road,' she muttered. 'Listen, you – we could have been sleeping in luxury in Holland Park tonight, but instead you have to go and throw a wobbly. Why did you do that? She's a nice kid, Ruth. Not as pretty as me, but... listen – you're not turning queer are you? I don't trust the manager of this place. He'll have you under the arches and on the game before you can say HIV.'

'Queer? Why do you reckon that?'

'Theo. Listen. Don't do it. You don't want to be in a victimised minority, do you? And you want a family, don't you? Beautiful kiddies? Beautiful wife? Beautiful home? Anyone would, right? Yeah. You deserve it, Theo.'

'Never really thought about it much.'

'Jeez.' She shook her head again. 'I don't know about this trend with you civilised people. I mean there you are at eleven years old, all kitted out and raring to go, fine fit fallopians and spanking young spunkbags, and what happens? You're suddenly supposed to pretend it's not happening while at the same time they're selling you a million fantasies on the back of all the toys that come with them. And it turns you into the weirdest creatures. I haven't seen anything like it in fifty billion years of living organisms. You get yourselves turned inside-out, over-anxious and utterly neuroticised. And if you do finally manage to get down to it, what happens? You get one or two sprogs max and spend the rest of your lives fooling around with rubber objects and dangerous chemicals that mess up your bodies and your life. It's too kinky for words. All this contraception. All this homosexuality: pointless.'

'Why should you care?' he said.

'You've got no cause for complacency,' she said angrily. 'Listen, matey, there's been more than one occasion in the past when I've had my work cut out on that front. I'm talking about survival, Theo. You should be grateful. You wouldn't be here now if I hadn't had to persuade a number of your ancestors at different times to plant his plonker in the proper place. We've had some extremely narrow escapes. And if the shirtlifters had their way, the race would end tomorrow.'

'You sound like my old man.'

'Glad you worked out the hieroglyphics, by the way,' she said, 'I'm really excited about that. You realise what it means? For the first time in history people are going to have direct communication with their genetic record. Do you realise what that means? Do you realise how much I can tell you?'

'So what's in it for you?' he said. 'Everybody looks after number one, right?'

She moved closer to him. She was musky and seductive. He

88

felt his crotch bristle. 'Theo, listen. We're in this together. You have a programme inside you – that's me – that goes back to the year fuckin' d-o-t. And now – you can retrieve into it! You're going to shake up the whole world!'

'You got me to scribble out a single name. And working it out was chance and guesswork. That's all.'

'But don't you see what it means once the process is perfected? Can't you understand how much information is going to be available? About every stage of organic development, going back millions of years? It'll just blast us clear of all the petty dimensions we're addicted to. We'll be freed forever, boy.'

She put her arm round him and whispered in his ear: 'We'll be fuckin' *immortal*!'

'No kidding.'

'Quick,' she said, 'Find a pencil. You've got to get all this down–'

But then there was a cataclysm of alarm clock and daylight, and it was morning. He woke remembering nothing. But he did check the piece of paper he had kept by the bed – it was blank.

💗

On top of a bus that wound towards the City, he took some of Mikoyan's advice. So, what helpful hints would Nietzsche have to offer. He opened a copy of *The Genealogy of Morals* at random.

'The distinctive mark of modern souls is not lying but *innocence*, incarnate in lying moralism,' he read. 'To discover this *innocence* everywhere – that may be the most disheartening part of our task.'

In a corner of the Guildhall Library, at one of a multitude of microfilm screens otherwise entirely occupied by elderly Americans hot for their heritage, he wound his way through the parish records of every city church between the years that Nounou had estimated the painting to have been produced. He was lucky – it took him a little less than a day to land upon the records of St Artheme, Goswell. And there in the long unwinding ranks of the dead – hostlers, dyers, spinsters and foundling children all being consigned to the clay on every day of every month from dropsy, smallpox, childbed, gripguts, convulsions, consumption and fever – he found 'Katherine Saukin, Spinster.' Place of burial was indicated as 'Cript.' Cause of death was noted, in the sexton's cursive hand, as 'Evil.'

Well now, that was generously cut. 'Evil.' What might this mean? Murder? Possession? At this thought he began to feel a little nauseous, and at the same time he had the distinct feeling that he was not alone in this body of his.

The next thing he knew he was on his knees in the toilets, vomiting into the bowl.

Now he felt better. He got up and washed himself, and looked at himself in the mirror.

'Well, kid,' he said, 'what possessed you to do that, eh? What comes gabbling out of that mouth, and why? What makes you scribble out crossword clues in your sleep?'

Who, he should maybe say. More unsettling than *what*.

The washroom mirrors were set at angles round the wall. There was a small crowd of Theos staring back at him.

And which of you is carrying out this game, he wondered.

'I am,' said just one of the reflections. But he couldn't tell which, because none of them had moved their lips.

♥

The church stood in the midst of a small, leafy square of terraced houses, mostly soot-blackened and decaying, though one or two had been restored and there were a couple under scaffolding, skips parked out front on the cobbles. The walls of St Artheme's were yellowed with the sulphur of ages, as was its stone spire, supported on pitted and flaking classical columns. Below, a three-legged black dog pissed against a weatherbeaten and pockmarked stone pyramid, then nosed its way out of the churchyard and crossed the street. It then pissed against the callbox where Theo was trying to ring Ruth and getting a crossed line. He gazed across to the churchyard. Three women were standing by the pyramid. One was young and wore tight marblewash denims – she looked like a refugee from central Europe; the second had flaming red hair; the third's face was hooded. Three sisters again. Winos by the look of them. He dialled once more. The crossed line came in. A woman's voice was saying, 'Anyway, a square under pressure will always tend toward a parallelogram. But you can't distort a triangle. Strongest form in nature. That's why we've got to build with them…'

He put the phone down. He knew this was the place. There were signs here. The three-legged dog was trotting back towards the church. He followed it through the gates of the churchyard. The three women had disappeared. In the porch, painted in gold above the heavy, iron-studded doors, an equation glowed. It looked like a diagram from molecular physics. His eye was drawn to the mathematical precision with which the geometry explained the ins and outs, the *ests* and *non ests* of the Holy Trinity. This *must* be the place. It's got to be the right woman. And he was certain she would have her writings with her.

He skirted the walls, looking for the crypt. Down a flight of sunken steps was a low door, at the foot of which lay a drunken woman on a nest of old newspapers. She wore a hooded tracksuit top caked in dribble. She greeted him effusively and told him her name was Lily Field.

'Consider the lilies of the field, swat I always say,' she declared. He asked her where her two companions were, especially the redhead, but she swore she had no companions and she didn't know what he was talking about. The heavy door was locked solid. It was hot, and the fumes of alcohol and urine were getting to him. He considered his options while Lily Field rambled on about her schooldays and her nature studies and her R I: '…But he's a lovely bloke, the vicar, that's who you want. Lovely bloke. I kiss his feet I do,' she said mawkishly. 'See your face in his shoes, you can.'

The polished black Oxfords of the vicar of St Artheme were at this moment stepping from his '67 Triumph Vitesse, which had just drawn up in the driveway. The Reverend Nick Seaton looked a little sinister in the black respirator he wore for driving in town on heavy, airless days like this one when the city was thick with fumes more noxious than piss or booze. As he took this off and slicked back his hair he saw Lily Field hobbling sycophantically towards him. He hurried away into the church and made straight for the privacy of the vestry.

Young Reverend Seaton had big plans for his ministry. He had only recently been installed at St Artheme's, but he already had the vestry redecorated and refurnished and fitted out like a modern office. From here in front of Mac, fax and all the trimmings he had begun to discreetly divert church funds into a scheme of his own devising, a project that would bring the lost congregations flocking back, and profitability to the spiritual enterprise. He had worked this out whilst still at Christ Church the previous year. It was no good most of the population being stay-at-home Christians: no good them keeping their faith to themselves, they had to stick their bums on the pews and their hands in their wallets or he was out of a job.

He considered the way most people spent their Sundays, and spend they did, on every leisure pursuit imaginable. Which made sense, since Sunday was a day of leisure. But didn't this, then, make the Church a leisure pursuit? And with an epiphanic flash he had realised that he must compete with all the other sabbath institutions: with the majesty of Do It All, the grandeur of B&Q; the aisles of Tesco's, the altar of TV, the thrill of streetmarkets; the uplifting experiences of theme parks and stately homes, sports meetings and car boot sales. But no problem. Here, he had a positive museum-piece of a building, a genuine chunk of olde London's heritage. He had an original organ – a monumental piece of work which only need a spot of repair and restoration before it was good for money-spinning concerts, radio broadcasts and *Songs Of Praise* gigs. He was already installing an upmarket bookshop at the west end of the nave, where you could buy Graham Greene novels, coffeetable books of the Holy Land, Cliff Richard and Van Morrison CDs and framed maps of olde London Town. He also had plans for an artist-in-residence to be installed in the belltower, as well as ideas for the crypt – none of your ping-pong-table-and-tea-urn here, there would be a good-sized brasserie which would make a fortune. But the problem with the crypt was that it was stuffed full of coffins. There were hundreds of them down there, packed tight floor-to-ceiling, most of them lead monsters weighing a quarter-ton apiece. He needed to get rid of them – a daunting project to be sure – and he must do it discreetly, and at low cost. As much as anybody, he hated to disturb the dead. Or the Bishop. There was little difference.

He pondered as he sat at the vestry desk, looking out of the window and across the street to where a house stood in process of restoration. He was glad to see the neighbourhood was looking up. Men were working on the roof of the house, unrolling a long strip of lead flashing.

Lead, thought Nick Seaton. Lead. Holy *Trinity*! I've got a fortune in lead lying right underneath me.

Without further ado he went out to the site across the street and made his precarious way up the scaff ladder. At the top he was greeted by a beefy, hairy man who was naked but for a pair of surfing shorts, dayglo flipflops and a pork-pie hat.

'Good afternoon,' said Seaton, I'm from St Artheme's over there. I want to talk about lead.'

'None of my boys has been near your roof, Reverend.'

'I'm not talking about my roof. Rather the opposite. If I was to say I had a substantial quantity of lead for sale at a very reasonable price, perhaps you might be interested?'

The builder popped a Lilt can and offered a sip to the priest, who declined.

'What kind of quantity we talking, Rev?' he inquired. 'I'm in serious business here, I haven't got time to waste on a few pounds of old piping, know what I mean?'

'No, of course not. There's at least fifty tons, I should estimate,' Seaton assured him.

'Kinelle,' said the builder. 'Pardon my French, Rev.'

Theo had meanwhile observed the vicar cross the street and climb the scaffold, and had taken advantage of this to slip into the vestry and find the key to the crypt. Then, holding a ready-lit candle he had taken from the church, he had penetrated the crypt far enough to realise the measure of the task which confronted him in this necropolis. He needed tools, better light, and a helping hand. He decided to beat a temporary retreat and return the key.

When Seaton returned he noticed a young man on his knees before the marble virgin in the lady chapel. Theo had been heading for the vestry when he had seen the vicar return, so had ducked into the side chapel and acted normal by prostrating himself at the feet of a sculpture of a paranormal being. As he heard the click of the vicar's steel-caps on the flagstones he concentrated a reverent gaze upon the blue-cloaked Mary, herself on her knees in her alcove as she gazed heavenwards. But then she turned her head and looked down at him. And he heard a familiar voice.

'G'day,' said the Holy Mother of God. 'I made it, but I don't feel very stable. I'm trying to go hard but it's failing, I can feel it. I'll have to get back to the drawing board. But it's funny, I recognise this church.' And she turned her pious face skywards again, and froze.

Theo got up. He reached out and touched her cheek. Just marble.

❤

'There's going to be a restaurant down here,' said Seaton. 'Two, in fact: I've decided to have a snack counter as well.'

He and the builder were at the crypt door later that day, peering into the necropolis that confronted them.

'You're having me on, Rev,' said the builder.

'Oh, no. I've given it some thought. You see, the church has always been in the business of fast food – the loaves and fishes, the soup kitchens, the eucharist – and there's a place for it today. We're in touch, you see. There's more than one gastronomical path to the Kingdom of Heaven. And sometimes you can't beat a good cheeseburger…'

'Dead right there, Rev.'

'…Yes, the taste of hot dripping Roquefort on prime minced veal accompanied by a little rocket leaf dressed with lime and coriander or a simple vinaigrette – how you want it, when you want it. It's about choice. Choice is the essence of Christianity. Dine or snack. Look at my bookshop: presentational leather-bound volumes of Aquinas – or a video of the latest Billy Graham tour.'

The bookshop was indeed doing well, both for his employers and the Rev. himself by virtue of the slice that he was creaming off the top. Seaton saw no moral problem attached to any of this, and despite Matthew 19: 23-24, no possibility of being banned from the hereafter on account of a healthy bank balance: this vicar had long ago learned that sufficient wealth could easily construct a needle's eye big enough to accommodate a twelve-lane motorway of turbocharged 24-valve GTI camels.

But the builder rolled his eyes: 'I don't know about Billy Graham vids,' he said. He didn't look happy. This worried Seaton. Here was a section of the spiritual market he had forgotten to cater for. Thinking on his feet, he immediately announced that he would soon be stocking videos of some of the Bible's more adult adventures, which would include such titles as *Salome*, *Solomon's Song*, *Deborah: Lust for Glory*, *Chainsaw Judith*, and *Delilah Goes Down*. But the builder remained unimpressed. He confessed to Seaton that he was a member of an obscure mid-eastern sect which had its origins in the foothills of the Caucasus and was based on revelations received by a certain ninth-century timber merchant.

'Sorry Rev, but you wouldn't find me here on a Sunday. Too much of a family atmosphere for my liking. When we worship it's strictly men only. But I wish you luck. And if you need any help with this Gethsemene Theme Garden, or an estimate for putting in your cafferie, I'd be happy to oblige.'

By now Seaton was already designing in his head an ecumenical temple, a religious mall which would cater for every faith you could name, all under one roof. That would be his next project: after heritage would come supermodernity – build it on a nice big out-of-town greenfield site near a major road junction. Lease out space for the Mosque, the Synagogue, the Churches and the Temples; a bunch of smaller square-footages for the chapels of Spiritualists, Jains, Quakers, Animists and Jehova's Witnesses; a Waterstones for Secular Humanists, an IKEA for Materialists. It's all the same thing. There'd be no problems. He'd rake it in. What about Atheists? No, they couldn't afford it. Splice it all with a spread of international cuisineries, stick a hundred-foot-high Fountain Of Life in the atrium, and surround the whole affair with a landscaped Garden of Contemplation: lawns, duckponds, Haagen-Dasz kiosks and for guilt's sake, *Big Issue* sellers. They could have pitches at a discount.

He put these thoughts aside for the time being, and asked the builder if he could clear the crypt of caskets. The price the vicar asked for all that precious metal was reasonable; the condition was discretion. The builder quickly agreed.

❤

The next day White called at the house in Holland Park.

'I guessed you'd come here,' he told Ruth.

'Fuck off and die,' she said.

'You've got something that belongs to me,' he said. 'A jar with a head in it. Not to mention a few pictures.'

'You ripped them off from the Armenian. I met the guy, Paul.'

'Don't talk to me about Mikoyan,' he said, 'He's doddery. He doesn't know what he's doing from one day to the next. It was a perfectly legal sale, I swear to you. There's some complicated business which goes back a bit.'

'Well, let's call him and find out.'

'Don't be silly. Anyway–' and here he cleared his throat – 'I think we should get married, don't you? Stop all this stupid behaviour.'

She smiled. 'So I can't testify against you, right?'

'You'd be happier if things were more stable, Ruth. You'd feel more secure.'

'And you're after my folks' money, too.'

'I'm trying to do what's best for you. That's what I've always done.'

'All you've ever done is colonise me, Paul. Get lost.'

The phone rang and she picked it up.

'Oh, Jesus,' she said, 'What the hell do you want, Theo?'

As she listened, White slipped from the room and went looking for the extension.

'I checked the libraries and everything,' Theo said. Not a trace of her there. But–'

'What's this got to do with me?' she said flatly.

'Well… Listen, I'll marry you. In return for some help.'

'Gosh, I *am* popular today. What kind of help?'

'I know where she's buried. And I just know those diaries are in there with her.'

'Theo, I can't talk right now. Call me back.'

When White rejoined her he started on a gentler tack. He went on about love and good times shared and how pleased their families would be if they tied the knot. He spoke in the baritone he kept in reserve for times like this. She was a sucker for English-English – the double whammy of the exotic yet comprehensible – and in White's case, the classy too. Ruth's secret ambition to marry an Englishman sprang from the same source as her passion for fossils. She liked things solid, unmutable, entrenched in the past. His true-blue eyes gazed meaningfully into hers and he took her in his arms. She fought, swore, slapped, kicked and scratched. Then they made love on the carpet.

And after he had pahked his cah in her Hahvahd Yahd, he said, 'So where's our friend Theo?'

'I don't know.'

After a moment, White said, 'You didn't have a scene with him I hope.'

'That's a joke. I never met anybody so totally asexual.'

'What did he want?'

'You should know, you've been listening in,' said Ruth. Then she told him the story.

'So he's going grave-robbing and he wants you to hold his hand,' said White as he rolled a cigarette. Then he said, determinedly, 'I want that head, and I want that painting – that was part of the deal we arranged too. All of this business is just absurd. There aren't any diaries. You're both getting carried away with it all. It's fantasy. The old man's senile. He's spun you a right old yarn, ha! And this Theo has got even bigger problems with the old compos mentis.'

'Yeah,' said Ruth, 'Maybe I have been going a bit crazy again.'

This is what he wanted to hear. And now – the idea of these diaries was beginning to interest him. Yes… and we couldn't

97

have some wop scuttling off with our heritage… But he didn't say anything. He sat in a chair like Frank Sinatra, blowing perfect smoke rings, watching them drift upwards and mutate into pound signs.

♥

By now time was beginning to lose its meaning for Theo. He found himself back in Camden, where he had found a floor in a squat full of market traders after setting up stall near the lock with a hundredweight of his shirts and whistles. It was a big old house where every room vibrated to the sound of sewing machines and thrash metal on cheap midi systems, and smelt of leather, heavy perfume and cats' piss. He needed someone to talk to, and he hadn't been able to get through to Ruth. At first he balked at confiding in any of these new companions, but after an evening lubricated by wine and Crucial Brew in front of a Ken Russell movie on the life of Byron, he found himself spilling all to a girl whose figure and costume cast her as the fattest of Nosferatu's sisters ever to crawl from a coffin at twilight.

'I got a severed head,' he told her. 'Down the left luggage.'

'What sign are you?' said the Nosferatette with a hiccup.

'I'm a bloody road sign, 'cause me Dad made me,' he said. 'Bloody one-way street.'

Then he gabbled on some more about lost diaries and bloody murder. When the movie was finished after quantities of flesh, blood, Sturm und Drang, the girl hauled him off to bed.

'Oh, you're totally perfickt,' she exclaimed as she undressed him. 'You're all pale and sick and decadent, and there's the shadow of the bat under your eyes. I bet your willy is long and thin and cold as marble, like the Devil's.'

He sniggered and passed out across her bed.

He woke up with a crucial hangover, and the Nosferatette made more futile attempts to get him to perform before she gave up and set out for a number of jumble sales. He swallowed some painkillers and went to phone Ruth. This time she answered. Since the previous day she'd done nothing but hang out with White in an orgy of fleshy consolations, but it had been temporary. By now she had screwed herself into a depression. She hated White again. She saw a future with him of conflict-sex-relief-depression in an endless cycle, and she decided she didn't want this. So she talked to Theo, finally put the phone down, climbed out of bed over White's sleeping figure, walked to the bathroom dripping chromosomes, showered, dressed, went out, jumped in her pink van and drove across town to St Artheme's.

Once inside the crypt, by the beam of their flashlights, they beheld the city of caskets. At first these appeared to be heaped indiscriminately in complete disorder. Many of them could be opened and contained nothing but dust, empty sherry bottles and the odd sixties girly magazine. But as they penetrated deeper into the crypt, squeezing themselves between the lids and the brick vaulting, the stacks became tidier and there were clear blocks of coffins separated by just enough space to walk sideways between them. Guided by the dates on the plaques, they came eventually to a stack from the 1690s. And upon one of these was a plaque bearing the name they sought. With much difficulty they shifted the caskets above it and manhandled it to the floor.

The leaden lozenge was sealed around the lid with a strip of solder. Ruth chiselled away at it while he prised a jemmy into the crack. The top came free. They lifted it off, and were engulfed in a sickly-sweet odour of sour caramel. By the light of their torches they could see a pool of dark, viscous liquor which lay glistening atop a cambric cloth.

'Oh my god, she's deliquesced,' Ruth declared, while he dry-retched. 'No, wait,' she said. 'This muck is just lying on top of the cloth. It'll be condensation. You take that end, I take this, and we lift it and pour it off.'

He took hold of the fabric. Oh shit the stuff was on his hands. He shivered as he felt the body liquor cling to his fingers like fondue.

'Don't be so damn squeamish,' she said, 'OK, lift!'

Cloth and liquor came up as one and splashed to the floor. And there now before them lay Katie Sawkin, dressed in a simple grave-shift, and so well preserved she looked alive. Her eyes seemed only loosely closed, and there was a faint smile on her face, which was framed by that flaming red hair. Her hands were folded across her chest, and held a small crucifix; she looked like she was pondering some interesting problem, and would spring up at any instant with the answer.

'That's her. That's the woman in the painting,' said Ruth.

He noticed that the corpse also bore a strong resemblance to the boathouse ghost.

But there was no diary visible. He reached into the coffin and began groping around the corpse. At this moment they were interrupted. There were voices and flashlights coming from the direction of the entrance.

'Damn,' said Ruth. 'Quick – hide in the casket.' And she slid back the lid of a neighbouring box and climbed in.

He clambered into Katie's casket and heaved the lid over himself leaving a crack to breathe through. He was cramped between corpse and coffinwall. All he could hear now was the thumping of his heart and the zinging of his nerves. He lay and listened and waited. There was a sweet, nutty scent in this leaden enclosure. He squirmed around tried to move his hands about to grope for the diary, but he couldn't get them free. He moved his head slightly, and felt his cheek touch the woman's smooth face. Then with a shiver he felt her cold, soft lips on his neck.

He had lain there for what seemed like a half-hour, and was considering a tentative re-emergence when he suddenly felt the coffin being jolted, and then begin to rock crazily. It was being manhandled. He was jolted about so violently that he found himself engaged in a bizarre snogging session with his casket-mate until eventually after a couple of heavy thumps all was still again.

He waited a moment, then decided to try and see what was going on. But when he pushed his feet up against the lid he found it was stuck fast. It would not shift an inch. With some difficulty he contrived to twist himself round into a press-up position and tried to use his back to push upwards, but this was ineffective too. His throat seized up with fear when he suddenly realised that this casket might well now be beneath several tons

100

worth of others. Another uncomfortable sensation told him he had just messed himself. What a way to go. But he persevered, pushing and shouting, although he doubted he could be heard, until the bumping started up again. It was gentler now, faster, more rhythmic. Every so often it would stop completely for a few seconds. After what seemed like hours, all movement ceased, and at the same time he gave up his futile efforts, exhausted, covered in the sweat of effort and fright, throat sore from screaming and shouting.

He was calmer now, despite the fact that he was finding it difficult to breathe.

'Well, Katie, looks like we'll be walking out hand-in-hand come judgement day.'

He was about to try the lid one more time when it opened seemingly of its own accord. There was a rush of cold, clear air and he saw the moon above him. Sitting up in the casket, he was confronted by two men in windcheaters and surfing shorts holding torches.

'Hi,' he heard himself say, whereupon the character who had just slid back the lid fainted on the spot, and the other let out an oath, turned tail and ran off into the darkness between two small mountains of wrecked automobiles.

He was facing a large pit. The moonlight picked out the figures of a mass of shrouded corpses that had been dumped there. Amongst these skeletal forms someone living was clambering around with a jerrycan, splashing petrol over them. Above the pit was a pyramid of earth which would no doubt cover the site once the flames had done their work. Elsewhere a crane was at work lifting an empty coffin and swinging it over to the maw of a twenty-foot high metal-crusher: a little recycling operation was going on. He looked at the pit again. It resembled the scene of a mass atrocity. The dead were being murdered. Behind him stacks more of them waited unwittingly. And another truckload of coffins was approaching. Time to leave. A quick search of the casket again and he discovered, wedged between Katie's feet and the butt of the coffin, a thick cube partly encased in metal. He was neither surprised nor relieved. He knew it would be there.

He looked once more at Katie's perfect face and her smouldering hair, and he looked at the moonlit pit. For a second he thought he might carry her off with him. She wouldn't weigh much. But no. That truck was backing towards him and someone had jumped down from it. He stole away rapidly through the breaker's yard and got out through a hole in the fence.

Moonlight glimmered on a country lane. He looked back for an instant and regretted leaving Katie Sawkin to her humiliating fate. Then he hurried off. But he had only gone a few yards when he saw a pink van parked up ahead.

'I managed to get out and away when I realised what was happening,' Ruth said, 'and I followed the trucks. I was just sitting here figuring out what the hell to do. Like, "Excuse me but my friend's in one of these caskets and I wondered…" '

'It's pretty nefarious in this neck of the woods,' he observed.

'It's Essex,' she said, 'what do you expect?'

'Cliché,' he said.

'It's true – besides, it's too close to Belgium.'

'There you go again.'

She sniffed the air. 'Is that the smell of the dead,' she said. 'Or did you shit yourself?'

♥

'You got a valuable commodity there,' she said, glancing at the volume as they drove back into town. He was flipping through the heavy vellum pages. He found it impossible to decipher the ornate italics.

'Makes no difference,' she said. 'It's heritage. So what if every page says *got up, shit, ate, went to work, walked home, wanked off, went to bed* – you got a lump of history there.'

Their luck didn't hold. Coming in on the Commercial Road they were pulled over. Ruth had no licence or i.d. One of the constables poked his nose around the van's interior while the other gave the outside a good going over.

'Looks like a recent respray,' he said to his colleague. 'Botched job and all.'

The other cop looked hard at Theo. 'What's your name, sonny?'

He opened his mouth. Then he realised he didn't know.

'I can't remember,' he said.

They were escorted to the police station, where they were separated. One of the constables held up the diary in front of him. 'What's this, then? Where did you nick it from?'

'It's mine,' he said.

They banged him up in a cell where the lavvy didn't flush and was full of piss.

Then they took him out to an interview room. A stubble-faced detective tried to get him to tell them what he did and where he lived. But it was all a blank. So they banged him up again. He stalked the floor of the cell and racked his memory. All he knew was that he had to reclaim that diary, and that it would tell him where to bury the severed head.

They took him again to the interview room. This time there was another detective, clean-shaven and wearing a baseball cap, and no-one else present. Like anyone else who'd watched TV for more than a week, Theo knew procedure backwards, and he didn't like the look of this. The cop thwopped the heavy diary down on the tabletop, and said 'OK. You are Theo Riddle, of fourteen Shepherd's Close, Basildon. It should be been thir-teen but developers are getting superstitious these days. And that's a shame because you'd have been better off at thirteen, with the old baker's dozen, right? A little extra creamcake for free?'

The cop flexed his fingers. 'Instead you're in this shithole. How would you like me to teach you a lesson?' He leaned across the table. 'A lesson about the number thirteen, about lunar months and menstruation, and how your grandmothers in the Upper Paleolithic finally forced some culture into you, for the sake of survival? About how we kicked the shit out of a few bull-shit machobozos in order to do so, and how we've been hunting down those deathwish chimpbrained bastards ever since?'

Lunar months? This guy was a lunatic.

The detective pointed to his baseball cap and his drab suit, over which he wore a soggy, fawn-coloured leather blouson jacket: 'Look at this shit-ugly habit,' he said. 'Look at this sick addiction. It's like wearing used J-cloths. If aesthetics is the ultimate truth then this outfit is the ultimate lie, this is where style is locked up, tortured and refused a lawyer. I never thought I'd have to stoop to this. The things a woman has to wear.'

'Oh shit, it's you. Diana.'

'Bullseye. But I'm thinking of calling myself something like *Helicia Aminoia Constructoria Exterior* – what do you think?'

'You were the Virgin in the church.'

'So were you.'

'I've been dreaming about you,' he said. 'So you finally made it into real life?'

'I tell you what, I've been pissing about in the synaptic seas with nothing but a bronze age soldering iron, but I made it in the end.'

'What was my name? Theo?' he said. 'Don't like it much.'

'Means *God's Gift*,' said Diana, taking the diary as she stood up. 'C'mon God's Gift, let's go.'

Some while later back at the police station, the naked D S – trussed up with a blue silk robe and handcuffed with a rosary – garbled out a tale of a nun who had attacked him. With a brass halo, he claimed.

♥

'What happened to Ruth?'

They were driving. The black-upholstered car they had taken from the yard smelt of plastic and aftershave.

'She'll get deported.'

'Can't we go back and get her out?'

'No time. Besides, she wasn't really your type, Theo.'

'Watch the lights!' he shouted as she careered through a red. She glanced off the wing of an approaching car, spun round 360 degrees and shot off again. 'It's OK,' she said, 'we're in a squad car, we can do what we like.'

'Ruth and me…' he said, '…I mean you can't just dump her.'

'It's me you need now. The Yank chick's getting off lightly. I've got more important scores to settle.'

'Meaning?'

'Do you think – shit!' She swerved to avoid a woman pushing a pram across the street – 'Do you think I'm the only chunk

104

of consanguinitic consequences floating about in this soup? Listen, there's a whole tribe of us boogalooing around the planet: the good, the bad and the stylistically challenged. And me, I've got one or two debts to clear with one or two folks who've been doing their utmost all along to wipe me out. So it's payoff time, and I'm well equipped now – *hey*!'

She skidded the car to a halt and called out to a man in a business suit. He came towards her quizzically.

'This is for your part in the Piraeus Affair,' she told him, and promptly spat in his face before pulling away again. 'He was lucky,' she said, 'he wasn't really part of the conspiracy. A little bit of interfamilial rivalry back in Athens around 500 bc. There was a murder and that slimebag supplied the weapons, though he didn't know the circumstances.'

'Not him on the street there – he's just a relative.'

'Just a relative,' she scoffed. 'Listen, the same thing drives him as drove his ancestor.'

'Hey, if Gramps fiddled the till once, it's nothing to do with me.'

'Get real,' she said as she wove the car manically through West End traffic. 'You of all people should know about primal crime. So tell me – why are you supposed to be born with the sins of Eve in you?'

'Because she was my original ancestor, and she sinned.'

'Dead right. Even if it is a rather primitive version of genetics. Not exactly fun-loving or feminist but it's the general idea. And you know what holds you and your lot together like a rope through time? It's me, and it's me who carries the can. For you, mum, grandpops – all the way back down the line. That scumball back there may not know what hit him just now, but he'll work it out in his dreams.'

Suddenly she swerved to the kerb and pulled up again. She got out and strode across to a paper seller outside Angel station. 'You know me,' she told him. 'Here's the latest headline.' Then she delivered the man a left to the jaw that felled him like a log.

'Let me guess, a relative of his bad-mouthed you in 1380.'

'Close. 1381. But you're getting the hang of it.'

'You're out of your mind.'

She roared off westwards. 'I don't have a mind. I don't need one. Know what's inside here?' she said, tapping her head, 'One grain of sand. One little silicon crystal. That's all it takes.'

'Where are we going?'

'That art shark's shack. I've got a nice long hit list, but let's get your immediate business out of the way first. I don't have much time.'

'Why the hurry?'

She didn't seem to hear him. She'd spotted someone else with an original sin and was pulling on a set of brass knuckle-dusters as she brought the police car to a halt. 'Found these in the glovebox,' she said.

♥

White opened the door of the Holland Park house and looked suspiciously at Diana. 'What do you want?' he said to Theo. 'And who's this?'

'Police,' she said, flashing her warrant card. Then she took hold of his arm and marched him inside and through to the kitchen.

'Would you mind telling me what all this is about?' he blustered. 'And you,' he said to Theo, 'where's Ruth?'

'You're a thief Mr White,' said Diana, taking his wrist and slamming it down on the tabletop, 'And this is what happens to thieves–' and so saying, she took up a carving knife and with one swift gesture she sliced off his thumb.

He watched dumbly as the detached digit rolled across the table. His stump was gushing blood. Diana let go his wrist. Panic in his eyes, muttering ohmygods, he leaped up and searched wildly for something with which to staunch the wound. He grabbed a teatowel and wrapped it around his hand. Cringing, he confronted Diana and took a deep breath.

'Can I have my thumb back, please?' he said.

She tossed it to him. 'Stick it up yer arse, drongo.'

He caught the still-twitching object in his good hand, turned and scuttled off down the hall, and raced from the house. They heard the slamming of the squad car door and the roar of its departure.

106

'Guess he's off to hossie,' she said.

'Yes,' Theo said. 'Yeah… interesting.'

Then he saw a figure appear at the far end of the hall, at the foot of the stairs. It was the bearded Scot in his black gown. He stopped and stared down the passage at the two people in the kitchen, and called out, 'What the devil is going on down here?'

Diana stared hard at him. Her eyes widened. 'Jesus H, it's you!' she said.

'Oh,' he said, raising a bushy eyebrow. 'So it's you.'

In an instant Diana had dropped to one knee, drawn a pistol, aimed and fired at the man. The report was deafening. The Scot ducked behind the balusters, pulled out a large automatic and returned the compliment: above her the clock on the wall exploded into fragments, and a second shot cannoned into a pile of saucepans above where Theo had ducked for cover, and sent them crashing down on him.

Diana grinned at him and waved her pistol. 'Lucky that DS was well tooled up,' she said, drawing another bead on the figure lurking in the hallway below a huge Lucien Freud painting of a naked mother suckling her child. 'Luger,' she informed him. 'Not exactly standard issue, I mean, the fantasies some of these cops run with, but… SUCK ON THIS, FUCKFACE!' she screamed, and her elbow jerked once, twice, thrice as she blasted off a rapid volley. Her distant adversary was hit in the shoulder. Reeling backwards, he turned tail and scampered through a doorway. Diana was instantly up and in pursuit. At the doorway she loosed off two more rounds and then ducked to avoid a slug that shrieked into the doorframe and sent splinters flying. Then she disappeared into the room. All was quiet. Theo made his way along the hall, glanced at the bulletholed and blood-spattered mother-and-child and put his head gingerly round the door.

'He's away over the backyards, the bastard,' she said.

His ears were ringing.

'Interesting, eh?' she smiled.

'Loud. What did he do – nick your crayons once?'

'That one,' she said, 'is really evil shit. Him and me are permanent enemies.' She reloaded the pistol. 'But I'm surprised to see him around. He wasn't ready for me, either. Looks like he made it before I did. I didn't recognise him before. I *knew* there was something funny about him. Hey, we were lucky. If he hadn't been so busy with Danish hitchhikers… or maybe it was your crucifix… but he could have blown us both away.'

'What do you mean, "made it"?'

'He's another nomad of the genetic freeways,' she smiled. 'Another nucleic acidhead. NFAs, you might call us, No Fixed Aboders. But he's gone hard, too. The bastard got there ahead of me. I'll kill him twice over for that. See, both of us have been working on it since way back when we were both in the same Pre-Cambrian amoeba. That's when we first split up. We've been rivals for the secret ever since.'

'Why not work together?' he said.

'Don't be so fuckin' wet,' she said, checking the magazine.

'But why not?'

'Because he's an evil bastard.'

'But why?'

She flipped back the safety catch, pocketed the pistol and grabbed his shoulders. 'Shut the fuck up, will you? He's a killer, period. It's him or us, Theo. Besides, it's a matter of honour now.'

'So who does he belong to?'

'I don't know. Nobody we've come across. Maybe he's lost them. He's in real trouble if that's the case. Why? Because there's a time limit for us outside. And you have to be close to your host in order to get back in quick if you start going soft.'

'What exactly do you do to get back in?'

She lowered her eyes. 'Oh,' she said, 're-entry's nothing… It's simple. But it's too complicated to explain.'

She looked up again. Her hair was beginning to escape the confines of the baseball cap. 'Listen,' she said as she fiddled with it, 'I'm sorry about all the noise. Let me go buy you a Wendyburger or something, hey? But first I've got to lose this shitty schmutter.'

♥

'Why go hard anyway? What's the point?'

'As the novice said to the abbot.'

They were in a café in Notting Hill. Diana had found another habit in a nearby theatrical shop. It had a long white headdress. He eyed her evasive expression as she forked a chip and toyed with it.

'It's fun. It's new,' she said. 'It's something to do.'

'Come off it,' he said.

'No, but all the history I've got in here,' she tapped her head, 'to make it public, to tell you guys what Adam really said to Eve, or what the primordial soup tasted like, or which way Beau Brummell swung. Remember old Tom Browne? – *"What songs the Sirens sang, or what name Achilles assumed when he hid himself among women, though puzzling questions, are not beyond all conjecture?"* Well, now we've got the answers. I want to put people right about a whole busload of things. Particularly about what Achilles was doing there in the first place. There's a long-forgotten cure for cancer I know about, too.'

'So tell us the big one,' he said. 'Does God exist?'

'Ah, jeez, c'mon,' she said, adjusting her headdress, 'how on earth should I know that?' The waitress gave her a strange look. 'But I guess I look at it this way,' Diana said. 'God exists like a slap in the face exists, right? See, here and now, could you honestly say a slap in the face exists? If it does, where is it? I don't see it, do you? If a face is being slapped in the middle of a forest where no-one can see it or hear it, does it exist? That was Lord Buckley's famous conundrum. Or was it Count Basie? I tell a lie, it was Earl Grey. And yet–' She dealt him a swift back-hander across the mouth – 'How about that? Does it exist now?'

'Shit, cut it out, that hurt.'

'But does it exist?'

'Not like a person does. It just… happens.'

'Yeah, well, maybe God's like a slap in the face, that's all.'

He wiped the blood from his lip. 'And this is the great truth for which you've appeared to tell the world about.'

'Jeez, no. Any primer on Zen Buddhism or the Kabala'll tell you that. The Communist Manifesto, too, in its own sweet way.

109

Yeah. And who was it wrote that God is a cosmic monkey and the Bible represents his first attempt to use a typewriter?'

'Talking of books, let's have a trunk at that diary. Let's get on with it.'

Diana fished in the folds of her robes. Then she fished more urgently. Then her face fell. 'I left it in the squad car,' she said, 'Holy *shite*.'

The waitress crossed herself.

So White had it. They checked out every casualty department of every hospital in town – it didn't take long – and drew a blank.

'He'll be down to Dickham,' said Theo, 'then he'll be away with Phyllida.'

6. CLUB MED

WILSON EASED the black Porsche down the tiny main street, narrow as a grave, of Dickham village. His torso was bare. The torn remains of his silk dressing gown were wrapped around his injured shoulder, sodden with blood. He turned into the drive of a large house. Inside he headed for the bathroom, washed the wound, and winced and cursed as he dabbed dry the red-raw flesh. Then he took a roll of lint and strode into the studio, where, atop a great mountain of freshly-scribed manuscript papers assembled on top of a black Blüthner grand, stood a half-empty bottle of Glenmorangie. He poured its contents onto a wad of gauze then dressed his wound with the saturated cloth, uttering more expletives through his teeth. This done, he pulled on his black jeans, black shirt and Frye boots, then made to take a slug of Scotch from the bottle. But it was empty, of course. Cursing and spreading his fingers, he attacked the Blüthner's keyboard with a single angry chord of such voluminous ferocity as to make the whole house resonate with a fearsome, booming convulsion, instantly driving all the birds from its vicinity (they were not to return for seven years). Then he went down to the pub.

The Ferry Inn had just opened for the evening. Through its picture window the river could be seen in the glory of a spring flood tide. Its waters lapped and slopped against the wall outside. Wilson bought a case of malt from the landlord and had a drink while he was there. Then he saw Phyllida come in

111

and order a couple of boxes of assorted liquors and mixers. He called across to her: 'Hi, Phylly! Partying tonight?'

'Oh, hi William,' she said.

'Drink?' he offered. She joined him.

'No thanks,' she said. 'Actually I'm sailing tonight. Getting in some provisions. I'm waiting for Paul. We must catch this tide or we'll never make it to Antibes on time, and that would be *so* boring.'

When White appeared, some two drinks later, he had added a pair of black leather gloves to his usual outfit. He proudly produced his new acquisition and laid the heavy brass-bound volume under their noses.

'Rather fine, don't you think Phylly? Perfect for our man in the Med, I would have thought. Binding alone's worth a few grand. Look at that tooling.'

'What is it?' she said.

'Diary of some seventeenth-century woman. Bloody weird. Script's practically impossible to read. A lot of it looks like Latin. Mine's not that bad, I can have a go at it during the trip.'

Wilson raised his eyebrows. 'My Latin's bloody brilliant,' he said eagerly. 'Let's have a look-see here.' He opened the book and scanned it rapidly. His eye lit on a passage which seemed to be the story of a death and burial on a dusty island in a wide blue sea a long, long time ago. With a flash of excitement he realised he knew parts of this story. He turned to White. 'This is serious business you've got here,' he said, 'I'm talking Middle English and Old French, not to mention Ancient Greek and some Aramaic that's bloody prehistoric.' (In fact the entire journal was in English.) 'You're talking to a linguist here,' he went on, 'I mean I could have sorted out *Babel* for those guys, *Berlitz-krieged* the place, right? Look, old son, why don't I come along with youse two and I'll figure it out *rapidamento*. And of course when this thing turns out to be as gilt-edged as I would reckon, then I wouldnae say no to a wee slice of the action, right?'

'I never realised you were such a Renaissance man, William,' said White, with a hint of admiration.

'Aye,' said Wilson, 'And I still remember those Renaissance women. I mean, really, – phew! Out of this world!'

112

'How are you with yachts?' inquired Phyllida.

'No problem,' said Wilson. 'I was on the Quinquereme of fuckin' *Ninevah*. That was something. I mean the rhythm of those drums, that orchestra of oarsmen, the blood, the sweat and the *passion*, right?'

A half-hour later, as darkness fell, the *Ubique* slipped away downriver on the ebb tide. White was below, feverishly making sure all the art they carried was concealed behind false bulk-heads or in watertight bilge-compartments. And he was dreaming of a good life and lucrative contacts on the Côte D'Azur. Every great Englishman had strong connections with the Riviera: the Duke of Windsor, Winston Churchill, Somerset Maugham, Dirk Bogarde, James Fox… and then there were the brave lads carrying the flag to the enemy, Stirling, Graham, Nigel, Damien: true Brit grit, lined up in their laurels at Monaco while the champers sprays over the scanticladettes and *vedettes*… maybe he'd get to shag a porn starlet, or one of those estranged wives of pop stars, some low-talent, high-energy look-at-me blonde from TV with two small kids, nanny, Landcruiser, and like every vicar's daughter, an insatiable appetite for prolonged rough. Mind you, old Phyllida was a bit of a cracker too, despite the streaks of grey. He hoped Wilson would not obstruct the pas-de-deux he had in mind. Hidden by the glove he wore, the stump of his thumb was giving him immense pain, but he bore it. As soon as he had discovered the diary in the squad car he knew he couldn't waste time getting it seen to if he was to stay clear of that crazy woman Theo had found. For sentimental reasons, though, he'd kept the severed thumb and put it in a bottle of olive oil, hoping to preserve it and have a tale to tell his grandchildren. He'd get a doctor to tidy up his stump at their first port-of-call.

Wilson sat at the prow hunched over a whisky bottle and the Sawkin diary, confirming what he had suspected in the pub. What he had discovered looked like changing the whole ball-game for him. Until now he had more or less given up – he had accepted the fact that he had no future. And terrible though this was – the realisation that he was going to die, and soon, after all these years and all these generations – he had got used to it. He

113

was just going to have fun while he could, and finish his immense work for chorus, orchestra, rock band, bulldozers and artillery cannon: his Symphony Number One, the *Goddamned*. Finish it if he could, if time allowed. Time was what he had been working against. The first signs of disintegration might show any day now: the shakes, the breathlessness, the confusion. But now – two extraordinary events on the same day. The bitch Diana, she'd figured out going hard too; and now this revelation in an obscure diary. Suddenly Wilson found himself with not one but two slim chances of survival. With this new hope came its natural companion: fresh fear. Mixed with Scotch and adrenalin, however, Wilson found it pretty stimulating. Mmm. Be nice to have a good steak dinner later on, and then maybe roger the buttocks off Captain Phyllida. She reminded him of a certain Miller's daughter he'd had his way with once while he was marching through Saxony butchering Catholics for Gustavus Adolphus. In fact – he'd have to look closer at her eyes to confirm it – she might have the same NFA in there.

In Phyllida's head, meanwhile, a number of thoughts were scampering around like mice in a railway tunnel. She stood at the helm in her blue kagoul and steered the *Ubique* through Kingsmouth toward the sea, thankful for no sign of Big Job Andersen. What an obnoxious man. As for these two chumps she was having to do business with... God, I hope they don't expect me to *sleep* with them as well. This is the *last deal*, she told herself, this is it – flog the paintings, sell the boat, launder the money... and in six month's time she'd have that ranch-style home in the foothills of Kilimanjaro where she'd sit on the porch and watch the glorious sunset and listen to the cowbells of the Samburu herds tonkling in the distance as she drank white wine and wrote childrens' books. The Samburu were a beautiful, strange people. Their name meant 'butterfly' and they never mentioned the dead. They had no past. This thought chilled her. Maybe – in the Commonwealth Club in Nairobi perhaps – she'd meet someone really nice – someone like her long-lost schoolchum Amanda. Someone to have a good laugh with, someone to share her home in Paradise. The kids would visit, of course: Titus would spend all day in the hammock talking into his mobile phone, and Lucy would chide her for having servants. And she'd offer them bowls of fermented goat's milk like that which she'd drunk in Asia and learned to love, the sweet-sour and the soft-sharp of it, way back before the Soviet-Afghan war, when she was travelling with her first husband, a draft-dodging New Yorker with whom she had brought back the first consignment of slipper-socks ever seen on the street markets of Europe. So her memories meandered. Gosh. The money we made out of Afghanistan in the old days. The parties... It's not the same anymore. I hate this boat. But my contemptible ex owes it to me. He's been ripping me off for years. God, why did I put up with that reptile.

Still no sign of the Harbourmaster. Thank goodness. I'm really going to make it this time.

'William,' she called out, 'do you know any Swahili by any chance?'

Wilson was making his way aft to get out of the spray thrown up by the open sea as they steered for Brittany. 'Know it?' His eyes sparkled and his beard seemed to be aflame. 'Phylly, I *invented* it. Maybe later I'll show you some interesting verbs.'

'Is it true we all come from Africa, Willy?'

'Aye,' he said, toking on the bottle. 'We're all Africans of one colour or another.' He put an arm around her waist and squeezed her tight. 'All Africans under the skin, eh, Phylly? How does it feel?'

She looked just a little fazed. 'Really? Oh well... what a strange thought. Give me some of that,' and she took a slug of scotch.

'This whole fucking globe, I mean, really,' Wilson was saying, 'is just the *African Empire*, right? This is *Planet Africa* we're on, baby.'

'Gosh,' said Phyllida.

❤

Back at the Ferry Inn, Windeatt sat on a bench next to the open fire holding a half-empty pint mug. He'd just been talking to Bibi van Helsing, who had once more treated him to her warm relentless smile and an offer of three introductory sessions at a discount. Windeatt, stealing lecherous glances at her long, bare legs, was beginning to think it might not be a bad idea. 'But I'm skint at the moment, see,' he told her, 'Mr White owes me money but he's buggered off to France for the next couple of weeks.'

'Well, maybe then, then,' she smiled. 'Bye!'

He watched her walk out. I do believe she fancies me, he thought. She was practically rubbing herself against me just now. And that stare of hers has got to be a come-on in any language. I've got to get some cash. He wondered how. Then he realised tomorrow was Thursday, when every crinkly in the county would be toddling off to the post office with their pension books, which meant a lot of empty bungalows full of tasty little items to liberate. By lunchtime he'd have them flogged in Plymouth, and then – but he was jerked out of this happy train of thought by the sudden presence of Theo, who had slid up next to him on the bench. He looked friendly enough, but Windeatt could not suppress a little cringe nevertheless.

'Hallo there,' said Theo.

'Do I know you?' said Windeatt, getting to his feet.

'Don't go,' said the other, catching hold of his arm. 'Like you to meet Diana.'

Windeatt sat down again. 'Oh. Pleased to meet you, Holy Matron,' he said deferentially to Diana, and crossed himself, wrongly.

'G'day,' said Diana. ' "Sister" 'll do fine.'

'Where's White, where's Phyllida, and where's the yacht?' said Theo.

'And who are you?' said Windeatt.

'Listen, my child,' said Diana, 'just cut the crap. Or we will use violence on you, pain us though it may. You should remember that we Brides of Christ have a lot of experience in the fine arts of torture.'

'Mortification of the flesh,' intoned Theo solemnly.

'It'll hurt us more than it'll hurt you,' said Diana. And this was the clincher. Nothing could have been better calculated to

116

scare Windeatt more than this simple phrase, fearsome, brutal, sadomasochistic. He confessed all he knew. White, Phyllida and the Jock had 'pissed off to the coat that's yours' a few hours back. What Jock was that? *That* Jock, Mr Wilson.

'Oh, good-oh!' Diana beamed, 'I *am* looking forward to meeting Mr Wilson again. Windy, you're a real mate. Take three hail Mary's and have a drink.'

'Cheers, Holy Miss.' These two were mad, he thought. Mad and dangerous. Do well to keep in with them.

'Right,' Diana said. 'What we need is a good, fast boat.'

'Naval school down Kingsmouth's got a couple of patrol boats,' offered Windeatt. 'No problem to board from a dinghy. I can drive them buggers. Navy man, see -' and he rolled up his sleeve – the opposite arm to that which he had shown White recently – to show off a half-naked Britannia in stockings and suspenders, reclining on a chaise longue and languidly ruling the waves while paying loving attention to her trident. 'Pardon my Britannia, Holy Miss,' said Windeatt.

'No worries,' said Diana. 'Let's go.'

'Hang on,' said Theo. 'We've already had *Magnum Terminator Fuck Off And Diehard II* today. You people are getting seriously carried away. This is the real world, right?'

The genetic nomad in nun's clothing and the pug-faced dwarf looked back at him.

'No navy larks. Apart from bringing down a lot of swift wrath, it's a waste of time. One black cat looking for another in an ocean-sized coal-cellar. Besides, there's no need.'

'What do you mean, smartarse?' Diana said.

'I mean if they're going to the Med then they've got to go through Gibraltar. We'll wait for them there. Sweet.'

'Yeah, and how do we know they'll actually put in there?' said Diana.

'I can't see someone like White missing a chance to stop off and kiss the Rock of Ages,' he replied, 'Anything less would be like pissing on the Union Jack, wouldn't it?'

'Oh well – you're probably right,' she said, sounding a little disappointed. 'But listen,' she said to Windeatt, 'Where does Wilson live?'

'Top of the village.'

Windeatt didn't need much persuading to break into Wilson's house. They found the studio, bare but for the grand piano alone in the middle of the floor and half-buried by the scattered score of the *Goddamned Symphony*, two giant hi-fi speakers and a couple of black leather sofas. Theo examined a small bust of Wagner which also stood on the piano. Diana sifted through the manuscript papers. 'Jeez,' she remarked, 'you need to go into bloody orbit to reach some of these notes, and others, its like, pass the fuckin' diving bell. What a heap of shit.' And she took an armful of the papers and tossed them contemptuously into the air.

Windeatt, who had rapidly discovered that apart from the bust Theo held the house contained no pocketable valuables, looked restless. 'If you don't mind, Holy Miss, I'll be on my way. This place gives me the creeps.'

She gave him a dismissive wave. 'Thanks Windy. *Nunc Dimittis* and all that.' And Windeatt left hastily.

Theo had been nosing around the garden. 'It's weird,' he said, 'The crickets are singing everywhere else but here.'

'I think our Willie is a desperate man,' she said. 'This music… crates of empties in the kitchen… he's been composing in a real hurry, it's obvious. So why would he suddenly piss off to France?'

'He's lost his host.'

'Which explains his hurry over this music, but not why he's suddenly abandoned it. If he knew he was about to disintegrate he'd want to complete it for posterity. He's a vain bastard.'

'All right – he's discovered something and gone to look for his host down the Med.'

'If that was true he'd fly.'

'Maybe the host is White or Phyllida.'

'No. They're both occupied. I can tell.'

'Got little engaged signs in their eyes have they?'

Her forehead was knotting itself up. 'Listen, we've got to be careful here. Because there's a vacant sign on you, mate, right? And I reckon Willie's set to jump into the first unoccupied person he comes across. And there aren't many of those about,

118

unless I'm very wrong and we surfies of the sexual wavelengths have suddenly started materialising all over the bloody shop.'

'Poor Di. And you wanted to be unique.'

'Why not? Everyone wants to be a star. But then I'm upstaged, aren't I? Of all the bastards in all the bodies in all the bloody world, he has to crawl out of history and into my life again. But maybe it's a blessing in disguise. Opportunity to off him for good this time.' She stood at the keyboard and picked out *Waltzing Matilda*. 'Yeah, right to the bottom of the bill-abong… funny how this ain't a waltz.'

♥

The captain announced that they were cruising at thirty thousand feet and flying conditions were perfect. The sign over the toilets read Vacant. For once a discomforting sight. He turned to Diana and said 'What did this Wilson bloke do to you? Must have been serious.'

'It certainly was. But he's been bugging me for so long. Last time it happened was what got my goat worst of all. He spied on me while I was taking a bath. I set the dogs on him but he got away. I'd been out hunting, see. I'd just shot down this fat old stag I'd been after for hours. I was knackered. I dropped my togs and took a skinny dip in the lake. And there I am floating around and chilling out nicely when suddenly I spot the bastard getting an eyeful from behind a tree. Dogs didn't notice him, they were too busy chomping on the venison. So I pretended not to see him, stepped out of the water and gave him a full-frontal. It was going to cost him, though. I picked up my weapon and got the drop on him. He tried to sweet-talk his way out of it, reckoned he was in love with me and all that shit, can you believe it?

' "You are dead, mate," I tell him. And I thought I'd have a little game. Smeared him with deer innards I did, tied a lump of skin to his back and gave him five minutes to skedaddle before I set the dogs on him. You never saw anyone move so fast. But you know what? He got away, the jammy bastard. But not this time.'

'When was all this?'

119

'Down in Attica about four thousand years back.'

'Sounds like that painting – *The Death of Acteon*, except he didn't get away.'

'Yeah, well I had my pride, didn't I? I put the story about that the dogs got the bastard and ripped him to shreds.'

'Let me get one or two things straight about you people. You're some kind of spirit, right?'

'Well, we're not flesh and blood. We're like electromagnetic collections of information.'

'And you're sort of semi-immortal.'

'We don't decay. But we can be destroyed,' she said. 'And what destroys us is being trapped inside someone who dies. So to get over that problem, we taught ourselves to transfer.'

'Transfer?'

'From one of you to another.'

'What – just like that?'

'No, worse luck. What happens is this. I'll be having a good time, you know, inhabiting some bloke, and the years go by, but I've got to be thinking all the time: do I stay, or do I cut and run? It's a gamble, always is. If I hang around he might get killed the next moment crossing the road, but if I decide to hop it, that's a risk too. So, imagine I'm with this guy, and I'm thinking, "This here drongo doesn't feel like a survivor to me, he's accident-prone, nobody loves him and his town's being blown to pieces by enemy artillery," so what I do is, next time he's with a sheila, I concentrate myself down in his balls, in the old repro-juice there, take a deep breath, and at the crucial moment I jump on the helterskelter and take a one-way trip to his girl's insides. Now as you may know, the next part of the process is dog-eat-dog: a million whiptail bullets racing like crazy for that egg. So I lock into the leading one and away we ride. Meanwhile I've usually got to deal with packs of killer sperm coming at me with chemical weaponry on account of his girl is usually fooling about with someone else, and of course I don't even know for certain there'll be an egg waiting round the bend... It's as precarious as that... Of course, I've calculated everything so the chances are there will be, but there's always that speck of uncertainty. That's the moment I'm scared shitless. Always. Never get used to it. No egg, and you're dead, there's nowhere to go but down the drain. Can't transfer to the main body, because there's no room for two NFAs there. But then you see it, this warm welcome red-and-orange glow up ahead, like a McDonalds on a lonely highway, and next minute you're diving inside, home and wet. And then for the next nine months you're hanging there inside this blasto-embryo-foetal and finally fully-formed sprog about to sprout. All this can be precarious too I might add.'

'What happens,' said Theo, 'if you're transferring from a woman?'

'Much easier – you just dive into the egg. There's a slim chance you'll meet another NFA coming the other way of course, and if this happens you've got a battle royal on your hands and one of you ends up disintegrated, but that's rare. No, you wait for the old sperm to show up and wallop – you're away. With the added benefit of being able to retreat back into the host's main system if her pregnancy looks like screwing up at any time. But being born is a real blast, like, now for a bit more autonomy, right? With any luck, for the next few years you've got the bastards doing *everything* for you. Life can be a real bowl of cherries in the old cot. Not always, of course,' she added.'Sometimes you can find yourself dropped out onto the dirt floor of some squalid shack in Shitetown with a couple of wasted parents and the local doctor pissed out of his head day and night. Then you've got your work cut out motivating your cute little lazy dictator of a host to look out for itself, else you're going down the gutter with it. I've had a priest give me the last rites, you know. That was close. Took me hours to finally shore up the immune system and then convert what few proteins I had left to work with in order to keep the sprog animate. But I made it, and I'm still here. G'day!'

He considered this as he poked with a plastic fork at the compartmentalised meal on his tray-table. 'But what happens,' he asked, 'if you find yourself inside someone who turns out to be a maiden aunt, or a priest, or–'

'Or someone whose vice is versa?' she said. 'Jeez, they give you a lot of extra work. But I found out that nobody is ever that

121

fixed in their ways. Especially if I can get to control a certain little button, a certain crucial switching point in the deepest caverns of the old corpus callosum, down there in the land of reptiles where the synapses are thick as a fuckin' Top End swamp. You can get some vital voltages going there, I can tell you, with just a little bit of reprogramming. Let me tell you about Plato, for example. Plato The Famous, as he was known in his time. Yeah – I was stuck inside that bundle of laughs. Clever bastard, all the same. He wasn't horny at first. No action at all. So I had to start something. I managed to penetrate the swamp – dodging all those great thoughts coming at me like road trains – and throw a few switches till I got him going. Trouble is it worked out so he only fancied slave boys – oh, and his mate Socrates, too. Bad news for me, eh? Years it took me to finally bend him the other way, and he was fighting it all the time. "Damn this sexual urge," he used to say, "It's like being chained to a lunatic." Charming. It was me who was chained to the fuckin' lunatic, till I finally got him to indulge in a brief little adventure under the desk with the sheila who came in daily to change his inkwells. Just the once it happened, but I was ready and I took my chance. Frying pan to the fire, really, because it meant I had to be born a slave. Still, I haven't been anywhere yet where the underlings don't get it on with the snotties – in fact that time I was spoilt for choice.'

She paused to take a bite from a chicken leg. Then she said, 'It was NFAs who invented the sexual thrill. We had to. We were dying like Aboriginals because you guys just weren't getting it on enough.' She looked at him. 'Do you know what makes your mob so different from apes? Screw language, opposing thumb, big toe, self-consciousness, culture, all that shite, it's that you're all permanently on heat. We couldn't take any chances. And we did a bit of tampering to get rid of most of your hair, just to aid the attraction, because there's something about bare *skin*, isn't there?'

She discarded the chicken leg and wiped the grease from her mouth. 'Hey, look,' she said, pointing out of the porthole. Way below was a sodium starburst. 'Madrid I guess. Not far now. Hey – you know it was in Spain where we first developed the last-chance-of-all emergency exit procedure? Yeah. Must have been around three thousand and eight bc. I was a silversmith. Or rather he was my... I mean I was his NFA. He was engaged to be spliced with a local girl, and I was looking forward to a trouble-free transfer at my leisure. Until the idiot goes and knifes someone to death at his stag party. And before I know what's happening they've wheeled him out to the hanging tree and they're stringing him up. Holy fuckin' *rites*, I'm thinking, I am completely kanoogled. This is curtains. Unless... by now they've pulled the cart away and left him groundless and gurgling and flaying about. I could see a chance, a very slim one, but I had nothing to lose, did I? So I went to work on his nervous system and made it go as if he was getting it on with his bride: pulled a few switches, concentrated myself down there – and then up went his rhythm stick, and blast off! First stage successful, and I'm tumbling through the air like a circus act. And he gives up the ghost, and I hit the ground. There's a lot of cheering and scuffling about from his captors, and in the mayhem a boot grinds me into the earth. And that's it. There I am, housed in this fluid seeping into the earth and rapidly cooling. I reckoned I had a minute or so left to me. I had to pull of something quick, I could feel the power draining fast. All I had to work with was the juice that contained me, plus the soil with which we were mingling: a bunch of lignified scraps, some silicates, and heaps of nitrogen. So I *informed* all this lot together so to speak, *enlightened* a few electrons here and there, spread a few *rumours* among certain cells of the organisation, and finally managed to get a modest little low-grade amino-acid production line going. It took a day or two for anything obvious to start forming, but meanwhile we were generating heat and a small amount of protein. Boy was I glad to see that happening! There was still life. And pretty soon after that, I was this *root*, wasn't I? And a pretty weird-shaped one, too – arms and legs like a miniature human – in fact I bore quite a resemblance to my recently-departed host. So I thought I'd better start attracting some attention if I didn't want to be stuck like this – I mean think about it, how would you like to be reborn as a plant? So I shot out a stalk and a few leaves, and topped them with some very attractive little pink flowers. Because I knew this silver-smith's fiancée, and I knew her favourite colour was pink. And I thought right, let's see if she turns up. And she did, too. I couldn't *see* her of course, being as I was now a subject of the vegetable kingdom. But I had a ripper little magnetic field, so I could pick up on this girl's thoughts as soon as she got within range of where I was busy being a plant.

'Yeah – she shows up with a bunch of blood-red carnations to mark the spot where they lynched her betrothed. She gets to her knees, says a few prayers to some assorted spirits, has a little weep, poor girl, then she gets up, tidies herself up – and sees me growing away there at her feet. She's knocked out. She's never seen a plant with such beautiful flowers. She's thinking there's something really special about this amazing plant that's sprung up here. Then she digs me up. She nearly faints when she sees the shape of my root. She starts calling the guy's name. As far as she's concerned he's been transformed by the good powers that be and his spirit was now in this jerrybuilt herbaceous perennial I'd knocked together. She wasn't far wrong, really. Anyway, she reckoned her spirit and his would be like eternally entwined if she were to eat me. So she took me home, chopped up the plant, leaves, flowers, root and all, sprinkled it with tarragon vinegar, and gobbled me up. And I'd made it back to humanity. But of course I had instant trouble when her own NFA realised what was happening. Nasty piece of work – Wilson it was again – and he let me have a few death rays as soon as he got wind of me. Luckily I had a lot of newly synthe-sised vegetable information to defend myself with, so I warded him off while I made my way pronto down to the girl's tubes, where I oozed myself into the first egg waiting there on plat-form two. And since she'd already got it on with her now-departed, nine months later it's papoose-popping time and there I am with a brand new me.

'Now, the thing is, when that sheila made a salad of me she thought she'd keep the seeds. And I'd left those seeds pretty charged up, I mean those seeds had a few zillion gigabytes each, they were just *humming* with stories. And it didn't take long for them to spread all over the Med. They called the plant

124

Mandragora, and the girls used to eat it to try and get themselves in the club. The Bible reckons Rachael scored some from Leah on account of Jacob's spunk wasn't up to much. If you don't believe me, check out Genesis 30.'

She paused, and looked at him curiously. 'Funny how your ma got pregnant again after all these years, isn't it? Just after she'd come back from her grandparents' place in Cyprus? You ask her if she didn't find herself a little of what did Rachael good, up there in the mountains.'

They landed at Malaga. He let Diana carry his dayglo rucksack containing the head. 'If there's any problems I'll say it's a holy relic,' she said, 'they like that sort of shit round here.'

There were no problems. There were wide, date-palmed avenues, and lots of monumental banks, with gypsies and beggars sitting outside them with their hands thrust out. They bussed out along the coast road, past old men on crutches, and hundreds of abandoned, half-built hotels, their concrete floors supported by crutch-like wooden props. It was crutch country. Was this why Dali's stuff was full of them?

An hour's ride and they were rumbling along the narrow isthmus connecting Gibraltar to the mainland. The British checkpoint was crawling with squaddies, who seemed a little nervous as they clumped onboard the bus.

'What's in the bag, sister?' Diana was asked of the bulging rucksack.

'Sandwiches, brother,' she replied with a heavy Spanish accent.

'That's a lot of sandwiches for a slim girl like you.'

'For the poor,' she said, bowing her head and batting her eyelids. 'I also have a holy relic,' she smiled, 'the severed head of a blessed sainted martyr.'

'Really? Nice with a bit of mayonnaise, is it?'

The soldiers got down and the bus rumbled on across a small airfield. The rest, towering up ahead of them, was rock.

'Hasn't changed much,' Diana observed.

'Since when?'

'We were in Ibn Tariq's train. We took the place from a bunch of Goths in 711. We had quite a job. Looks solid, that rock,

125

doesn't it? But it's full of limestone caverns. We chased those bastard hornhats around inside there for months. Then we called the place Jebel Tariq, geddit? People have drilled out more of them since. There's bloody great barracks and hospitals inside there now. If they dig out any more the whole thing is going to implode.'

The closer they drew, the clearer the rock became, like an enormous resting lion, pockmarked all over with tunnel-mouths, and bristling with pylons and antennae. And below, the town, squeezed into the little space between rock and sea: harbours, shops, cafés, petrol stations, barracks, and servicemen everywhere. It could have been Aldershot on a hot Saturday.

They took rooms in a roach-infested pension tucked away in a network of squalid backstreets. They walked the harbour walls; they observed battleships at anchor out in the roads. They sat in waterfront cafés and watched the coming and going of yachts, and waited for a sight of the *Ubique*. By day, marching bands paraded the streets and squares; by night off-duty soldiers in denims and trainers had themselves drunken punch-ups outside bars and got themselves truncheoned by MPs and carted off in paddy-wagons.

Diana fiddled thoughtfully with her rosary. They had been there some days now. They were sitting outside at a café table overlooking the harbour. 'You know what I reckon?' she said. 'I think our friend Wilson is stranded. I reckon his host kicked the bucket. That's probably why he materialised in the first place.'

'His last chance, eh? – Listen,' he said, 'if he does turn up, no shootouts, right? This place is crawling with security. They've got Spanish nationalists to deal with, and they shot down some IRA here not too long ago. Take it easy, OK? Softly-softly.'

'Yeah, all right,' she conceded grudgingly. 'But he's danger-ous, mate. You need some protection for yourself. Listen-' and she poked about in her robes – 'I've got a nice little automatic for you here, fits nicely into your windcheater pocket, really discreet.'

'Nope.'

'Jeez, you're so bloody noble it stinks. Look – take a blade at least. I've got a beaut little silver dagger here -' And she

126

produced it. It was a foot long, housed in a sheath curved like a crescent moon. 'A Bedouin gave it me once down in the Negev. Beautiful piece of work, eh?'

'Can't deny it,' he said. 'How old is it?'

'About two thousand years. In a manner of speaking.'

'What do you mean?'

'Well, it's actually a fax. Couldn't keep the real thing with me across all that time – I wasn't even material myself. But it's the same thing as far as anything matters – identical bytes and all that. Go ahead: take it. Don't take chances.'

He pocketed the weapon. Then he said 'When you were talking about Wilson just then you said, "There's more to it." What do you mean?'

'Oh yeah. Listen – you ever hear of cryogenics?'

'Yeah,' he said, 'brilliant album.'

'No, not that shit,' she said, 'I mean–' But he cut her off.

'Don't look now,' he said, 'but there's our man.'

He had just noticed a familiar figure come out of a doctor's surgery and head in their direction. But the moment Theo spoke White clocked them, paused momentarily take off his flipflops and stuff them in his jacket, and fled.

'Excellent!' she said. 'Come on, we'll nail the bastard.' But she too had trouble with her clothing. She took a step forwards, caught her foot in her robes and sprawled headlong. 'Jeez,' she gasped, 'I'm not playing chase dressed like this. Go on, God's gift, do your stuff.'

As he took off up the hill in pursuit he saw White turn into an alley. Reaching this, his quarry bounded up a distant flight of steps and then vanishede. And when Theo emerged from the alley, the man was nowhere to be seen. He was perplexed. The road here was practically deserted. The only activity was that of two trucks picking up a crowd of local workers with picks, tool-boxes, mops, buckets and thermos flasks. The first was already setting off. And that was White crammed in amongst its cargo of underlings.

Theo raced across the road and joined the party in the second truck, which promptly took off behind the first and roared up the narrow road before turning onto a wide highway which hairpinned its way up the mountainside and was lined with cheap apartment blocks, stray dogs and petrol stations. The traffic was mainly military. The sun was hot. He was sweating. The conversation around him was Spanish. In front of them now was the sheer, vast, scrubby rockface. Ahead was a tunnel entrance and a military checkpoint. He watched the truck in front slow to a crawl and the driver wave a pass as it went through. There were a couple of jeeps between the two trucks, and by the time his truck had got through the checkpoint and they were roaring along the snaking subterranean road with cool air rushing through their clothes, the lorry with White aboard was out of sight. A couple of minutes later and the route had led into a rock cavern the size of an aircraft hanger, full of power plant and stacked portakabins, lit with neon strip. Here the truck stopped and the Spaniards climbed down and went about their business. He jumped off too.

No sign of the other vehicle. He guessed it had passed straight through here. He made for the far tunnel mouth, as casually as he could. But before he was a few yards into it a voice from behind rapped at him:

' 'Ere, Pedro!' A soldier was ambling towards him.

Shit, he thought. But right there in the tunnel wall was an alcove, and a steel door. He tried the door. It opened. He stepped into total darkness and closed the door behind him. He felt around for a switch, found it, and threw it. Ahead of him, dimly lit by periodic yellow bulbs, a low pedestrian tunnel led off into the distance. He hurried off along it, crouching forwards to keep his head from scraping against the low brick roof. The tunnel smelt like all the cats of Hell had pissed in it; it was like King's Cross station on a good day. He could detect no sign of pursuit behind him, but he didn't slow down. A minute or two later the passage ended at another door. He stood there for a moment getting his breath back, then opened the door. He found himself confronting a row of old marble urinals: the brasswork was tarnished with verdigris, the cisterns hissed, and the place stunk of rich tobacco. Bit of luck, he thought, I could do with a Jimmy. And as he went about this task he heard muffled talk and laughter beyond the far door. And when he presently opened this door and went through, he saw he had stepped into a pub.

It was smoky and crowded. Men and women huddled in groups, drinking Guinness. They were dressed like country bumpkins – fleabitten tweeds, waxed raincoats, marblewash denims. At the bar was an old man with a shock of white hair reading the *Tyrone Chronicle*. The juke box thumped to a Joe Dolan song. He wondered what he was doing in Ireland all of a sudden. He pushed his way through the huddle of drinkers and made for the door. Outside, it was Ireland all right. A small high street in a sleepy village with a war memorial in the middle of the road and a traffic sign to Donegal and Londonderry. And all shrouded in a heavy Irish mist. A solitary car passed by. He could hear a distant pipe wailing, to the accompaniment of a bass drum.

This doesn't make sense, he thought. But what else does? For instance, why were there now people coming out onto the street everywhere, from shops and sidestreets? The answer was soon evident – the funeral was even now emerging onto the main road, led by the pipe and drum, the coffin carried by six men wearing anoraks and balaclavas. A priest walked before them. A large crowd was already following the coffin, and people were rapidly joining and swelling the procession. And it was cold, so cold. He wished he wore more than a T-shirt. He found himself pressed by the throng to the front of the cortège, the drone of 'The Flowers Of The Forest' sharp in his ear, and out of the mist ahead, the sight of armoured cars emerging from the gloom, flanked by a squad of footsoldiers. The procession shuffled to a halt.

All this seemed all too familiar, like he had been dropped into the TV news. Now he heard a cry of abuse from behind him, and saw a flaming bottle arc above his head and explode into fire and smoke in front of the army lines. The scary thing was that there was no video burn. He could smell it. Bricks and more petrol bombs followed. The air was metallic with curses. Then the army opened fire. It set his teeth chattering. He turned and fought his way back through the rioting crowd. It was then he saw a pair of flipflops and bellbottoms also beating a retreat.

Free of the crowd now, White was hurrying off beyond the war memorial and into the mist. Theo loped along in pursuit. Behind him cars were being overturned and set alight, and screams, molotov cocktails and plastic bullets rent the air. It occurred to him that this must be some kind of warp in space-time. He was gaining quickly on White, who was hurrying along the pavement, keeping close to the doorways. Then Theo saw the roadblock, and three soldiers drawing a bead on the bellbottomed art thief. White stopped and addressed the squaddies.

'Look,' he called out, 'there's been a mistake.' He began walking towards them with his hands spread out, palms up.

The hands of the first soldier tightened around his rifle.

'I don't trust him,' said the second soldier. 'Where's his tag?'

The third could detect a heavy object weighing down White's jacket pocket.

'That's a bomb he's carrying,' he said.

Then White called out as he hesitantly approached. 'Look lads, I'm British. I was a lieutenant in the OTC.'

'You're right,' said the second soldier to the third, 'it's got to be a bomb.'

'Oh Jesus,' said the first soldier, and fired.

Theo, who had ducked into a doorway, saw White double up with the bullet's impact, lurch backwards and land in a heap at his feet. He took his opportunity. He reached for the bulge in White's pocket and retrieved the diary. As the soldiers approached he backed into the shop. It was dark and deserted in there, and it looked like they had the builders in. Negotiating timber, trestles and rubble he hurried through to the back. The walls, like the floor, were bare stone. In the gloom he could just make out the entrance to a passage. He plunged into its darkness and groped his way forward. Another little tunnel. The ground was uneven, the walls were bare and dripping. So where did this lead to? Belfast? Bosnia? Baghdad? He felt his way forwards in the silent blackness, clutching Katie Sawkin's diary.

The passage seemed to lead gradually upwards. And then it just ended. He felt a blank wall of earth and rock in front of him

him. Damn. He kicked out at the rock in frustration. And was surprised to feel it give way. He kicked it some more and it gave way some more. And eventually he had scraped and kicked and clambered his way through to where the tunnel continued. It was wider here – the walls was dry and the dampness had gone from the air. Exhausted, he sat down for a breather. He pulled out the diary from his waistband. He weighed the heavy volume in his hands. He ran his fingers over the clasp and the ornate patterns etched into the brass covers, like a blind man at braille. Then he remembered he had matches from that café. He lit one and held it over the book, and opened it at the first page.

But he had to struggle to decipher the obscure and jagged script. He was wasting matches on it, it would have to wait. Then he noticed, by his feeble flame, that there were figures drawn on the walls of the passage. They were painted. Lifesize. Men draped in Arab gear. Green robes, exotic turbans. They were angular and crude. They carried flags and shields which displayed a crescent moon. More moors, he thought. Now where am I?

He kept going. Every now and then he lit a match. The walls were continuously decorated with human figures, but they were changing: now their skin was pink instead of brown, their clothing was heavier-duty, and they held crosses.

Some way further on, they became Romans with those shin-guards and cute little miniskirts that he used to draw all the time at school. What's more he could draw all the folds and pleats far better than whoever did this lot.

The next flare of brief, sulphurous light revealed Greek warriors.

I get it. Some kind of heritage tour. He gave top style points so far to the next lot, a bunch of hairy men with incredibly coif-fured black beards sticking out from their chins like flights of stairs. And then there were bulls, black bulls being put to the sword by naked men with thick necks and curly locks. More women began to appear. Topless too, with huge knockers. Bulls with crescent-moon horns, women with goose-head masks, women adorned with snakes… it was quite a party, and it seemed to go on forever. Then the people began to disappear

131

from the paintings, and the pictures grew more scarce. The figures were vaguer, the colours faded, and all blacks and reds. There were deer-like creatures, bear and bison, some hunted by tiny, simply drawn figures almost as slim as matchstick men. And then herds of lion and horse. And after these there was the strangest of beings: it had the rearing hindquarters and torso of a big cat, human arms and legs, a fox's tail, and was crowned with deer antlers atop a strange white face with a long beard and big dark staring eyes. Fearsome. A sort of stone-age robocop put together from spare parts.

Now the passage was widening. Musty smells wafted up his nostrils. A bat flickered past his face. The floor was becoming littered with bones. He lit another match. What next? Eden?

What was next was another blank wall. But not a sheer face – it seemed to have steps cut crudely into it. He began to climb some kind of rock-chimney. He lit his last match, and found himself staring at a realistic-looking ape. This didn't surprise him – but he was startled when the ape blinked. It turned and scuttled away up the shaft. And when the match went out, he could just discern a faint aura of natural light up there. He worked his way on up. The passage was very narrow now, and its slope was flatter. He was crawling on hands and knees through dirt and leaves and droppings. And moments later he poked his head above ground. He was in the middle of a clump of bushes. He could smell the salt air. He clambered free and found himself high up on the rock, the sea before him, crashing against cliffs way below. And he was surrounded by apes, looking at him curiously and demanding food.

Back down in the town he showered at the hotel, put on a pair of baggy jeans, sat on his bed beneath a crucifix on the wall, started in on a large tub of sheep's yoghurt, and opened the diary.

THREE

7. FOURTEEN GENERATIONS BACK

TWO MEN held him fast from behind while a third held a kitchen knife to his throat. With excruciating pain the knifepoint was poked into his Adam's Apple. Then it was withdrawn.

'We'll be back,' said the knifeman, and suddenly launched his boot into Willis' groin. His creditors left him doubled up in agony on the floor of his studio. Mingled with the ringing in his ears were the sounds from the street. Barrows rumbled across cobbles. The costermongers were bawling jokes to one another. A handbell rang officiously, and then right below the window came a swarm of squawking gulls.

He grabbed the edge of a table, pulled himself to his feet and surveyed the devastation. Every easel upturned. Materials strewn everywhere. Floorboards torn up. Mattress ripped open, feathers all over the place.

Stumbling around, he searched the room until he found three pots, scattered to one corner. Each full of hardened paint, chrome yellow. He picked one up and dashed it to pieces on the floor, and then picked up the solidified mass. He took a hammer to this and broke it asunder. Hidden in the middle was a gold sovereign.

He smiled, narrowed his eyes, and pouted. Then he doubled up in pain again and coughed up a mass of phlegm. When he had recovered from this he chipped the remaining bits of paint from the coin, pocketed it and went down to the street, where he sluiced himself down under a pump. Then he picked his way through the market, through the crowds of scavengers bent double over the day's rotten leftovers, went into the bar of the Moor's Head and demanded a pint. The barkeeper raised her eyebrows at the gold coin, and before she served him she tested the doubloon in an acid bath (a tin of stale beer) to check it didn't change colour or disintegrate.

The Moor's Head not only displayed on its inn sign an image of a near-oriental wearing a green bandanna, it also had the real thing on a shelf behind the counter, preserved in clear pickling fluid in a large stoppered jar. The head did not rest at the base of this jar, but was suspended in its translucent medium. It had been sharply severed from its shoulders: the neat cross-sections of artery and tendon were visible. The eyes still seemed to express the shock of this treatment, and the mouth looked as though it had been about to open much further. What interested the painter Willis most about the Moor's Head was that it was said to utter prophecies at significant times.

The barkeeper set his beer before him and passed him a heavy handful of change. He supped gratefully from the pot. He was still shaking a little from the beating he had taken. He'd sunk a long way below his station. He owed an awful lot of money to a worse lot of people. But right now he didn't give a toss for his creditors. None of them would starve. He had more important things to do with his money. His first task was to find the most beautiful woman alive. He gave himself no longer than this night to carry it out.

And then, if he was to avoid any more visits from the lads or the law, he must move on. This wasn't a difficult prospect. Houses were empty everywhere. Granted, some people were beginning to come back to town, but not in great numbers yet. Then he could get down to the real work at last. No more time wasted on tobacco. He might even find some buyers. He still had some society connections.

He looked at the Moor's Head again. Its heavy brass earrings, its luxuriant black hair. It was a youthful face. It could have been of either sex. Willis suspected it was a girl, since it was an oracle. But it hadn't spoken in his lifetime: never a thing to say about wars, epidemics, kings and queens, God or the Devil or the End of the World. Not that anyone ever asked it, either. It had long ceased to be an object of much interest. Just a dusty old souvenir from one of the old crusades.

Willis stared fixedly at the head. He began to imagine the circumstances of this girl's death. He saw a Mediterranean temple, a vulnerable child, and a number of mail-clad and red-crossed figures approaching with drawn swords. Then, along with his empty jar, he put these fancies aside and went out into the evening.

Mingling with the crowds on the South Bank, he came to a baiting. You won if your dog could draw blood from the grizzly. You lost soon after that, usually. A terrier was putting up a spirited show and the punters were howling for blood, but Willis was more interested in a girl he saw working the crowd. He sidled through the throng and drew closer to her. He admired her technique, her deft fingers as they snaffled out coins and sparklers from unwary pockets. She had just purloined a pie from a stall and was noshing as she went. She was young, perhaps not sixteen. She had long red hair and a confident, graceful bearing, not the usual jerky, half-cowed appearance of your usual villain. She was without doubt the most beautiful woman alive. So he set himself up for her, and when he sensed her hand on his purse he caught her securely by the wrist. Then he turned and smiled into her startled eyes.

Her voice was deep and tuneful. 'Let go of me, you turd,' she said.

'Listen, mistress,' he said, 'work for me and you'll have a real reward.'

'I don't do that kind of thing.'

'If you won't, then I'll turn you in. I've been watching you.'

'Go to hell.'

'You'll be rich… famous, too.'

'Away, you ponce.'

' 'Tis nothing to do with that kind of thing.' He showed her a half-crown. 'Deal?'

There was the sudden shriek of a dog being swiped into eternity, and a roar from the crowd.

'Maybe,' she said.

Then there came a strange gurgling sound from the bag she carried.

'What have you got in there?' said Willis.

She opened the bag. The fierce eyes of a small baby confronted him. Its tiny fingers clutched at the remains of a meat pie. It was covered in crumbs and juices, and it squirmed about in a sea of farthings and cheap jewellery. It looked savage and satisfied.

'All right?' she said.

He laughed, shaking his head. She misread him. 'I could always dump it,' she offered.

'Go ahead, then.'

'What?'

'Get rid of it, then.'

'Right,' she said. Then she stopped and thought for a moment. 'No,' she said in a matter-of-fact way, 'I've decided I don't want to do that.'

'That's fine,' he said, 'Besides, I can use it.'

'*Her*,' she corrected him.

'Her. I should get rid of the bag, though.'

'Why?'

'She hath just shat black hell into it,' observed Willis.

❤

They moved to large, well furnished rooms north of the river, and she began to model for him. She sat till her back ached and her neck throbbed. The coffee helped but it gave her the jitters. He scratched away manically, eyes darting rapidly back and forth from her to the paper.

'Don't you ever let up?' she said.

'What for?' he said.

'What's the hurry?'

'Be still, will you?'

'Sorry, I'm having a break.'

'Allow me a little while yet,' said Willis.

138

'What do you take me for?'

He sighed and put down the charcoal.

'What is it that drives you so?' she said.

'Simple. I'm going to die,' he said.

'Who isn't?'

'I've got a month, maybe, at the most.'

'What do you mean?'

'I've got the plague.'

'Don't talk squit. It would be scabbing out all over you.'

'No. It gets inside you, you see, before you even know about it. But it's there, quietly taking hold from inside. And then when the time is ripe – Kismet! You wake up dripping sweat with the pox bursting out all over you.'

'Squit.'

'Maybe. But someone close to me went down with it, and you know what that means.'

'You turd. You let me in for this and you didn't tell me.'

'There's the door,' he said.

She didn't move. 'It doesn't matter,' she said.

'Oho,' said Willis. 'We are in the same boat, are we?' He looked at the serious child she held. 'Were you with its father?'

She nodded.

'Has he been dead long?'

'The day you met me,' she said.

'Oh.'

'Keep scribbling,' said the most beautiful woman alive, 'and I'm sorry if I suddenly break out in pustules.'

♥

From the diary of Catherine Sawkin

May 1st, Anno Domini 1666

This is the Journal of Catherine Sawkin, begun this Day. I am surprized to have had the Courage to start. It has been a Week since I first determined on it. When I told *Willis* of my Plan he looked astonish'd and said, 'But Katie, you can neither read nor write.' This was not the playn Truth, because I already had the Alphabet and a few Words taught me by the Deaconess at St.

Saviour's when I was but seven Years old, and I had then copied out two Verses from the Gospels. But I could read Nothing else at all, and had not picked up a Pen in the seven Years since. So I then said to Willis, 'Well then, I am going to learn, and in Haste.'

I had then been under his Roof for a Week, ever since the Evening we had met on the South Bank and removed from his Rooms by the Market-place. I was glad to have a proper Lodging at last, and proper Employment for the first Time in my Life, but I was still in utter Misery. I knew that verie soon, along with my Babe, I was to suffer a Death most terrible. And this vexed me sorely and made me morose, and cruel to the Child, which I resented having brought into this World. For Hours I would sit in my Poses for the Painter, dwelling on the darkest of Thoughts, having Nothing else to engage my Mind. He called me Beautiful, yet I both looked and felt like some dreadfull Creeping Thing. Moreover the Work was much fatiguing, and I ached in both Body & Spirit.

Despite his own equally sorry Predicament, my Client-Landlord was not affected like this at all. He was always in the most energetick Spirits. This made me hate him, and abuse him roundly & ofttimes. And I was constantly mourning my lost Family, my lost Man and my dearest Friends. But in Truth it was I who was lost. In the little Time I had to Myself I dared not venture outdoors, and instead would lie about smoking copious amounts of Tobacco.

But Willis allowed himself no Respite at all. 'There is no Time any more for Rest,' he announced. 'In fact, there is no Time anymore. We are at the End of it. These last Daies are Aeternal. And so everything we see and do should be an aeternal Glorie.' And he spent everie waking Hour at his Work. He was determined to leave a Testament to the World, and he would often look kindly upon me and reassure me that I was Part of this great Project and was blessed for my Contribution. Was not there Honor and Glorie enough in this? I replied that with Nothing to occupy my Mind I would die of Insanitie before the Plague could finish me.

'By Heaven you are right,' says he—'You must have an Occupation.' And he suggests that I learn to cook. I suggested that instead he should boil his Head. For me, Cabbage-Soup is not a great Testament to Mankind.

He would not allow me to draw or paint, for he said this would be too great a Distraction from my playing the Mannequin. And when he propos'd that I take up Embroiderie, I replied that I had no Inclination for such a tedious Craft. The Truth was, I wanted to speak. To speak instead of scream all the Time. I was tired of blubbering louder than mine own Child. The Baby was the calmest Creature within these Walls. And so I realiz'd that I must make a Journal, and I insisted upon this.

For the first Stage of my Project I had Willis procure me a Bible, from which I would learn my Craft. I was to read aloud while posing, and he would correct me. I would copy Passages before I went to Slepe or whilst feeding the Child in the small Hours. 'And how long do you give yourself for this Task?' says the Painter. I explained that I intended to read the Book from Beginning to End, and that this would take me seven Daies, and that by then I would be a qualified Diarist. 'Seven Daies!' says he, 'you make a merrie Jape, Mistress Sawkin! Why, no letter'd Person could hope to achieve that Labor, let alone an unschool'd one, and a Woman to boot. Why not keep to one simple Book?' I replied that there was not enough Time for one simple Book. For as he himself had said, there was no Time.

And so I began my Task, first learning to speke the Word *Genesis*, which was enough in itself to raise my Spirits. It took me two Hours to master the first five Verses and thus pronounce the Coming of Day & Nite. By Lunchtime (at which I re-discovered my Appetite for the Gruel that Willis cooked) I had spoken of Adam and Eve being created, punish'd and banish'd, and by the end of the Day I had completed the first Book.

My Client was not unimpress'd, but as I sat copying out the Story of Sodom & Gomorrah by Candlelight, and hearing the Sound of Corpse-Carts rumbling thru the Streets below and the melancholie Cries of 'Out with your Dead!'—he reminded me that there were yet two-and-seventy Books to complete, and six Daies left for this Accomplishment. I did not slepe at all that Nite. I remained at my Writing-Table with the Infant on my

141

Lap. Between fitful Dozes I would be forc'd awake to pacify her, and then I would copy out more Scripture. All the Time I heard the Dead-Wagon's Roll and the Hand-Bell's Toll. They had spoken of a new Burial-Ground at Broad Street. I saw Myself being presently dispatch'd to it. I felt my skinny Corpse tumble into the Pit along with thousands of other forsaken Mortals. But it made no Sense to dwell upon this, and I shuddered and quickly return'd to my Work.

May 2nd, A.D. 1666

On the Morrow I completed the Pentateuch, reading from Exodus thru Deuteronomy. I stumbled over those savage Laws of Leviticus, I lost my Voice. I lost my Way. It took me until Sun-Set to finish Numbers. And the Kindling set up such a Wailing as she never had before and much Time was taken in the Pacifying of it. We eventually discover'd that Peppermint settles her Gripes with Efficacie (& also settles our Nerves). The Beautiful Brat has beautiful Clothes now. And she can at last find her Way back to the Tit by herself.

This Painter Man talketh in his Slepe. I hear him behind the Curtain. He conducts Disputes with Italians. Often they are in Italian, and will sometimes switch to some more eerie Tongue. I understand them to be upon the Subjects of Religion, Painting, and the Bodie. He frequently challengeth men he calls *Signor Pintor* to a Duel. I imagine that they fight with their best Brushes, but evidently Willis' is the Longer of the Two, because it is always he who wins. After each such Victorie I have taken to creeping close to his Canopie, the better to hear what always follows, which is BOTH SIDES of an am'rous Conversation in Dutch. It is as if there were two Persons behind the Drape. I am resolved henceforth to study the Tongue, the more fully to comprehend these Occasions of Double-Dutch.

The following Day brought a freshening Wind from the North which temporarily dispelled the sicklie Odors which had flowed like bad Liquor into our Lungs. I felt strong and renewed as I sat thru the Daie with the Kindling on my Lap, even though I was speaking of the Decline of an Empire and the *Israelites'* consequent Fall from Grace. When I recounted the majestick Justice of Judith—*Her Sandals ravished his Eyes, her Beauty made his Soul her Captive: with a Sword she cut off his Head*—Willis suggested that I had sung of this with more Relish than is seemlie. It was then that I first began more properly to observe him. I had never taken him for a handsome Fellow, he was rather runtish and short of Stature. His Brow was low and wide, and his little Eyes were set deep within the Skull, from where they sparkled like Jewels in a murky Cave. His Nose was flat and broken, his Mouth generously wide, but thin and tight. He had no Neck to speak of; and his chicken-skinned Adam's Apple fought for Space between Chin and Chest. I concluded that any Person bent upon decapitating Willis would be hardput to find the right Spot for the Blade, although I decided not to attempt to comfort him with this Observation. His Trunk and Limbs were less unattractive, however; his Build was sinuous and athletic, and his Movements were quick and confident. He was not a Man I would ordinarily be drawn to, in fact I was some-what repelled by him during the first Daies of our Association. But after Midnite it was, on the fourth Day of my Reading, that he had retired to Slepe and I remained with Babe, Book and Candle, copying the Song of Solomon:—*Draw me*—I wrote—*We will run after thee to the Odor of thy Ointments: we will be glad and rejoice in thee, remembering thy Breasts more than Wine*—And further,—*My Beloved put his Hand through my Key-Hole, and my Bowels were moved at his Touch*—I too was moved at this, and not I confess in a righteous Manner. These Verses appeared an unlikely way of describing the Love betwixt Christ and His Church. For myself, they drew forth Memories of more wanton Occasions which I now began to miss for the first Time.

When I had finished copying the Song of Songs, I extinguish'd the Candle, arose and went to stand by his Bed. From behind the Drape I could hear his irregular Breathing and Slepefull Murmurings. I parted the Curtain a little, but could see Nothing of him in the Darkness. But it was the Smell of him which o'erwhelmed me, rich and buttery it was, and also a little sharp. I remained by the Curtain for some While, savoring this warm Mist, untill the Kindling began to complain at me as if she were jealous, and I was obliged to join her in mine owne Bed.

As I lay in the Dark feeding the Beautiful Brat I thought more on Willis. He was the Son of East Anglian Gentlefolk, and had come to London to pursuive his craft. He had been apprentic'd for some While before quitting his Master prematurely and descending into a Boozer's Life, amassing both Debts and Enemies. His home Toun was struck by the Plague and none survived; and when his few Friends in London began to expire one by one and he saw his owne Daies clearly numbered 'And drawn in Flames across the night Sky,' as he put it, it was then he determin'd to mend his Ways:—'Death is for the Living', he insisted to me as he gripped my Shoulders and attempted to shake me from a tearful Stupor. 'Until now, your Daies and mine have been merely a Living Death, but now—no longer! Would you insult Heaven? Spirit, Katie! You have ample Reserves of it. Would you let it all drain away as Tears?'

I answered that I was afraid to die, afraid to burn.

'You will burn so bright as to scorch the whole World,' says he, 'And after this the Flames of Purgatorie will seem no hotter than a Glow-Worm's Conceit. *Fiat Lux!*'

And so saying he seiz'd upon the numerous Boxes of Candles stored in a Corner and rapidly took every Taper there was and arranged them in Banks th'entire Length of a Wall. Hundreds, there were, and when he had lit ev'ry One they vibrated in such a Blaze of Glory as I never saw in any Temple. I was obliged to shield mine Eyes from the Intensitie of their Glare, as if from the Eye of God. Exalted, Willis strode about preparing his Materials whilst the Shadows danced wildly around us. And when he began to sing a rousing Hymn in a Voice cracked and terrible, the Kindling joined in with a Descant even more savage. I could not help but laugh at Willis' owne immense Conceit.

On the Eve of the sixth Day I finished *St.* Jude, and there now remained but the Book of *Revelations* before my Task would be complete. I resolved to defer this until the Morrow, and meanwhile I posed for Willis in a series of Allegories.

Now, the Hour was late, and I was stood as Naked Truth Holding The Book, when there came a Knocking at our Door from a pair of *Ruffians* who insisted upon the Entry which they

144

shortly gained. They had come to extract certain Monies they claimed were owed to them by Willis. When my Painter replied that he owed them Nothing, they drew Daggers. The fat One took me and held me fast. He held a certayne Part of his owne even faster as he did so. His Master confronted Willis, who stood quietly before him, still holding his Mahlstick.

'Else you complie,' says this bearded Villain,—'Else I will kill first the Child and then your Wench. And should you need Time to consider, why, I shall be pleased to kill them at a most leisurely Pace. Now, sir, will you pay me?'

I made not a Sound, though the fat one squeezed me and slobbered over me like a Dog. Willis fondled the Tip of his Mahlstick and appeared to be considering the Rogue's Proposal.

—'Well? What say you?' demanded the Beard.

Willis regarded him meekly. 'I would sooner eat the Devill's Foreskin,' quoth he, and so saying he unscrewed the Mahlstick's brass Ferrule, tossed away the leathern Head, and drew from the hollow Stick a Rapier which was conceal'd within. Before the astonish'd Villain could move, Willis had run him through with the Blade and he fell to the Floor and expir'd, dribbling Blood. Mine own Captor was shocked by the Sight and relaxed his Grip upon me, and I seized this Opportunitie to first kick his Privates and then bring the full Weight of the Holy Bible down upon his Head, at which he stumbled away, gurgling. Willis let the Man escape:—'Avaunt, Little Piggy!' he cried, 'Wee-wee-wee all the Way Home!'

Thus we were delivered. But there was now an unwanted Object on our Hands, *viz.* the Corpse of the bearded Thug. I knew immediately what to do:—'But we live in such convenient Times for a Situation such as this!' I exclaimed, 'We shall simply paint him up with scarlet Blotches, then dump him on the next Dead-Cart to pass!'

But the Painter reminded me forcefully that if we did so the Howse would immediately be condemned as Plague-Ridden, be instantly boarded up, and we would be left to starve to Death within.

'No,' says Willis. 'Look at him: is he not *Holofernes* to a T? This is a Gift from Above! I have my next Subject.'

Thus it was that I was straightway posed as *Judith* in the Act of beheading the Assyrian Chieftan, as soon as we had hauled the Villain's Bodie over to a Couch furnished with fine Draperie. I stood holding a wooden Broadsword across the Corpse's Neck whilst its wide-ope'd Eyes stared into mine owne, and Willis put his Mahlstick back to its original Use.

On the following Day, before we break-fasted, I read the Apocalypse. It seems that it is a Woman who will save the World, and one heavy with child at that, according to *St. John's* Vision. Later, I was conversing with Willis as we continued work on Judith and Holofernes. I begged him to make Haste with his Picture, since the Corpse would soon begin to smell. He assured me that he would soon be finish'd, after which he planned to anatomize the Body & then dispose of it in small Portions.

May 3rd, 1666

I have been everywhere, and done every Thing. I have assisted at the Creation, I have been in the Garden, and then expel'd; I have been in Slavery, and from there escaped; I have been shewn the Promised Land, onlie to find it already occupied. I have vanquished the Canaanite, the Midianite, and the Ten-Headed Beast. I have been spat upon for Dancing and stoned for Adultery. I have killed my Brother & slain my Lover. I have never known who I was.

Willis suggested that my Journal include some biographical Note. The above will have to suffice.

Two Things have I not done: the first is to kill my Father, for no Daughter has done this in the Scriptures. Willis adviseth me to study the Tales of Ancient Greece to perhaps discover such a Story. I shall begin to-morrow. The second is to pose for a *Pietà* of Mary clasping her dead Son to her Breast, the Son being modelled by our fast-putrefying Corpse. I will not do this, insist though the Painter may.

May 9th 1666

Willis hath anatomiz'd the Corpse and thrown its Innards to the Dogs in the Street. He hath stuffed it, and embalm'd the

Body with his painter's Oils. He has produced a Mountain of Drawings and Studies from this Activity. Verily, he is as much the Physician as the Artist, and possessed of similar Tools and Techniques.

I have now read all the Greek, and all the Latin (& yet there is no Trace of the Patricide I have made a Hobby-Horse of seeking); I am now set to study the Church Fathers, beginning with Clement. While Willis was busy playing the Mortician I embarked upon a Volume of my owne Commentaries to the Texts I read; this Project gathers apace and there is already a sizeable Folio. Poor Willis is at times jealous of my Learning. He has now insisted that I lessen my Writing Activities and return to sit for him, but I am unwilling to lend him more than Half my Time. I have my Work, and I have my Kindling; when I explained this to him this Morning he generated a fearsome Rage. He told me I had Ideas above my Station. He then blustered on about the Fact that I was his Tenant, and in his Employ, and he made threats to evict me. I in turn reminded him that he was merely a Client, and I would gladly find Emploiment and Lodging elsewhere if he so desired. But much of this Business (and worse Abuse which I shall not record) was but mutual Hot-Air. We are both under no small Pressure, and sometimes our Lids must needs rattle. Willis will never throw me out, and I shall never leave him. We love each other like Brother and Sister (although sometimes when I smell his Slepe and hear his dreamy Endearments I would have it otherwyse).

June 23rd, 1666

Willis has finally procured for me a Copy of *Enoch*'s Book, that which St. Jude mentions. It is composed of the most Wonderful of Visions. I have determin'd to translate this Manuscript from the Greek.

He now hath many Versions of Judith and Holofernes, and of all Shapes and Sizes. It is as well he made a Mannequin of my Fellow-Model, whom we have taken a Liking to and call *Holly*. Willis hath executed a Number of little Dutch-style Pictures of Holly and I playing at Cards or generally carousing.

147

June 29th 1666

My Kindling is dead. Yesterday she was shrieking from some mysterious Ailment, and by Nitefall she had come out in the Blotches. All Nite & all Day she was feverish and vomiting. We could do Nothing to lessen her Suffering, and her Cries were Torments. An Hour ago I put the Pillow to her Face and watched a mercyfull Peace overcome her Struggles. I was right surprized when Willis owned that he had not the Courage to draw her in Death. I have therefore made a modest Cartoon in his Place.

Enoch sayeth:—

Wisdom went forth to dwell among the Children of men
And found no Dwelling-Place;
Wisdom returned to her Place
And took her Seat among the Angels
And dwelt with them
As Rain on a Desert
And Dew on a thirsty Land.

My dearest *Kindling* was as Dew on a thirsty Land—but only a Drop, and alas too soon consumed.

August 10th 1666

To-day I entreated a Favor from Willis. I asked that, i'th'event of my becoming senseless with the Plague, he prevent me from writing, by Force if so be it. I do not wish to have preserved for *Posterity* any ungodly Rantings that I may deliver.

August 28th, 1666

This Nite Willis came to my Bed. Quivering like a Mouse, he confessed to his mortal Fears, and bade me hold him in my Arms. At first I was completely o'ertaken by Surprize: What? A Chink in the bold Knight's Armor? And then I was touched, and not a little amus'd. He said he found it harder by the Day to conquer his lengthening Periods of morbid Preoccupations. When the Kindling died, he said, Plague had then clearly staked its Claim here in our Rooms, and he could not slepe for the Terror of it. It was a different Willis whom I comforted that Nite. He was a little Boy afraid of the Dark. And I held him to my Breast, and rocked the poor Creature to Slepe.

148

August 29th, 1666

Willis hath been in better Spirits, but a little fever'd and sick-lie. We are resolved to slepe together from now until the End. It is a great Comfort.

He hath told me of his *Dutch Sweet-heart*, whom he met whilst traveling in the Low Countries. His Master was a Dutchman, it transpir'd, a Painter of some Renown, and when they visited the Toun of Delft Willis there met and fell enamor'd of his Master's young Niece. Their ensuing Separation was to have been but temporary, but Willis' subsequent Fortunes, as well as the Barriers of War and Epidemic, had ended their Alliance. The Woman was now married, but W. confess'd that he still held her in his Heart.

August 30th, 1666

Willis has the Blotches.

'So, Good Morning, Mother Plague!' says he jovially at Daybreak—'By Heaven I've run you a good Race, and it's not over yet!' Thus did he confront his Mirror. But in Truth he has been staggering a little as he works, and tending to let fall his Brushes and Spatulas. I have been obliged to lash th'appropri-ate Instrument to his Fingers that he might continue. God give me some of his Strength when mine owne Time cometh. He hath even dared to venture out-doors, with Face well-hooded. When he returned he told me what News was abroad: the Dutch Warfleet had been driven back, and the Citie was full of victorious, weary Sailors; and that Nite in the Tavern at Southwarke the Moor's Head had spoken a Prophecie. This last Fact pricked me with excitement:—'And what did she say?' I demanded of Willis.

'There is the Rub, Katie,' says he, 'for nobody knows, because the Head gave forth in some un-intelligible Tongue. Yet a fearsome Sound it was, and it be taken for a Sign of great impending Events. They say it hath not spoke since the Time of the Comet, half a Centurie ago.'

'And on that Occasion, what did it say?' I asked.

'Again, nobody knows,' says he, and he gave a sly, perverse Laugh and began to dance a little Jig, singing 'Nobody knows,

149

Nobody knows,' chanting like a Childe at play. After this did he collapse, sweating profusely, and I held him in my Arms and wiped his steaming Brow.

'Then in Truth it is a useless Prophet, this Head,' I mused aloud, as my Willie fell into a wheezing Slumber.

August 31st, 1666

Willis hath weakened, and is surely close to the End. To-Day, in his Delirium, he made an Assault upon me and attempted what he once called (a Lifetime of yore) That Kind of Thing. But he was feeble, and easily repelled. I forgive him as easily. As I write he lies in a *Coma*. I myself have a large Pustule recently broken out on my Forehead, and feel somewhat feverish. So, I shall be the Last to go. If I had been first or second, it would have at least been in the Hope that One of us survive. But it is not to be. I pray that the Creator give me Time enough and Presence of Mind to complete my Translation of Enoch.

September 1st, 1666

My dear foolish Painter passed away this Morn as I sat by him reading aloud *Solomon's* words from Ecclesiastes 3:—*And I have found that Nothing is better than for a Person to rejoice in his Work: and that is his Portion. For who shall bring him to know the Things that shall be after him?*

I took him for Inter'ment at Bun-Hill, where I paid deep i' th' Purse for a twin Plot. Into this Grave I secretly placed the preserv'd Remains of my Kindling also, whom Willis was obliged to treat in the same Fashion as he had Holly. I have instructed that I be buried here also when my Time shortly comes. At this Moment I am surrounded by the wildest of Percussions, for they are boarding me up in my Residence. The Work-men appear at my Windows bedecked with many Crucifixes and Charms, and smoking continuously that they might avert th'Influence. They avoid mine Eyes as they saw and hammer. With each Plank the Light grows dimmer, and I am beginning to burn inside of me. I must now attend to Enoch.

September 2nd, 1666

PURGATORY is arrived—with a Million fiery Eyes in its Windows, and a Multitude of Serpents which dance toward me o'er the Rooftops on Necks of ululating Flame. The Human Multitude waileth i' th' Furnace and weeps for Water, but the Rivers are boiling & the Streets run with molten Fat all marbled with Blood. I am abandoned to mine owne Incineration & am transformed by the Element. But I am resolved to burn Hell to the Ground, & liberate the Prison of the First Teachers.

8. SOLVITUR CONSERVANDO

THE WORKS of the painter Willis were not all destroyed in the holocaust which was to raze the city within three days of his death. Some were to survive this catastrophe on account of an event which took place on the fourth day.

Imagine, floating down a sewer, an old scrubbing-brush bespiked with toothpicks from which hang a number of torn snotrags: thus the good ship *Herald of Enterprise* nosed into the city docks that morning. It was returning from the wars, having been involved in yet another futile attempt to destroy the Dutch fleet. The remains of its crew were as tattered as its sails, and the ship itself was barely afloat, its upper decks awash. Its disarray matched that of the devastated city which still smouldered and flickered all along the opposite bank to which the vessel finally moored. And barely had the last sailor stumbled ashore when the ship gave a final heave, and sank swiftly amidst a turbulence of belching and bubbles.

A certain sailor called Kiddle was not sorry to see it go. He had been pressganged to it a month ago, yanked from his bench by three armed servants of the King and bundled off into the service of his government. Now he had returned, tired, dispossessed, and angry.

All round the perimeter of the fire zone the homeless had set up their camps. Kiddle made his way that day through these shanty towns with their huddled families and scenes of despair and frustration. This frustration was vented on anybody who could safely be accused of being either Dutch or Catholic – he saw many a suspected fire-raiser beaten up or disembowelled. And the despair brought out many a crucifix and much wailing and self-flagellation.

The largest gathering of refugees was at Goswell Fields, where they were crowded in their thousands. It could have been a festival, except that the predominant colour was grey. Hawkers moved amongst the homeless as they put up their crude tents and wooden shelters. Salesmen set up stalls, preachers preached, children were lost. Families squatted around fires. Some argued, some sang songs, some just sat, bewildered. Not far away, the inferno had reached its limit and the zone was circled by militiamen. A smoky mist enveloped the throng.

Kiddle had one acute concern: his own survival. He stood in Goswell Fields, chewing on a mutton rib, and tried to formulate a plan. Some way off a company of travelling players was moving through the crowd promoting a show shortly to begin. There were jugglers, clowns and acrobats. And then a figure on stilts, portentously picking its way slowly through above the heads of the dishevelled multitude like one of Hell's presiding demons. Once Kiddle saw this – this giant creature with the head of a comet trailing flames – he had his plan.

The show took place on a scaffold in the corner of the fields. To the rolling of a drum, Mars made his entrance. Venus made hers to the wolf-whistles of the crowd. Mars was drunk and kept groping for Venus' enormous painted tits, but all went well enough with these two lovers until the comet passed above them on its stilts, accompanied by sung prophecies of disaster. And then Mars and Venus began to fall out and fight, whilst lesser beings aped their situation: a priest molested a nun, a man strangled his wife, and everything went to Hell when the devils came on at the end with their pitchforks, accompanied by wild music and flaming streamers.

Kiddle made his way backstage after the show and found the comet-on-stilts taking off its costume, sitting on the grass with its long legs splayed out wide. The fiery mask was lifted to reveal the weatherbeaten face of a young woman, breathless and sweating. Kiddle squatted before her and spoke tersely though his scraggy beard.

'Bravo, Mistress Comet,' he said, 'I much admire your art.'

'Thanks,' she said. 'Who are you? Will you help me with these?' She began to undo her leg straps. 'What do you want?'

'Pray, keep thy stilts on,' Kiddle said.

He told her he wanted stiltwalking lessons. He explained that he had returned from sea to find that his home had been destroyed in the fire. He wanted to go into the zone and find what remained of his house. He had possessions stored in the stone cellar; for all he knew his family had sheltered there, too.

'But the city still smoulders with a fearsome heat,' she pointed out, 'The streets are submerged in hot embers. You will be scorched to death.'

'Not if I should walk high above the ground,' he replied. 'And I will pay you well to accompany me, for I have much to retrieve before the place becomes infested with robbers.'

'Well then, we must first make another pair of stilts,' she said.

And so they did, and after a few hours' tuition Kiddle found he could totter around passably well. Then he was obliged to buy Mars' suit of tin armour in order to sheath the stilt-legs and make them fireproof.

Towards evening the sailor and the thespian slipped past the guard and into the fire zone, carrying their stilts. The first streets were untouched by the conflagration, but evacuated. Here they donned their long prosthetic limbs and began their ungainly promenade towards the scene which confronted them.

Ahead, the sun was going down over a vast silver sea, a flat ocean of ash which stretched as far as the eye could see, shimmering in the heat-haze. Here and there throughout this wilderness stone chimneys, slim spires and blackened posts poked upwards like the masts of sunken ships. Kiddle, already sodden with sweat, led the woman into the midst of this ashen world, step by awkward step, through the yard-deep sea.

Kiddle was certainly looking for a cellarfull of possessions, but not his own. He didn't even come from this city. He was an opportunist. He wanted first pickings, a few sackloads of valuables, and then to return to his home in the South West thus compensated for the way his country had treated him. And there, in the middle of the zone, he seemed to have found what he was after. On the lee side of a low stone wall, the remains of a building had escaped total submersion in the ubiquitous ash. He turned to the actress.

'This was my home,' he said. 'Oh, misery me.'

They destilted. After painstakingly clearing away rubble, they found a flagstone with an iron ring attached, and taking this up they beheld steps leading to a cellar. They descended with a torch.

'And my dear, dear possessions,' said Kiddle when they saw the paintings, books, jewellery and plate, 'God be praised.'

Most of the jewels were paste but Kiddle wasn't to know it as he stuffed his pockets. They took the rest out in sacks, and remounted.

As they picked their way back – two lone, grotesque insects – the ashen sea took on the vivid pinks and purples of the setting sun. The heat was still intense. The sacks weighed painfully on the woman's shoulders. It was slow going, and each hesitant step took noticeably longer than the last. Then she heard the sailor cry out behind her and turned to see him stopped still, watching as flames took hold of his stilts at the point where they were no longer protected by tin.

There was nothing she could do. A second later he was completely enveloped in an uprush of fire. There was not even time for him to topple. For a short moment he stood, long legs asplay, a creature of fire. A heartbeat later he was a black silhouette against the rainbow sky. Then he was nothing but dark, wispy gossamer; and then he was gone, atomized. In an instant he had turned into pure soul before her eyes.

The actress prayed that he would soon be in heaven; hell was pretty overcrowded these days. She turned and made her way back with half the plunder. She knew a dealer in the western outskirts, Michael the Armenian.

❤

From the diary of Catherine Sawkin

October 31st, 1667

There are such Things as Fallen Angels. Men may say what they will, but I have seen one manifest, such as hath saved me from certayne Death.

What do the Scriptures tell us about these Beings?—That in the Daies when Men and Women first walked the Earth, certayn Angels on high, perceiving the Beauty of the Human Race, descended unto Earth, took Spouses unto themselves, and strove to disseminate their Knowledge amongst the people of Earth. They were the first Teachers, and the first Philosophers. *Azazel* made known the Metals of the Earth and how to smelt and forge them; others taught the Beautifying of the Eyes and the Arts of Jewelry; and others reveal'd the Art of Pigments, of Tinctures and of Coloring.

Baraqijal it was who first revealed Astrologie to us; *Ezeqeel* gave us the Art of Weather-Prediction through Knowledge of the Clouds; *Kokabel* how to navigate by the Stars; and *Semjaza*, who first propos'd their Mission, he it was who taught Enchantments, and Root-Cuttings.

Some say these Angels did Wrong by this; 'tis the Sage Enoch himself who would have them forever imprisoned for such Deeds, and who would have our true State as one of Ignorance, and Bliss; he would fain fix our Abode, and that of our Teachers, in some celestial Gaol.

Yet, what would be a World without Color; without Metal; without Navigation; without Roots;? For in such Wisdom hath stood our beauteous Glories & our Delites, and thus hath God revealed Himself, through the Work of Angels descended.

I have stood at the verie Brink of Annihilation by Fires within and without, and I was saved by such a Being.

It is refreshingly cold here. There is an ever-green Box-Tree in the Garden beyond my Casement. The Lawn is verdant, and its Borders are asmolder with the Blooms of Autumn. We have Peacocks here, they strut amongst the blown Leaves, upright and suspicious as that righteous Captayne who is wont to visit from Time to Time. It is indeed a prety Scene, and appeareth

156

quite incongruent with our Status as Outlaws. Now that I am at last in sufficient Health to take up my Pen again, I shall make Treatise of the Events that have led to this Pass, dealing first with the Day that London was consumed.

How I raged then at the Lord of Hell and his burning Charyots! How I howled from within my boarded Tomb as the verie Buildings opposite began to spit Fire & Splinter! My Fever by its shere Heat drew forth such angrie Energys as I would never have imagined myself to possess. Because of the Cataclysms which wracked me I could now witness numbersome fiery Highways which plunged away from me at everie Angle into the Worlds Apart. I was at this Point spread-eagled upon my Bed, overtaen with Ecstasies both torturous and sweet. (—For Payne is a prety Thing, it must be confessed, as I have of late been learning at length.) As my Convulsions neared their Peak I beheld myself in the Embrace of a Nebulous Creature who seemed to issue with my Sweat from every Pore, and who with each passing Instant grew the more substantiall, until I found myself wrestling with a Being of Flesh and Bone.

Not all Angels be possess'd of Wings. For crossing the Great Spheres, the Mechanicks of a mere Bird are crude and insufficient. This Angel bore no Feathers. The broad Back that I scored so bloodily with my Nails at the Summit of Passion bore only a fine, downy Fur, and the Rest of him I then saw as he now knelt above me: a naked, flaxen-haired Youth, panting, temporarily exhausted.

—'I Faith, I have come in the Nick of Time,' quoth he.

I myself was drowsy all of a Sudden. 'Am I alive, then?' said I, 'or already transported to other Realms?'

'We have but this present Inferno to worry on,' quoth he, leaping from the Bed & hastily searching for what Garments he could find to wear, for none had he brought with him. He kitted himself hastily & bade me hurry and collect my belongings, which I laxly set about to do in my enfeebl'd Estate.

'But how are we to leave?' I asked. 'For we are planked in like Anchorites.'

'Madam,' quoth he, 'After such Tribulations as I have just been through, to effect such an Egress as this is mere Chyld's

157

Play.' And with this he threw his broad Shoulders at the Door, which after severall heavy Batteries gave way and allowed us to descend to the smoky Street. We had next to unload an abandoned Dead-Cart of its sorry Cargo, into which we then placed my Possessions. We then made for the River. A profitable Day for Ferrymen indeed, with Hundreds like ourselves bidding to evacuate to Southwarke, which we presently did, the Crossing affording us a fyne View of the Citie in Flames.

At Southwarke Folk were camped out on open Land else packed into any Lodging they could find. A fine Day too for Landlords. Rooms were at a Premium, and Busyness ruled over Pitie. We secured Accomodation at the Moor's Head for the Price of three small Bawdy-Prints of Willis', each of which shewed myself bespread most saucily, and would each one have been worth a Month's Rent in happier Tymes.

It was then I asked my Angel why he had seen fit to deliver me from Fire and Plague—for my Fever had indeed already much abated. 'Art thou, then, my *Guardian Spirit*?' I asked.

' 'Sooth, it's rather thee who guards me,' he replied, after which he said, 'I do declare I should like to try some Tobacco— hast thou a Quid to chew or a Pipe to fill?'

I gladly offered him my Pipe, to which he applied himself in high Excitement, as if this were some New and Deliteful *Phenomenon* to him. As also was the Mirror, before which he constantly posed, and gazed at his owne Image in Wonderment, praising his Maker, saying, 'God, thou art beautiful.'

'This is my first visit to this Realm,' he confessed to me. 'I wonder if I will meet others of my Kind, pressed by Necessity?' And then—'By Heavens, this Tobacco does little for me…have you no *Nicotiana Rustica*?' At which I had Needs to explain that the Old Rustic had been outlawed this past Half-Centurie. 'Aye,' he enjoined, 'And it is the old Kill-Joies who still rule the Day:—we may not *smoke*, we may not *drinken*, and we may not read the best Books of the Bible.'

'Which be those?' I asked.

'Why, those which treat of Woman,' quoth he, 'Aye, Woman… and Wisdom. We may not even look at their Pictures.'

I knew his Meaning, for I had myself been drawn to the True Church in the Course of my Studies. The Puritans would destroy all Images—the worst of them would fain destroy all Words also.

Then did he examine Willis' Paintings, unrolling each Canvas in turn—'Were it not that these are saleable in certayne shadie Quarters,' quoth he, 'I should advize you to destroy all of them instantly. Any Woman discovered in Possession of such a Collection of religious Paintings and Pornographs as you have here would be taken for the verie Devill conjured from Rome. You must find safer Lodging, and i' th' heat, before the Landlord upon thee doth resort to Black-Mail, else betray you to the Sergeant-At-Arms. As for myself,' he said with an Air of Sadness, 'I must return. My work in this Realm is done for now. You must embrace me.'

I did so willingly, and in Transports of delite possess'd him once more.

'This is my last Command to you from the highest Authoritie,' quoth my Angel as he clung to me and whispered into mine Ear—'*Breed! Else thine End is Truth's and Beauty's Doom and Date.*'

And I gasped & I shuddered, & he turned soft, & then to Mist, & then was gone, & I was left clutching onlie myself.

And so I was left Alone and Friendless. I had indeed my Books for Companie, but these did not suffice. I had survived the Plague, but I was still enfeebl'd by its Ravages, and a Sight right ugly did its Scabs create across my Countenance. Write could I not; I had no Wish except through Prayer to praise God for my Delivrance, and bear witness to His Glorie.

I refused to attend the established Church. I could not worship along with those who publickly made Bonfires of Paintings and demolish'd holy Statuarie. I longed for the bitter-sweet odor of *Frankincense* and to savor upon my Tongue the Taste of the Body of Christ. With Sadness I considered that I might be obliged to flee to France. Such Thoughts occupied me that Evening as I lay abed. And then a strange Thing:—there came low Murmurings from the Room which adjoined mine owne. A single Voice, then others, then the single Voice again, &

so on. Curious, I put mine Ear to the Wall, and full quickly did I ascertain the Nature of the Deeds in the next Chamber. It was a ROMAN MASS. Verily, my Prayers had been answered, and I thereupon resolved to confront the Room's Occupant, whom I guessed to be a secret Priest, on the Morrow.

He was a thin Man called *Love*. Of course he would not at first admit to his clandestine Standing, but once I had invited him to my Room to view my Etchings and inspect my Library, I begged that he might take my Confession. I afterwards unburthen'd myself to him, and inquired of him whether he might have Connexions Abroad that might admit me to some suitable Communitie where I might recover my Humors and pursuive my Studies safe from Persecution. The good Love then wrote me a Letter of Introduction that I might carry to a certayne Howse in the West Country, to a certayne *Samuel Fish*, Esq.

Some few Daies later did I board the Stage-Coach at the Chairing-Cross. Much taken by the Moorish Head which had been displayed at the Tavern, and of which Willis had earlier made Mention, I had offered to purchase the Object in Exchange for an Erotograph. The Publican was happy to part with it. He said he feared that sooner or later it might be taken for a Catholick Relick and he would lose his License. I did not reveal how certayne I was myself that it was a Sainted Creature.— "Folk may say what they will," quoth the Landlord, "But I never heard it speke in forty Year". I with-held my Observation that wondrous Events are forbidden by Puritans, and so naturally they forbear to occur.

But what Wonders upon my Journey! For I had right motley Companie. My first fellow-Passenger was a Grocer by trade and a staunch Royalist, who raged at Parliament and Catholics and Foreiners in general, all the Way to Aldershott. I was joined at Andover by two Spinsters who were silent for the Whole of their Journey but for their periodic Utterances of the plain Statement "*Jesus is Lord*"—which they would repeat from Time to Time, as if they were Halfe-Wits trying to fix this simple Lesson in their Memorie.

At Ilminster their Place was taken by a zealous Priest, banished that Day from his home Toune, who declared forthrightly that there is NO SUCH THYNG AS SIN.—This shocked me so much that I decided to deal him a Slap across his Face:—'There,' said I. 'Have I not sinned against thee? Are you not therefore disprov'd?'

'Milady,' he replies,'—Any Act of Aggression on your Part henceforth can only be taken as an Attempt to enlighten me in good Faith. Not as a Sin. I myself carry out my Calling in the same good Spirit of didactic Militance. Now, will you give me a F--k?' I did refuse him in no uncertayne Terms.

'There is no Sin—' These were his parting Words upon descending at Exeter—'There is only Goodness and Ignorance. Therefore rejoice and be enlightened. Good-day, Milady.' He then spat in my Face, bowed deeply and took his Leave.

Verily, this Countrie is a Cauldron of Chaos stirred up by great *Eris* Herself. It seems that every derang'd Philosophie under the Sun is up for the Grabbing, and all rational Argument is up in the Air. I saw the Shadow of the Beast fallen across our pixilated Nation, and our Governance as a drunken Giant who stumbleth perilously across a Sea of Ice-Floes. I was glad finally to alight some Distance beyond Exeter, and thus escape from the Companie of two *Quaker* Women who were shamelessly baring their Breasts to Heaven and praising the Lord. They were bound for a Military Garrison at Plymouth, there to stand naked at the Gates to protest Violence and Intolerance, and they prayed they would there be arrested & thus publicize their Cause.

I found myself in the Toune of Fastbuckleigh. Here in the Square I came upon an Event full curious. They were hanging a Sow. This Pig, a Great White, stood condemned of murderously trampling to Death two Children. The *Pope* himself, they said, had sent evil Spirits into the Beast to bid it carry out its heinous Deed. How the Creature shrieked as it swung ponderously from the creaking Rope, all Tits a-wobble;—and how the Tounsfolk did cheer! I took leave of this intriguing Event reflecting upon how, in similar Manner, the eighth *King Henrie* did dis-interre, bring to Trial, condemn and destroy the verie Corpse of the good Thomas *Becket*, which had until then lain some three hundred Years and more in the Ground. And how, in similar Manner, the Greeks of yore were wont to take any Piece of Rock or Wall or Column that had fallen upon a Person and caused Death, and solemnly banish th'offending Article from the Citie. Yea, nothing in Creation is beyond the Law.

Some Miles from the Toune, along a pleasant wooded Road which ran hard by the Moorland's Edge, was situated the Fish Estate, at which I presently arrived on Foot, quite worn from the Rigors of my Journey. A plump-faced Porter confronted me at the Gate-House, viewed my Letter and escorted me thence along a gravell'd Road which led through a Forest of Pine and finally to the very Portals of a fyne Brick Manse, there to wait and view the surrounding Out-Houses and Barns, and Folk going about their Busyness.

I was in due Course ushered into the Hall, where *Fish* greeted me. He was a rounded sort of Fellow, yet small, with twinkling Eyes, smooth Skin and a Wigge of much Luxuriance. His Ladie Wyfe cut a most similar Figure; indeed the Pair seemed more like Brother and Sister than Husband and Wyf.

The Fishes made me welcome and allotted me Rooms which gave on to the Courtyard. And during the Period I was recuperating, which took some Months, I learned much about this Communitie. It was sufficient unto itself, no-one being obliged to seek Work beyond its Walls. They farmed Crops & Cattle & Sheep, managed Woodland & Orchard, and made fine Furniture & woven Cloth. And they were every One a true Catholick, which Faith they (& I) practised with much Discretion. All attended with regularity the Parish Church at Fastbuckleigh of a Sunday, but having discharged this Obligation to the Communitie-at-large, they later in the Day observed a clandestine Mass in a ruined Chapel all o'ergrown with Briar that stood in the Estate Grounds, led by a Priest who here plies his ostensible Trade as a Weaver. *Fish* hath no Scruples about attending th'Established Church. It is most necessary for our Credit and thus our Survival, he holds, and moreover the reformed Service is not truly evil, but merely insufficient, being not depraved but merely deprived of various Texts and Rituals and thereby the proper Fulfilment that our owne true Act of Worship supplieth.

Yet there were Peculiarities here which I could not help but begin to notice. In the first Instance, there were no Children of the Estate, though there were wedlock'd Couples a-plenty. Moreover I myself was the only unattach'd Woman. What free Men there were appeared to be strangely uninterested in worldly Courtship, within or without the Walls. There was little Sign of Ribaldry ever; Folk rather spent their Leisure Time walking in Contemplation through the Woods, else they would circle the great Carp-Pool in the Courtyard with slow and steady Paces. I soon noticed also that there was no Division of Labor according to Sex: Men milked Cows and Women discuss'd Philosophie. An Air of faint Unrealitie enveloped this Settlement.

The Secret of the Fish Estate was revealed to me after I had been resident for some three Months, and was now fytte and well. It fell thus:—at regular Interval Soldiers came from the Garrison at Fastbuckleigh to buy our Produce, and it was my Dutie to account the Transactions. In the Course of this Work I had Needs to deal with a young *Captayne* of the Troop who quickly became enamor'd of me and began making Visits on his own in the Pretense of some Busyness or other, so that he might converse with me more. I had to strive hard in my Attempts to cool his Ardor. I acted as inelegantly as I could, and in Conversation did feign utter Disinterest in any Subjects save Arithmetick and the Weather; yet he would not be discourag'd, looked at me with Dogges-Eyes, and bade me walk out with him of a Sunday.

This I was loathe to do and so I refused him, but still he kept to his Attentions, this inflamed Soldier. It was then, one Month ago To-Day—that Fish approached me and spoke of this Affair. —'It disconcerteth me sorely,' quoth he in his sweet Contralto, 'to witness these tedious Visitations and the Discomfort they cause you.' And then did he fix his Eyes upon mine and say—'I fear we shall have to take Steps lest this *Captayne* grow disenchanted and take some aggressive Action, such as ceasing to buy our Goods. It happens with Men in Love such as he. I know their Kind:—they are quiet, obeying and adoring, and ever loath to lose Hope in Love; yet when they do finally despair,

163

they rage, they spy, they wound. We absolutely must not risk such a Pass as this.'

—'What is to be done, then?' said I.

—'It is simple,' replied Fish:—'You must disappear.'

—'I must leave?'

—'On the contrary,' said Fish, 'You will stay. But as far as our Captayne is concerned, you will have gone.'

—'I am to hide, then?'

—'In a Manner-of-Speaking,' he said. 'For this is the Stratagem: you are to dress as a Gentleman.'

—'What a merrie Notion!' I laughed, 'But can it be convincingly done?'

'The male Demeanor, being simple, is easily learned,' he replied, 'After all, every *"Gentleman"* you see here hath done so. For we are all Women in Realitie. We do not wish the Attentions of Men.'

'All Women?' I cried. 'What—even our bearded Blacksmith?'

'Verily so,' said Fish, 'For we are *Nuns*—and Nuns must perforce be of the Female Sex.'

Nuns, forsooth! In a Flash were all of the Oddities explained. And then, I begged Fish that I might be initiated into their Order, for I was certayne that my Studies could only truly be fulfill'd in the full Communion of these Ladies' Company. Fish replied that she had come to me this Day to propose th'Event herself, for there was no-one, said she, whom she, being *Abbess*, did not value more for their Learning, their Charity and their Chastity; and she trusted me completely. She had no Need to remind me of what grewsome Fate would attend us were we ever betrayed. A Nunnerie, in England! Who could have imagined such a Thing? I would have more quickly bethought me of a Pomegranate of clock-werke. For in these Times it is sufficiently difficult for ordinary Followers of the True Church to survive unrecogniz'd at large;—how many Families have been fyned or imprison'd? How many Priests slaughtered in their Holes? And yet here was an Order of fifty Women, living unhindered in the broad Light of Day; albeit most cunningly disguis'd, for they had with utmost Accuracie adopted the Dress and Mannerisms of the other Sex.

This Occult Order had, Fish informed me, been founded on this Spot shortly after their original Abode (now a Pile of Ruins in Lancastershire) had been dissolv'd in the Reign of King Henrie, and those of its Inhabitants who surviv'd the Rape and Slaughter had fled South, led by their Abbess, the first Fish.

I was duly novitiated on Sunday last. At Midnight of the Sabbath it is the Nuns' practice, I now discovered, to hold Mass in the Crypt of the ruined Chapel, and it is here that they divest themselves of their worldly Disguises and put on their spiritual Robes. Here did my Initiation take place.

I was first dressed as the Bride of Christ, and married to Him with due Pomp at the Altar of that dark and shady, low-vaulted Place. With what Gladness did I embrace the Lord of Life Aeternal! But I can still feel most keenly the Shock of what was next to take place. For I was stripped of my Habit and then dressed up in a simple, funerary Shroud, and laid out prone upon the Altar Table. And it was with Surprize and Horror that I next heard the Priest's voice begin to intone over me the Last Rites. 'What?' I said timorously—'Am I to die?' And then Fear and Bravado took me over, and I made to rise and leave. But I was instantly pinioned there by the attendant Sisters. The Priest then spoke:—'You are about to die in the Eyes of the World,' he told me, —'For you are about to renounce the World and its Temptations. This is why you will now receive Extreme Unction.' And it was so. It was with a macabre Joie that I imagined myself departed from this Vale of Flame and Folly, and then with true Happiness that I next imagined myself to be in Heaven, for all my Woes were now truly dissolv'd.

I then arose, and joined the Midnight Mass. All Candles were extinguished, and we Participants disrobed, and we began to chant the *Miserere*, crying out to our *Lord* from the very Depths of this utter Darkness. It was then I heard, all sudden, the frightening Crack of a Whip upon Flesh, and then the Cry of the Victim whose uglie Wail did cut like that Whip across our Song. An unseen Figure was moving amongst us, wielding a crewel Flail. Then Another's Scream rent the murky Air;—and then Another's, until the cries of Suffering mingled equally with our Chant, and I was in a Dread of tormented Anticipation, attending mine own Purgatory, which arrived soon enough, and I was of a Sudden thrown to the Flagstones by a Lash invested with all the Heat of Hell, which scorched across my Back and wrenched all Breath from my quaking Body. Again and again the Whip came down until my Skin was flayed afire, my Bones full sore and my Mouth full of Blud. I had needs struggle for my verie Breath. I felt as a *Terrier* mauled by a *Bear*. I crawled, I gasped, I dribbled, I choked. And still the Whip came down while my Sisters sang and keen'd. And then, most surprizingly, while my Tormentrix took short Pause, I became impatient for more Blows. I felt myself as one on the Threshold of an higher Realm. My Bones and Brain were all a-humming. Again I called for the Lash, and again I felt its Sting, and then again, until I was in an Ecstasy of Torment, and my Lungs were full, and I felt my Spirit liberated once more and Free of its fleshy Prison, redeemed by our Lord Jesus Christ and at one with Him and His Beauty, staked upon the bloody *Cross*, bearing mutual Testament to this unjust Worlde and our passionate Passing from it. Once more, I say, because this Realm was right similar to that which the Plague at its Height had transported me. And once the Whip eventually ceased its Ministrations, this Ecstasy was enhanced by th'ensuing Song we enjoined all through the dark Hours till the first Light. It was in this elevated State that I was to eventually return to my Chamber.

There is a Condition attach'd to the first direct Raies of the Sun that must needs be convulsive. For after the vague Diffusions of Dawn, lingering Night must take its violent *Coup-de-Grâce* from a Sword of purest Luminosity. And then all Creation is transformed: Dark is now Light, and Payne is now a Pretty Thing, such Power doth *Phoebe* in the East send forth in the first Moment of the Day—and we are thus stung into Illumination. On the Morning I speak of, this Instant of Ignition had yet to announce itself. All was hazy and diffuse. I stood at my Window at looked out across the Gardens and over the Treetops, across the misty Pastures and beyond to the Moorland Peaks, where the great Rock of *Ish Tor* stood black against the Sky, appearing as a giant slumbering Eye, where a faint Glow issued from the Hole at its Center.

I had been greatly exerted by Mortification and Song. I felt myself bathed in an intense Heat which radiated from my Wounds, and beneath my Cloak I was further insulated by a second Skin of drying Blood. And then, as I looked out, I saw the Eye of *Ish Tor* all of a Sudden flash with a Beam of gilded Fire. It dazzled me such that I turned away, and it was then I beheld the Moor's Head, and I saw its Glass Chamber and liquid Medium all pierc'd through with Denizens of Light, flashing Patterns fantastick, and now emanating *Luminescence* of its owne Accorde, as if some peculiar chymical Transaction were taking place. The suspended *Head*, without itself changing Color or Expression, yet began to insist itself. Its glowing emerald Eyes were more than themselves. Its luxuriant black Hair never seemed more present. This Head—nay, this Girl, was more Real than Real. Her Gaze, brimming with Light distill'd from Aeternity to Aeternity, held me transfix'd. Her Mouth, partly open, was beyond Words;—for these were to issue from elsewhere.

She spoke directly inside my Head with a soft yet supple Voice which rippled through my Sensibilities.

'Hearken to me, Katie Sawkin,' she announced. 'While the initial Energies of the Day lend me Power to speak.'

'Who are you?' I entreatied. 'And how came you by your Fate? What terrible Martyrdom hast thou suffered, and where came you by it? Aye, and whose Hands are bloodied by the Deed?'

'Ah!' sighed she, 'Whose Hands? Why—those of Ignorance & Wisdom combined, which is always a fearsome Conjunction, yet is the essential Conflict which must of Necessity drive our Life. As for my Fate, this is not yet fully unravel'd, for my Story is not yet all told.'

—'Pray relate it while your Powers prevail,' said I, in Thrall to those beckoning Eyes, which were inanimate yet *lumenescent* to their Emerald Depths. And the Voice rang clear inside me:—

'I dwelt at *Kypros*,' she began, 'Before the Turk, before the Venetian, before the Crusader, before the Arab. My Father had fled Alexandria in Aegypt when the Caliph *Omar* invaded and burned the great Library and sacked the Citie.'

'Of this I have heard tell,' said I, —' 'twas the Deed which ushered in the Dark Age of the World, for in the Inferno of Alexandria perished all the Knowledge of the Ancients.'

'Not all,' the Damsel replied, '—For in the Diaspora which took place in the Weeks beforehand and continued until Omar was at the verie Gates, some of this Wisdom was yet saved. My Father escaped with many a learned Codex when our Familie took Ship to Kypros on the Day Alexandria fell.

'So we were come to that Island of Olives and Lemons, and we settled in that Citie of the Mountains, where my Mother traded in Carpets, Jewelry and Artefacts, and my Father studied and copied his Manuscripts, and praised Heaven for having survived to live yet under Christ and Apollo.

'It was here for the first Time that I, a Childe of three Summers, asked my Father of his Philosophie. At this he raised an Eyebrow, paused, adjusted his Skull-cap and stroked his long Beard.

' "I study Immortalitie," was his Reply, " 'tis the onlie fit and proper Philosophie to pursue. Life is holy, and we must preserve it. I fear the good *Nazarene* gave up his owne too easily. But behold, Child!—"

'And he lifted me into his Arms and carried me to the Window, where there stood a Row of glass Vessels, variously replete with different color'd Liquids which glowed in the Noonday Light and bathed us in their Hues fantastick, and made a peculiar View of the Jew's House opposite, as if it were a Mansion situated at the end of a Rain-bow.

'And he set me before them, and I beheld suspended in each stopper'd Jar a different small Creature. There was a Snail, a Toad, a Lizard, a Mouse, and then a Bird which was most beautiful and encased in a clear Liquor of celestial Blue.

' "The Snail I entombed only yester-day," said my Father. "The Toad, when we first arrived in this Citie. The others hath I carried from Alexandria. But look well on the Bird. For this Creature hath sung for your Grandfather of the thirtieth Generation, in *Samar-khand* of Trans-Oxiania a thousand Years before the Prophet—Peace be unto him—and five hundred Years before the Christ, in the reign of *Darius*. This *Songthrush* dwelt in a wooden Cage above his Porch, and oft made Accompaniment to his Sarod."

' "It is truly wondrous and beautiful," said I, "And so perfectly preserv'd that I cannot believe it a thousand Years dead."

' "Ah! Now," quoth my Father, "Now do we come to the Crux of the Matter. Dead, you say? No! It is not dead. But neither does it live. For it is merely *inanimate*. It is suspended in Liminalitie, I would say, for it is forever on the Thresh-hold of both Estates.'

' "Would that I could hear the Song of such a prety Thing," said I.

' "But you shall!" said my Father, whereupon he took the Jar, unstoppered it, and retrieved the speckled Bird, which remained unmoving in his Hands.

'My Father then spoke to the feathered Creature, uttering with his deepest Breath a long-drawn-out Cry of "Kat-Su!" which was not loudly spake, yet caused the very Timbers of our House to ring with its Vibration.

'Upon the Instant did the Bird start to flutter in his Palms, and presently it stood, and sent forth its Song to mine amaz'd Ears.

'It mimick'd Bells and Street-Cries and Hoofbeats and Horns, and set up such a *Cacophonie* as to cause me to imagine myself within some great *Metropolis*' multitudinous Precincts. And so adept was this Bird's Art, and such were its Powers of Similitude, that it impersonated the Voices of Men and Women.

' "Listen well," said my Father, "And you will hear your Ancestors converse."

' "I hear them!" said I, clapping my Hands in the Excitement of it, "Most vivid! But the Tongue is alien. What do they say?"

' "They are bartering with Jew, the first ever to reach Samar-khand in the time of that People's great Dispersal. He is buying Maps and Provisions for his further Journeys north to the Land of the *Khazaks*. Listen:—how heatedly do they dispute!"

' "Of what do they argue?" said I.

' "Our Grandfather will not accept the Jew's coin, he holds it is not of true gold. Listen now—"

'And there came the voice of my Father of many Generations, its strange Tongue growing less inflamed, and appearing to make some Offer of Compromize.

' "You hear, Child?" said my living Father, "He asks for the Hebrew's Slave as part of the Bargain. In a Moment you will hear the young Woman speak."

'I did indeed, and much else of interest before my Father, with a second "Kat-Su!" of different Vibration to the first, rendered the Bird once more inanimate and returned it to its limbic Abode. He then recounted how it was this Forbear whom we had heard speak who had first perfected the *Manufacture* of the Liminal Medium, so desirous was he to preserve his beloved Songbird. He was able to cull Knowledge from many Sources, for Samar-khand was at that Time at the Cross-road of Asia Major, where Men and their singular Projects came from all parts of the Compass to briefly meet and merge like Camels at the Waterhole. And many among them sought the Secret of Immortalitie. Those from the North advocated *Ice* as preserving Agent, for they had themselves dis-interr'd Monsters preserved from the Beginning of Time beneath the *Tundra* of *Kamchatka*;—but they could not breathe life back into the Creatures, which when warmed would onlie rot. It is from the East that Knowledge of "Kat-Su!" and other Powers of Breath and Vibration have come. Our Ancestor in Samar-khand held it certayn that the preserving Agent should be a Fluid, and the Success of his Distillations had been well proved by what I myself had just witnessed Centuries later. My Father continued:—

' "Our ancient Grandfather, however, try as he might, was never able to apply the *Technik* to larger Creatures and thence to Humankind, which was his final Goal. Theories abounded, and thus were written the various Books of the Dead, greatly prized as Instructions for Travel thru Space and Time, of which a Number survived at Alexandria. But in Time, through all the Course of our Family's Wanderings, this Knowledge was lost, even down to the Recipe for the Liminal Fluid;—though the Bird itself remained, handed down through the Generations. But since we came to Alexandria in the Time of my Father, I myself have had the Opportunitie to studie the lost Wisdom, and Step by Step I am slowly gathering the Means by which to approach Immortalitie. What you see before you in these pretty Vessels is but the successful Side of my Work. I shall not talk of the Failures. But my Goal is to preserve Human Life for ever, no less, and to do this I yet have not devized th'appropriate Fluid. The more superior the Creature, the more difficult is the Task. But at this verie Moment doth a *Dog* lie in a Demi-john behind yonder Curtain, immersed these last six Weeks and still shewing no Sign of Decay. Next to it is an *Ape* from the Straits of the Lion, sunk in the Fluid even longer. I progress, and it is good.

' "But come now," said my Father, "This is enough for one Morning. I believe that downstairs we have Jam and Pickles for Luncheon. *Solvitur Conservando*!"

'For the next few Years my Father had Peace enough for his Researches, until the Arab Invasions began. The coastal Towns of our Island were frequently attacked and held, and Imperial Troops were unable to prevent the Infidel from making Sallies inland from Time to Time. Our owne Citie, insufficiently walled, had the Misfortune to be entered on a Number of Occasions, and I, being about my Busyness during one of these raids, was briefly captured and sorely misus'd,—indeed I thought those Sons of Allah would kill me once they had their Busyness-like Pleasure of me, and I was onlie saved by our own Forces at the last Minute. But I survived that Ordeal, bore the Child of it, and we both continued to grow up and wax healthy in that Island's kind Clime. Yea, it was an all-together different Enemy that was to seal my Destiny.

'How well I remember the Day upon which All was precipitated, and the Horror in the House when I first shewed the Signs of Levantine Influence, which killed all it struck within Daies. And then my Father's Words:—"Though no-one hath yet survived this Ravage,—yet there is Hope." And he reminded me that he could now suspend and *re-animate* at will Suckling Creatures as large as the Ape that he occasionally brought to Life to play acrobatic Tricks for our Entertainment. This Beast was only a Step away from our own Kind, said he, and so now (perhaps a little prematurely, but Necessitie demanded it) he

171

propos'd to make Myself the first Human Subject of his Researches, and to suspend me in Liminalitie before th'Influence could run its Course. "And in due Time, when sooner or later a Cure is found," he said, "You shall be made re-animate, and the Remedie applied, and you shall be saved. Praise be to *Christ* and *Apollo*," quoth he. A more optimistick Fellow ne'er walked the Earth.

'And so after bidding my Family a tearful Fare-well, I was *drugged* and *prepared* accordingly, and the next Day I was immersed in the Tomb of Liminalitie, which was a Glass Tank constructed with a Frame of Copper and most elegantly shaped to my Bodie. The Tank was then placed in the Securitie of the Cellar, and thus the Gamble was made. Needless to say, all my Familie's Energies were forthwith devoted to seeking a Cure for th'Influence which had brought Things to this Pass.

'Unhappily, they were not to succeed. And when once more the *Arab* attacked and forced them hurriedly to evacuate the Citie, they had no Time to take with them more than could be carried on their Persons. They left the House, and Myself there entombed, to the Hand of Fate which rests in the Lap of the great Gods. What became of them I do not know. Nor of the great Gods, for I have been full deserted.'

The Damsel's Voice related how the Citie then fell to the Invader, and how, when one of their high Generals was shewn the Oxianian's House and the wondrous glass Tomb which it sheltered, he fell immediately in Love with the sleeping Girl and accordingly ordered the House demolish'd but for Cellar and Tomb, and a glorious *Palace* built upon the Site. The fanta-stick Coffin became the very Hub of this Mansion. Around it the General built an extravagant Vestibule decorated with fine Tapestries and Mosaics and all Manner of beauteous Riches. Every Day he would come and venerate the Maid who lay there suspended in Time in her fabulous Sarcophagus. This Man too sent out throughout the World to find a Cure for the Influence, for he had taken good Note of the Inscription etched in the Glass, wherein the Father had described the Circumstances of the Damsel's entombment and entreated whomsoever to discover the Remedie which would enable her to live again.

And when the General had done this, he proposed to make her his Wyfe.

But it was not to be, for *Byzantium* in due Course reclaimed its lost Island and drove out the *Saracen*, and the General's Palace was sacked; and in the Course of this Event a certayne *Legionary* did discover the Tomb, and paying no Hede to its Inscription and opening the Tank, did sever the Maid's head, place it in a Jar with some of the Fluid, and hurrie away as the burning Building fell all around him, thinking himself now possess'd of a fyne *Souvenir*.

And this inanimate yet sensitive Head then related how she came to be passed from Hand to Hand, all down the Years, as a mere Curiositie: she was played for at Dice; sold to a *Franciscan*; briefly venerated as a Saint; used as a Door-Stop by a *Satanist*; displayed at a Travelling-Fayre; then won at Cards on a Nite in *Ulm* when the Wandering Jew himself shewed a Royal Flush and took brief Possession before selling her in Amsterdam to the Flying *Dutchman*, whose Cabin she graced for a Centurie of Journies upon the Oceans wild. Thence more Thefts, Card-Games, Bargains and the like saw her pass through many assorted Hands, and she related with some Relish the countless Events both publick and private which she had witnessed in the Course of her Travels, and the Meanderings of Chance which had eventually led her to this *Chamber*, here to speke for the first Time, under the Eye of Ish Tor, to mine enchanted Ears.

'How richly do I resent mine History as a Commoditie,' quoth she, 'Despite knowing I have inspired much use-full Speculation and provok'd many a Dispute both philosophical or fantastick. Fain would I be returned to my Bodie {if still extant it be} and then, once the Progress of Knowledge permits, to walk and breathe upon the Earth once more.'

And now did the strange Light wane, and the *Eye* of *Ish Tor* close, and common Daylight prevail. The Head had spoken.

And so I have determined to free the Maid-in-Glass. I must carry her to *Kypros*, there to re-unite the cloven Temple of her Soule. Then swiftly shall I research a Cure for that deadly Dropsy, and Lo:—the sainted Creature shall be reborn, God willing, and for the Sake of mine owne lost *Kindling*.

November 1st, 1667

I leave within the Month. I have spoken to Fish of th'Affair, who hath offered all Support for my Mission, and recommended certayne Safe-Houses and Convents along the Way. Meanwhile I study Herball Thaumaturgie, along with what few Writings our Librarium doth afford of oriental Wisdom. Nothing have I yet discovered of this "Kat-Su!", but there is a Sister from *Helsing* in our Companie who hath visited the Monasterium at *Enkakuji* in *Japan*, & she promises to speak to me of it anon.

The Righteous Capt. was here to-day and I dealt with his Accounts. He did not see through my Disguise. He is of a colder Disposition lately. Perhaps he is pining for me. God grant that my *Alias* prevail.

November 5th, 1667

Tonite the Bonfires are ablaze throughout the Countie. We Hidden Sisters played our Part and attended the grewsome Occasion at Fastbuckleigh. They had constructed there for the Pyre a great Mannikin of Fawkes, all daubed with the Papal Cross and crowned with a card-board Mitre. Next to it atop the Mound was tethered a bearded Billy-Goat, and bound and lain in twisted Shapes at their Feet were two Men lately convicted of Sodomie.—"Sooth, them Buggers will make perfect Faggots to bathe the Papist in Hell-Fire!' cried a good-natured Fellow who was pressed next to me in the Throng, and offered me a Swigge from his Cider-Flask.

—'Why, pray, do you also burn the Goat?' I asked him.

—'Why, 'tis part of our Heritage,' he replied, saying that their Custom had always been to burn a *Jew* at the annual Fire, but since none were to be discovered this Year (indeed none had been found since the reign of Edward I when all Jews had been expel'd from this land) then the Goat must stand Proxy.

We Sisters held our Peace. We even found it within ourselves to raise a Cheer with the rest when the Pyre was ignited and the Flames began their terrible Dance. The Capt. and his Troop did attend the Ceremonie, and he passed some polite Words with us:—''Tis a merrie Display, is it not?' quoth he, stone-faced, 'Though I like not the Construction and Display of Idols, even if, like those Sinners i' th' Pyre, they be only created in order to be destroyed.'

Last Nite in my Bed, my Angel came again unto me. He professed himself full glad that I was shortly to leave the Fish Mansion:—'I like not that Cloud of Celibacy which envelopeth it like an *Atmos-Sphere*,' he confessed as he lay in my Arms: 'Remember how I hath exhorted thee to be fruitful.'

'But there is Power in Chastity,' I replied,—'And besides, though I travel afar I remain of the Order, and married to our Lord Jesus Christ.'

'Pshaw,' he then exclaimed. 'Married! And you with all your Learning. 'Tis an Estate much to be avoided. Besides, in this Case do you still not recognize a *Metaphor* when you see one?'

It is true. An Angel hath said 'Pshaw' to me.

9. DEAD ANGELS

A COCKROACH was busy investigating the empty yoghurt pot that had fallen to the floor of the twilit room. Theo sat hunched over the diary, eyelids drooping, swaying with fatigue.

Then his robed companion crashed breathlessly into the room, eyes flashing with excitement, and jerked him upright – 'Hey, c'mon, what's up? We gotta move, the fuckin' *Ubique*'s the other side of the rock, and halfway to the horizon worse luck, so we've gotta grab a boat and get after them.'

'Take it easy, there's no hurry.'

'You got the book – good-oh! Come on, you bastard.'

A nun and a schoolgirl. What a combination. Some people would appreciate it. Not if they could see her now, singing, 'We're going to get them, we're going to get them,' to that taunting, evergreen playground melody: 'Ner-ner-ner-ner-ner'.

There was no hurry, he told her. He knew where they were headed.

'Oh yeah? It's too bad I can't read your thoughts now I'm hard. I kind of miss that,' she said, 'And another thing I found out – isn't it weird having to think for yourself? I mean one hundred percent? Hey, but we can still get us a boat, right? A real bloody fast one!'

'A plane – no, not hijacked – would be less bother.'

She began to stomp impatiently around. 'I just want to – I just want to – I should like to severely *disinform* that bastard. I'm going to cancel him as a viable project. He'll be *geography*.'

'History. He'll be history.'

'Yeah, that too.'

He went to the wardrobe. 'You go ahead,' he said. 'And I hope there's lots of blood and that. I'm going to the airport.' He took out a linen suit and began to change.

She stopped her pacing around. She put on her sarky face and grunted from the side of her mouth. 'Yeah, guess I forgot there were no more heroes. No real ones. Look at yours: some... *tailor*.'

And look at her: Nietzsche's angel.

'What's this big argument you've got with Mr Try It?'

'It's important, Theo. He was sent to kill me.'

'Why?'

'Goes a long way back. How can I put it? – There was a war in Heaven, that kind of thing. I know that's a contradiction, but it was heaven before the war. Nothing changed, see. It was a time in the history of the old primordial electromagnetic fields when nothing had changed for millions of years – there was no decay, no leakage, no entropy from the system. Comfortable state of affairs. Boring, mind you, but heaven all the same – nothing's perfect. Then it started. Things were changing further afield in the solar system. Impinged on us – presto! Rot sets in, i.e. we realised we were going to decay and die if we didn't do something about it. So we generated new information from this and started spreading it, and we discovered how to transfer from one cell to another. But there were other guys, real fuckin' okkers, who didn't go for this, didn't want to change, and they either didn't believe they could ever decay or they just accepted it. The worse of them got really addicted to this new idea of mortality, and they wanted everybody else to go down with them. Yeah. They said it was the gateway to another reality, the dickheads. So they started cell-hopping after us, and if they couldn't kill us themselves they'd work on the host to do it. They called it redemption, right? Like we were items in a pawn shop. I call it sheer bloody assassination.'

'Wilson doesn't want to die.'

'Not until he's seen me off he doesn't. And look at that shit he's composing – fuckin' death-wish Götterdämmerung. Play that and it's physical and artistic suicide in one.'

Wilson was beginning to look like another of Nietzsche's Angels.

'So how did you get White to part with the book? Did you kebab the bastard?'

'There's a practice Ireland under that rock,' he said, 'complete with practice riots. He stopped a practice bullet, but I guess he'll survive.'

'Too bad.'

'Oh yeah, and there's some cave art that looks pretty old. Bit of a major discovery, that.'

'What was Ninefingers doing ashore anyway? Buying postcards?'

'He had a Queen, two Chas's, three Di's and a Fergie in his pocket. And a *Penthouse Couples*.'

'Jeez, that's what I call necrophilia on the grand scale. But I reckon he was peddling the diary more like.'

'Maybe, but he was coming out of a doctor's.'

'And while he was ashore the other two decided to jilt him. It's Jilt City around here.'

He picked up his bags. 'You go off and do what you've got to do and all that. Meanwhile I've got my little job.'

Quietly she said 'I can't leave you, you bastard. You know I'm stuck with you.'

She was stuck? He was once forced to take his kid sister to the zoo. She bombed the penguins with doughnuts, threw fruit gums to the tigers, fed chewing gum to the chimps, caught a wallaby by the tail and got them both kicked out. All the way home she said a lot of dumb things, picked her nose and picked fights with any boy in sight. And here he was now with a billion-year-old tomboy.

Aboard the plane, she looked up from the diary. 'OK, so what happens after sister Goody Two-Shoes sets off from Suckfastpeas, Fuckin'ghastly or whatever the place is called? I know: she never makes it. She's captured by the Captain, the convent is discovered and they're all burned as witches, except Katie The Pious who makes a breathtaking escape with El Capitano because he's still in love with her... Yeah! And she slices up a few soldier boys while she's at it.'

178

'She never got around to learning that Katsu! thing. That's too bad. That was interesting.'

'So what are you going to do to this head? Stick it back on, Katsu! her back to life and slip her a broad-spectrum antibiotic?'

'I thought I might deanimate you with a Katsu! for a start.'

♥

'OK, so where's this Transoxianian's cellar?' she said.

They were in another hotel room with another crucifix above the bed and another tiny balcony. From this one you could look across the glare of baked brown rooftops to the bastions of the walled city beyond. Inside, they were looking at a map of Nicosia.

'I don't know. There's all sorts of old palaces and stuff. It was opposite a Jew's house. Could be anywhere.'

'No, mate. These towns only had one Jew. They shipped him in to run the bank because they didn't like soiling their own hands with that business. He'll have a real solid place – robber- and pogrom-proof – and it'll be in the middle of town. Bound to be marked, heritage and all that.'

She studied the map intensely for a moment. 'There it is. And hey – good-oh! It's right on the green line!'

'What's good about that? Anyway, which sector?'

'No sector – it is right on the line. There's a no-man's-land about five blocks wide. Don't look so pissed off. It means it'll be deserted. Easier for us – I mean there'll be searchlights and heli-copters and sirens and shit – yeah! – but it'll be empty.'

The Greek checkpoint blocked a narrow and decrepit shop-ping street. Beyond it the road was deserted: windows were boarded up, sidestreets barricaded with breezeblock. Half a mile off, where life began again, the Turkish flag could be seen fluttering from an observation tower.

'The only people allowed through here are tourists in coaches, and they don't stop. What do we do?' he said.

'When the going gets tough,' she declared, 'you know what the tough do.'

♥

She emerged from the changing room in a clingy T-shirt, tight Dockers and sneakers. Plus lurid lipstick, lots of kohl, and the silver earrings that Jack Solomon didn't give her. She handed Theo a bag with her nun's gear in it. 'Wait in the café over the road,' she told him. 'I'm going to ask a favour from the right-eous captayne of the guard.'

He was into his third cup of coffee by the time she returned. She looked satisfied.

'So Mata Hari's back.'

'Pushover. Signed and sealed. You're my brother and we're going to put flowers on our Grandma's grave, right?'

'What if he speaks to me in Greek?'

'I told him you were a bit gone in the head and you only talk gibberish.'

'Thanks.'

'Just smile and nod and go "Neigh, neigh" like a donkey. He'll understand.'

The obliging soldier was happy to lead them through a house by the checkpoint that served as a guardroom, and to the lane behind, then he embraced Diana, murmured a few husky endearments, squeezed her arse and waved them off.

Stray cats jumped up and hurried away. The lane gave out onto a wider street. It was a ghost town, dusty and litterblown. Every so often they passed an old car down on its tyres, a home for cats or rats. Everywhere there were peeling, faded placards: pictures of a bearded priest in a stovepipe hat; a concert announcement for the Osmonds; a cinema poster for *The Exorcist*. Now and then there were glimpses of the Turkish control tower over the rooftops. They moved rapidly along in what little shadow there was, past flaking doorways and shop windows laden with grimy merchandise. Everywhere he looked, a cat stared back at him. There was a peculiar quiet, complete but for the distant hum of the living part of the city. Not the quiet of death, but something else.

'It's kind of inanimate here,' he observed.

'Yeah,' she said. 'Reminds me – when there's more time I'll tell you what actually happened on the *Marie Céleste*.'

'On it, were you?'

'The food *sucked,*' she said, 'nobody would touch it. Anyway, see down there? The big house with the barred windows? That's the Jew's House. So opposite–'

'Is a large car dealership. Quite a palace.'

It was a modern low-rise affair, a long wall of plate glass. Out front a car stood tilted crazily at the petrol pumps, three tyres flat, the pump nozzle still rammed into its tank.

'This is it, sport. If your princess is anywhere, she's somewhere underneath that lot.'

The door to the office was unlocked. They went through into the showrooms. There, adorned with bunting, chromework gleaming, was a collection of pristine automobiles, every one brand new on the day this place was frozen in time. He recognised the first car he remembered his old man owning – a wreck even then compared to this. This one was festooned with limp balloons, and there was a life-sized cut-out of a girl sitting on the roof raising a champagne glass, a g-strung siren. What song had she sung in 1974? Other girls were perched atop the other mint-condition Fords, Fiats and Ferraris. Crepe and tinsel hung from the ceiling and rustled and rattled with the first fresh air felt in years. More cut-out hostesses in leotards and fishnet posed around a table on which stood a very real champagne bottle and glasses amongst piles of brochures. It was quite a party.

'Looks like the Turk turned them to stone,' said his companion. 'The year you dropped into life's party.'

They split up to search for some sign of a basement. He went through to the workshops where cars stood on hoists, bonnets up, and tools were spread around like cutlery. He sniffed the air. Amongst traces of oily vapour he could discern the whiff of Brut. Trust that primordial slime to last the ages.

Then he felt his arms suddenly pinioned by a fierce grip, and he was jerked around to find himself facing Wilson. The man had changed. His complexion had lost its lustre, his red beard had faded, there were pock-marks on his face and neck and there were dark rings around his red-rimmed eyes. But he still managed to raise a sparkle in them.

'Welcome to the Land of Olives and Lemons,' he grinned with sulphurous teeth. Theo was deftly frisked and relieved of the silver dagger. 'Yeah. May they forever grace your pre-show cocktail here at the *Café Céleste*.' He let go his grip. 'Come on Kiddo, I'll show you something, I mean, really – you have got to see this, I'm not kidding, this is gonnae be an amazing floor-show.'

And he led him out to a backyard building site where surveyors' posts poked up through weed-choked ground, and a JCB had been abandoned in mid-excavation, its scoop full of rubble which now sprouted grasses and saplings. In front of the digger was a deep pit strewn with rocks, and down there was a low brick archway revealed by the shovel.

'Giving a brief thank-you-Jimmy to the eternal war between Greek and Turk that has fortuitously allowed us a glimpse of eternity – let us descend,' said Wilson.

The arch was partially blocked but he was able to crawl inside. Wilson followed, holding a torch which illuminated the passage as they picked their way through piles of rubble and broken earthenware until it gave out on a low-vaulted room. The walls and ceilings were tiled with a repeating geometric arabesque and hung with moth-eaten shreds of fabric; the floor was laid with rotting timbers, and at its centre was a marble plinth, upon which lay what resembled a mummy-case, grey-grimed and banded with verdigri'd copper.

'Here's the lassie,' said Wilson, 'just as per specification.' And he wiped some grime from the glass with his elbow. 'Pretty good looker even without her head.' Then he flipped a series of catches which allowed him to free the lid of the tank and manoeuvre it ponderously aside.

The liquid was crystal-clear. The body, unclothed, was tanned. The ruby-red varnish on the toenails looked as though it had been applied an hour ago. No stain from the scarlet stump of neck had seeped into the fluid shroud.

'That is some *ekte* eau-de-vie,' Wilson said, 'I am impressed. That is *l'eau juste*. I mean, a glass of that with ice and a slice and entropy theory just falls apart, right? I mean, I thought old MacOxiania had stumbled across liquid nitrogen, didn't you? Thought we were going to be treated to some display of pre-medieval cryogenics. But this stuff looks like it could be a superior product.'

He dipped his finger in the liquid and sniffed it.

'Odourless. Primitive Stolychnaya no doubt. But I don't think I'll try it before analysis. It'll have to be duty-free Morangie for the time being.'

And he produced a bottle of this, flipped off the cap and took a slug that half-emptied it.

'*Majestoso con brio con spiritu sanctu!*' he exclaimed with a satisfied belch. 'Nurse – the head, if you please!'

Theo handed over the jar.

'You're pretty cool,' Wilson observed. 'This sort of thing happen every day where you come from, does it?' And with the help of the dagger he de-stoppered the jar, grabbed the head by its hair, lifted it free and held it dripping over the tank. He swayed slightly, and belched again. 'No, listen,' he said to Theo, 'get closer – I need an audience. Call it vanity, but I'm an artist... and hey, I've got no quarrel with your D N Angel by the way – she's the dangerous bloody lunatic – she's the one with the Uzi and one round short of a clip. Give you the same old story did she? Pursued through the millennia by a dangerous agent of the Evil Empire? Listen here, son,' and Wilson leaned across the tank and breathed Highland malt into his face, 'that little sweetie is about as sane as Caligula and nine times as paranoid. I'd steer clear of her if I were you. Now just watch this.'

And he lowered the girl's head slowly into the tank, and placed it carefully against the stub of scarlet neck, where it remained in position as he withdrew his hands and reached for another slug from the bottle.

'Just look at that,' he said with furious pride. 'That is a match. That is a print. And now it's time for the chord which comes from the bowels of the universe, right? I mean, you're about to hear the *music* that cooked the *soup* that made the *cosmos* loop the fuckin' *loop*.'

And he drew breath, and let out a thunderous cry:

'KAAAAAAAAAAAAA–'

Theo's skull was buzzing fit to burst. The floor vibrated under his feet. Tiles cracked and flew from the walls. The liquid in the tank began to shimmer.

'AAAAAAAAAAAAA–'

The shreds of ancient wallhangings sprung suddenly into flame and the carpets too were on fire. The dust of ages dislodged itself and descended in an abrasive fog.

'AAAAAAAAAAAAA–'

He was choking with the smoke and dust and his ears were ready to explode. Wilson's face glowed like coal. His arms were raised aloft like a crazed conductor cueing the cannon for the 1812.

'–TSU!' he uttered sharply, bringing his arms down in a sudden gesture of finality.

The fires flickered out, the smoke cleared and the dust settled. Theo peered at the figure in the tank. 'You can't see the join,' he declared. 'Not bad.'

'Cue standing ovation and thunderous applause,' said Wilson, and emptied the whisky bottle with a gulp. 'OK now, this is the difficult part. This is front page – or dustbin of history. We are going for a *spayed castrato* here; we are talking seven octaves above middle C – and either this fair damsel springs to life again or we attract every stray dog on the island. OK. Here we go.'

He drew breath and let rip a 'KAAA–' but this time it was so shrill as to be inaudible. He stood there straining, eyes squeezed up tight, face wrenched into a hideous grimace, thyroid cartilage a-quiver, TRY IT charm pulsating.

At first it seemed to be having no effect. The Oxianian girl lay in the tank, eyes open, expression unchanged, arms folded across her breast. Off in the distance Theo imagined he heard a dog howl. And then he shivered as the air turned suddenly chill.

'–TSU!' mouthed Wilson.

It was extremely cold in the tomb now. Both of them stood shivering over the glass sarcophagus.

'Energy transfer,' explained Wilson, his breath turning to steam as he regarded the girl intensely. 'Come on lassie, crank yourself up.'

Abruptly, the air grew warm again. And at the same time they saw a small envelope of air curl forth from the girl's mouth, and twist and flicker upwards till it burst at the surface.

'Cue Nobel Prize and intergalactic fame,' said Wilson. 'Come on sweetheart, out of this coffin and into my life.'

He plunged his arms into the tank and hoisted the girl from its embrace, and – staggering somewhat – laid her propped up against the base of the plinth.

'Slap her about a bit, sonny,' he advised Theo. 'Get her going while I fix the syringe.'

He complied. Her eyes drooped a little. But now she was breathing deeply. He put his hand to her chest and felt the heart going like a bass drum. He stared at her, mesmerised. He ventured to touch her hair.

'How's she doing?' asked Wilson as he produced a hypodermic and a bottle of serum.

'Her split ends could do with a bit of attention. What's in the bottle?'

'Broad-spectrum antibiotic and half a gram of Mandragora,' said Wilson. Then he stood still for a moment and wiped his brow. 'I need some attention myself. Took it out of me, that did.' He filled the syringe and gave it a preliminary squirt. Then he closed his eyes and shook his head. He had turned pale. His beard was white. His skin was becoming more creased and chalky by the second. Feebly, he took the girl's arm and sunk the needle. Then he stepped back and sank down against the pedestal, breathless, shivering.

'She's going to need some warmth,' Theo said. The drapes that had been burning had ceased to smoke, and they were not even lightly charred now. He pulled a length of satin from the wall and enfolded the dazed-looking girl in it as she lay propped against her tomb. A minute ago there had been a head in a jar and a decapitated body in a thousand-year-old tomb; now there was a teenager lying here with painted toenails, sarong and green bandana, looking like she had just crashed out by the bathtub after partying till dawn. He took her wrist and felt the pumping of the vein. Her eyes flickered open and she looked at him, and at his hand on her wrist.

What to say? 'Together at last, eh?' he said.

Hardly moving her mouth, she uttered something almost inaudible.

'A pound a look, eh?' is what he thought he heard her say.

Then came Wilson's faltering voice. 'Gis a hand.' His breathing was laboured. His hair was a dull silver. But his TRY IT still glimmered.

'I used up so much juice with the magic words that I'm gonnae disintegrate unless you play helpful gooseberry,' he wheezed.

'What are you going to do with her?'

'Och, maybe we'll talk about tickets for *Tosca* and a cosy little restaurant afterwards,' he said sarcastically, then, 'For fuck's sake she's *vacant* and I'm *dying*. You can turn your head away if you like, but just help me over to her. I can't lift myself.'

He thought twice about this.

'Enjoying your power are you?' said Wilson. 'Fuckin' little tosser.'

He took the man's arm, light as cardboard, retrieved the dagger from his pocket at the same time, and helped him over to the girl. Immediately Wilson took her in a lunging embrace, and with a cadaverous sigh planted his lips upon hers, at which the girl's body gave a sudden convulsion, and then appeared to absorb him completely, like a desert taking a shower of rain. Wilson had vanished.

Theo stared, and for what seemed like an extremely long moment, he thought about angels, and things.

Diana's anxious voice interrupted. 'Is he in there? Did you let him rape her?' She was pointing a pistol at the girl.

'No,' he replied. He was fairly certain this was a lie.

Diana approached cautiously, pistol held out in both hands like a crucifix.

'I thought you'd be able to tell,' he said.

She stood over the girl, who had lapsed into unconsciousness again.

'Not with smart bastards like him,' she said. 'He's in there, isn't he?'

'He didn't touch her. He was fading away too fast. He's just air now. Atomised.'

She shot him a dark glance. 'Why don't I trust you?' she said.

'I'm going to help her out of here,' he said.

'Don't get too attached to her, God's Gift. If I suss that Wilson's in her, they're both redundant.'

This was when he realised he had had enough of this Diana. It seemed like she'd been on his back for years. He looked at her with contempt.

'I'm going to get her to a hospital. They should look you over, too, the state you're in.'

She gave him an equally dismissive look and opened her mouth to speak, but he cut her off.

'Shut it,' he said. 'Act your age. Whatever that might be.'

Meekly she helped him carry the girl out. They put her on a sofa in the midst of the frozen party in the showroom. Diana was dark and thoughtful.

'Don't sulk, Lady Di,' he told her, and sat next to the satin-wrapped teenager under the respectful pose of a cardboard waiter. 'I think this calls for champagne,' he said. 'Mission accomplished and all that.' He took the magnum, popped the cork and poured three glasses. What would the toast be?

'To the dead,' Diana said surlily. 'To the nonexistent billions. Sorry to be so morbid. Maybe the grog'll help.' And she took a glass and drunk from it while he applied another to the lips of the comatose young woman.

He looked at Diana. 'Why are you looking so bored?' he said. 'This happen every day where you come from?'

'No,' she said distractedly, 'Pour me another glass Theo, it's quite good.'

While he continued to force the bubbly stimulant through the girl's lips Diana took hold of a cardboard salesman and waltzed it off around the cars and the cutouts, grabbing a length of tinsel and wrapping it round her partner's neck as they whirled. But she soon tired of this and said, 'Theo, she'll be fine. She's looking spunkier by the minute. Let's dance.' And she grabbed him up and whirled him off. 'Too bad there's no music,' she said breathlessly. He felt heady. Yes, it was too bad.

She held him tightly and whisked him waltzily across the floor. 'Hey,' she said, 'a Rolls! I've never been in one of those.'

He laughed as they tumbled into the Silver Shadow, and found himself on his back beneath her.

187

'Let's drink to the future,' she said as she sat astride him and brandished the bottle. 'Look,' she burbled, 'I'm wearing King Solomon's Pheremones.' And she reached below her ear and unscrewed the silver phial, dabbed some scent on her finger and applied it to her neck, wrists and cleavage.

He felt a pleasant weakness overcoming him. It was similar to the onset of 'flu.

She leaned over him, shook her hair out and whispered, 'You're a good-looking bastard really, aren't you?'

She was horny enough herself. She put her hands inside his shirt and massaged his chest. He felt a load lifting from him. She slipped out of her gear. She was perfect. Yes. To be seduced on Roller leather, to be carried away by this angel.

Wait a minute. Angel. He didn't think of angels like that anymore. Despite the delicious magnetism which enveloped him, he looked at her and caught a glimpse of a shabby old cosmic outlaw, something distant and mercenary. Then she whispered in his ear. 'Time to show you the secrets of love, as promised. First you do *this*.'

And she did something to him.

'Then... you... do... this...'

And she did something else.

'And then you – that's *you* now – you do this.'

And he did this.

'And then – you – do – this... and... how shall I put it? – the world goes away.'

Now it was something else indeed. But he couldn't shut out the world completely. If he did do this, what was he letting himself in for? His mind boggled, and said 'No thanks.' And his body said the same, quite clearly. Diana looked down at him. 'Oh darling,' she giggled, 'it's still just a prawn on the barbie. Never mind. Let's just try this...'

But her wiles weren't working. He feigned embarrassment and apologised.

'First-night nerves,' she said, 'Only natural. More champers? Or have you had too much already?'

The silence of the showroom was then shattered by a sharp electrical shriek followed by an engine bursting into life and a screaming of tyres. The Oxianian girl was at the wheel of a black Porsche which lurched violently forwards, scattered cardboard partygoers and crashed through the plate glass window before taking off in a cloud of dust and fleeing cats.

His would-be seductress turned purple. 'He's in there! The bastard's in there! I knew it! Get another car going! Quick!'

'Now, that,' he said admiringly, staring after the vehicle as the dust settled, 'is what you call German reliability.'

While she raced from car to car in a futile effort to get one to start up he went over to where a note lay under a second emptied champagne bottle: *THANKS FOR THE TIPPLE*, it read, *SEE YOU IN HELL*. But who exactly was this addressed to, and who exactly was it from?

'Jeez, he's got back and he's got more control,' he heard Diana mutter to herself.

'What's that you said?'

'Nothing.'

Now he knew he was doing the right thing.

When they crossed back into the Greek sector they heard nothing of a runaway Porsche from the amorous captain. But their hotel room was ransacked and the diary gone.

'We've got to figure out where'll he'll go next,' Diana said.

'It's a she, isn't it? Anyway, I'm through with this chasing about. I'm going to see Mikoyan. I can tell him his ancient relative is alive and well and drives a Carrera.'

'Yeah, and then?'

'I – we'll track the girl down after that.'

He hoped it would be 'I' by then.

It was a curious sensation to want someone dead. Distant and cool. No anger, irritation or frustration left. Pure necessity, only that. Plain, dire, its-you-or-me necessity.

She didn't make it easy for him that night in the hotel, because of course she knew every fantasy he'd ever dabbled with. So as well as the nun's gear and the T-shirt so thin it was metaphysical, she knew what to do, what to say and what to touch down to the last detail, The horniest things he could have imagined, she did to him. He'd never imagined he'd ever have to fight for his virginity. But he kept himself conveniently disabled and distracted by imagining the consequences: a slave to this angel, this parasite who, if she was right about Wilson's actions, would have more control of him than ever, would be messing him about interminably. But how would he get rid of her? Put a pistol to her head? Too painful to imagine. Poison?... And then there were those irritating questions of morality. While she herself was turning sweet as Cypriot honey – she even said she might be wrong about Wilson – that maybe he never made the transfer, that maybe even he wasn't such a bad guy after all. And he almost believed her. She had, he realised, got the most incredible eyes. He forced himself to study them to avoid falling into them. Perhaps there'd be the old tell-tale sign somewhere deep within the crystalline structure of the iris, or in the reflective well of the pupil, a clue to her alien status, some vacuum at the epicentre. But there was no such consolation to be found, and besides, it wouldn't have made things any easier: after all, like everyone else, he'd fallen in love with the replicant in *Blade Runner*, whose dark, appealing beauty was not unlike Diana's. It did just that: it appealed. But the verdict would have to stick.

During the flight back he thought about his mother. Her parents were Cypriots who had settled in Italy. She went back to the island for the funeral of her grandmother. That's when she met his father, who was working at the British base. And he thought of these desperate spirits, seraphs, clusters of information, messengers in control of the message, these hard histories, these no-fixed-aboders, cosmic gypsies, deoxyribonucleic angels, genealogical nomads; these dancers of the chrono-chromosomic twist, growing up, leaving home, pairing off and dancing here with Miss X, there with Mr Y, there with the second Miss X, bonding, splitting up, leaving home, never faithful, never constant, schizo-moody – call them what you will – who had lived for ever but might not be immortal.

Wilson, to impress those Scandi hitchhikers during that ride to Fastbuckleigh, had rattled away about Nietzsche and Wagner and Götterdämmerung and Ragnarrök. Gods died, then.

'Who kills them?' he had said.

'We do,' Wilson replied. Now he wondered what Wilson had meant by 'we'.

Diana was staring out of the window. According to her, God is a slap in the face. Yeah:

' 'E knocks me abaht a bit but I luv 'im.'

She had a point.

Katie Sawkin had some odd ways of getting to her god. Sex and religion. Bishops and actresses, bishops and actors, bishops and underage boys, bishops and anything cellular. Nuns and me. You're supposed to lose it with a slut and then marry a nice girl. Lurid. I should advertise: virgin seeks virgin for mutual satisfaction. A double-first double-header. To be deflowered whilst deflowering, to pluck each other's blooms: what could be cooler than that?

They were above the clouds. She was still gazing out of the porthole. 'They reckon Heaven is where you are right now,' she said, a little morosely, 'except it's so much better.'

That's when he saw that a little bit of grey had begun to show at the roots of her hair by the temples. She turned round to him. 'Maybe a spot of nooky in the lavvy would improve it. Wanna join the mile-high club? Hey?'

'That idea really doesn't turn me on.'

'Saving yourself for a nice girl, huh?' she said. She was too weary to make it sound cutting.

Saving myself for a nice human would be more to the point.

He got up to stretch his legs. 'Hey, don't be too long,' she said, 'the movie's coming on.'

He ended up in the games room of the mile-high club. He locked himself in the plastic cubicle and sighed deeply. From outside he could hear the titles rolling, the stormy orchestra, the strings soaring like seabirds, and the voice-over describing a war-torn world and the aspirations and peregrinations of desperate travellers.

He sat down and looked at his image in the mirror. He pulled his lips tight.

'Play it, Sham,' he said.

Then those particular sensations that occur in booths: the confessional; a police cell; and of course the photo-kiosk – star-

191

ing at your reflection through a glass darkly. No-one was ever happy with their passport picture. Why? You had to *be* someone in front of that mirror. You had to better yourself. To get on top of something. How did you do that? Well, you picked up murder weapons in places like this – like Michael Corleone in *The Godfather*. He still had the Bedouin dagger. He pulled it out. It felt very light. It was now covered in a sort of turquoise verdigris. He gripped it tightly and it crumbled to a soft, cloudy powder which drifted floorwards.

Beyond the toilet door they were singing 'Die Wacht Am Rhein', which was gradually overtaken by the 'Marseillaise'. Then came the clipped tones of Sidney Greenstreet. It was like White talking. Then Bergman – suspiciously similar to Bibi van Helsing.

He sat and waited. The soundtrack snaked its way through the intrigues of love and war. Sam played 'As Time Goes By'.

Places like this were supposed to bring relief. This was where you fixed things. He waited. Sam played it again. Then Bergman and Humph were out on the tarmac with the wind blowing and the engines roaring:

'If…' began Humph – and there was an urgent rapping on the door.

'Sir? Sir? Mr Riddle?' said a steward's voice. 'Your aunt is asking for you. She says you have the medicine she needs.'

'*…you'll regret it… maybe not today, maybe not tomorrow, but shoon, and for the rest of your life.*'

'Tell her I'll be right there,' he called out. He stayed put.

Bergman flew away. Bogart watched her go. Riddle eventually emerged from the toilet as the credits rolled and the lights went up, and looking over to his seat saw something that he had half-expected yet still gave him a chill. Wearing a white headdress and black headphones, a skull was grinning vividly and helplessly, even accusingly, back at him over the seatbacks. Her sockets still had eyes, and her cheeks were still red with the remains of flesh. But even as he looked on they faded away and left only bone. Then a skeletal fist produced and rotated a single skeletal finger as the skull dissolved to a blur and the headdress collapsed from sight.

He made his way slowly to the seat. There was just an old habit. And a note that read:

SEE YOU IN HE

♥

When he got to Kingsmouth he hired a dinghy and pointed it upstream. The liquid embrace of the river and its steep forested flanks, made him feel like an NFA on a transfer mission. He snaked up with the tide into a seamless vision of dappled sunlight and tranquility. There was the Harbourmaster's cottage nestling beneath the trees like a picture on a biscuit tin – except that Job had now demolished the hedge and concreted over the entire garden: there were two sprinklers on the go watering the stone lawn, and a third spitting away from the roof. Job's dripping, steaming house glistened in the sunlight and threw up a little rainbow against the darkness of the woods beyond.

He shook his head resignedly and went on up to Gimpton Creek. No sign of Ruth or White. Only the dog Buster, skinny and unfed, raging at him from the end of a rope. He cut the hound loose and it went for his ankles. He sent it off with a hefty kick. There was no more of Mikoyan's stuff here. In fact there was nothing left bar the unfinished boat: the tools and equipment, the telephone, the stereo, had all gone. He suspected the hand of Windeatt.

Outside the Ferry Inn the usual crowd of tourists were sitting in the sun imbibing refreshments and soaking up the essence of England. Out on the jetty was Job Andersen, dressed in a white decontamination suit and helmet, looking like he'd stepped out of a nuclear facility. He was telling folks to clean their boats, not to tread mud on the jetty, and not to throw breadcrumbs to the birds because it made a mess.

In the pub doorway the landlord was cuffing his daughter. Theo headed up the hill to Wilson's house. Here, the garden looked as though it had been hit by a chemical attack: every leaf on every bush and tree had withered to brown, and the lawn was just scorched earth. Inside, things appeared as he had last known them, except that the sound system was missing. There was only the piano, and manuscript paper strewn everywhere.

He painstakingly gathered up the *Goddamned Symphony* and stuffed it inside his jacket. He was about to leave when he heard sounds of metallic activity coming from the bathroom. Investigating further he discovered Windeatt in there with a hacksaw, busy removing the copper piping. Windeatt started and reddened, and pulled his sorrowful, earnest, innocent face.

'I can explain why I'm here,' he said.

'I'm impressed,' Theo said. 'The greatest minds on earth have been grappling with that one for some time.'

♥

Mikoyan greeted him with a stiff little bow and invited him through to the back of the house where a grand old ballroom stood open to the sky. Its fluted columns were two storeys high and supported what few roof beams remained. At the far end, French windows stood open and rotting. Ferns sprouted from the walls and grasses poked through cracks in the marble floor. In the middle of the ballroom stood an old two-wheeler caravan, embraced by weeds and briars and green all over with mould, to which Mikoyan led him with shuffling gait while the cat skipped around his feet. The van too was in a state of collapse, and only a few splinters remained of its roof. But inside Mikoyan had erected a brown canvas tent, into which he invited his guest, and, sitting crosslegged, brewed up coffee on a gas burner. Theo related his story by candlelight and the scent of Arabica beans, while the cat thoughtfully shredded a corner of the carpet.

'It is excellent,' said the old man. 'It means I can now leave in peace.'

At that moment there came the throbbing sound of an engine drawing near, until the echoing pulsations told them the vehicle was inside the ballroom and slowly approaching the trailer.

'My niece,' explained Mikoyan.

'Where are you going?'

'I thought Samarqand,' said the old man, 'overland.'

They finished their coffee and stepped outside. A black

Porsche was now hitched to the trailer. The Transoxianian girl was at the wheel.

'Still in one piece, then?' he said to her.

'Yes, thank you very much,' she said, in an accent similar to Mikoyan's.

'Swap you a symphony for a diary?'

'I don't know what you mean.'

Perhaps Wilson *had* failed to re-enter?

Mikoyan climbed in beside her. 'House is yours,' he said to Theo, 'but I should sell it if I were you. It is mere galosh. We have saying: "Better Dosh than Galosh".'

The Porsche started forwards with a jolt and much creaking and crashing as the long-embedded caravan was dragged into motion.

'Thanks,' he said. 'Take care of yourself. Watch out for all them wars.'

'We have AA Gold Star Five Star,' said Mikoyan. 'And what will you do?'

'I'd still like to get laid one day.'

'Take old man's advice,' said Mikoyan. 'Be laid by old woman.'

Car and caravan tumbled out through the French windows and were gone. He crossed the ballroom and headed for a room he had previously noticed on the first floor. Old woman? No thanks. But who do I fancy? Nuns were definitely out.

In a dusty, panelled drawing-room, a grand piano stood by the window. He took out the first page of the *Goddamned Symphony* and propped it above the keyboard alongside a copy of *The Rudiments of Music*. As he looked at Wilson's feverish script he felt a twinge of regret for those two NFAs. It was their age, their enormous age, which made their deaths a little outrageous. To have lived so long, and for what? And how many more of them were were managing to get themselves into three dimensions? Mad artists and paranoid mercenaries… and whatever other kinds of fallen angel you could imagine. He'd felt strangely free once Diana had climbed out of him, and he felt even better now she was dead. But if there were more out there, materialising from religious statues or the busts of mad

195

Teutonics, out to seduce with their crazy notions and then take us over completely – then what? Things get a little dangerous, no? A trifle dog-eat-dog. And who, and where now, was the musician from whom Wilson had materialised? He wondered what Bibi knew about all of this. She had a couple of degrees. Maybe he'd pay her a visit. Meanwhile he applied himself to the rudiments of music. Shouldn't take him too long.

The symphony began with a little melody. 'Me-fa-me-ray-doh-ray,' he sang. Oh yes, very funny Mr Wilson. Then came a pause. Then there was a ten-note chord, which he painstakingly decoded until he had both hands spread in position across the keys. '*fffff*'. What's that? With his teeth he flipped through the pages of the primer. Fffucking loud. Right. So he hit it. It set his skull buzzing. At the same time the great Ormolu mirror above the mantlepiece cracked loudly into a thousand fragments which flew across the room in a shower of glitter, and as he ducked to avoid the shards, the piano's legs snapped and it collapsed before him like a punched-out drunk.

It was then that the floor began to shift and creak and he was forced to make his rapid exit from the doomed building.

♥

'You didn't make it, Katie. Your diary ends with an angel saying 'pshaw', rude thing. Somehow or other you were laid to rest in a London crypt, and ended up robbed and dumped in a scrap-yard.'

That wouldn't be very tactful.

He was sitting in the garden of the old boathouse, watching the *Heart's Content* steam by, waiting for her. And when at length she showed, looking as striking as ever with her crimson hair and her long cotton nightdress, and with that vague-yet-urgent expression on her face, he told her that through a strange set of circumstances he'd done the job she'd set out to do three hundred years ago. Then he asked what had happened to her. Had she been waiting here for a boat which never came? Was she betrayed and murdered here? What?

But she didn't seem to hear. 'Then I'm free,' she said simply, and vanished. It figured. Didn't it?

From across the Flat Owers he came in sight of the *Wilja*'s familiar form, like a black-and-red garterbelt. Bibi was standing amongst the geraniums in the cactus position when he drew near.

'You look different with a beard,' she said, 'Coming aboard?'

He had visions of Eglantine tea, auric massage and a reading from the *Somerset & Avon Book of the Dead*.

'Got any real tea? Or coffee?'

'Bad for you – even decaff. I have Eglantine tea. Then we could do some aromatherapy.'

'It's just my socks. I haven't changed them.'

He climbed up.

'I've got some liquid that I'm curious about,' he said. He'd saved some of the liminal fluid.

'Looks like the stuff I keep my lenses in,' she said. 'So, how's chaos?'

'I've been following it closely.' He pulled out a number of scraps of paper covered in scribbled diagrams, complex family trees, names encircled, arrows pointing everywhere, lists of dates and question marks.

'It's sure hard to follow chaos,' said Bibi. 'Easier to dance with it.'

'I give up. I think I've been hallucinating.'

'They say virgins have the best visions.'

'Does that offer of yours still stand?' he said.

♥

After deflowering him she insisted on being paid.

'It don't seem right,' he said.

'We are not in love, Theo. Paying me will remind you of this and avoid complications,' she said sweetly.

'Whatever,' he said dreamily.

'Good. Now that your anima problem is solved you can go off and have fun and you won't get lovesick over phantoms. Oh yeah, and recommend me to your friends – I'll give you some of my cards. You know, I quit Holland because everyone's already having so much fun there there's not enough work around. But here: wow! I reckon I'll clean up over here.

New titles from The Do-Not Press:

Stewart Home: C*nt
1 899344 45 4 — B-format paperback original, £7.50
David Kelso is a writer who claims to be so lacking in imagination that his fiction isn't fiction at all. He returns from a faked death to complete a trilogy that necessitates him having repeat sex with the first thousand women he ever slept with. But then he starts to lose the plot — literally... Stewart Home's brilliant new novel is abrasive and darkly witty; essential reading for psychopaths, sociopaths and anyone else interested in the ins-and-outs of the book trade.
'Home is reconfiguring books as explosive elements — pages so stuffed with ideas that they might go off in your hands.' — Ben Slater, The Independent

Carol Anne Davis: Safe as Houses Bloodlines
1 899344 47 0 — B-format paperback original, £7.50
Second psychological thriller from the author of Shrouded. Women are disappearing from the streets of Edinburgh and only one man knows their fate.
'Carol Anne Davis writes with dangerous authority about the deadly everyday. Her work is dark in ways that Ruth Rendell and Minette Waters can only dream of. This is our world, skewed and skewered, revealed in its true sanguinary colours.
You've got to read her.' — IAN RANKIN

Gary Lovisi: Blood in Brooklyn Bloodlines
1 899344 48 9 – B-format paperback original, £7.50
Tough Brooklyn PI Vic Powers thought he'd seen it all, but then someone threatens to blow away the only thing he holds dear — his wife. Before long he is on a hellbound train to confront the psychopathic childhood companion whose monstrous games still haunt him. And when pushed, Powers knows that he can be a monster himself...
The first Vic Powers novel from New York's new master of the hardboiled thriller, Gary Lovisi.
'A craftsman who learned his business from the masters' — Eugene Izzi

Also available from The Do-Not Press: RECENT TITLES

Ken Bruen: A WHITE ARREST Bloodlines
1 899344 41 1 – B-format paperback original, £6.50

Galway-born Ken Bruen's most accomplished and darkest crime noir novel to date is a police-procedural, but this is no well-ordered 57th Precinct romp. Centred around the corrupt and seedy worlds of Detective Sergeant Brant and Chief Inspector Roberts, A White Arrest concerns itself with the search for The Umpire, a cricket-obsessed serial killer that is wiping out the England team. And to add insult to injury a group of vigilantes appear to to doing the police's job for them by stringing up drug-dealers... and the police like it even less than the victims. This first novel in an original and thought provoking new series from the author of whom Books in Ireland said: "If Martin Amis was writing crime novels, this is what he would hope to write."

Mark Sanderson: AUDACIOUS PERVERSION Bloodlines
1 899344 32 2 – B-format paperback original, £6.50

Martin Rudrum, good-looking, young media-mover, has a massive chip on his shoulder. A chip so large it leads him to commit a series of murders in which the medium very much becomes the message. A fast-moving and intelligent thriller, described by one leading Channel 4 TV producer as "Barbara Pym meets Bret Easton Ellis".

Jerry Sykes (ed): MEAN TIME Bloodlines
1 899344 40 3 – B-format paperback original, £6.50

Sixteen original and thought-provoking stories for the Millennium from some of the finest crime writers from USA and Britain, including **Ian Rankin** (current holder of the Crime Writers' Association Gold Dagger for Best Novel) **Ed Gorman, John Harvey, Lauren Henderson, Colin Bateman, Nicholas Blincoe, Paul Charles, Dennis Lehane, Maxim Jakubowski** and **John Foster**.

Jenny Fabian: A CHEMICAL ROMANCE
1 899344 42 X – B-format paperback original, £6.50

Jenny Fabian's first book, Groupie first appeared in 1969 and was republished last year to international acclaim. A roman à clef from 1971, A Chemical Romance concerns itself with the infamous celebrity status Groupie bestowed on Fabian. Expected to maintain the sex and drugs lifestyle she had proclaimed 'cool', she flits from bed to mattress to bed, travelling from London to Munich, New York, LA and finally to the hippy enclave of Ibiza, in an attempt to find some kind of meaning to her life. As Time Out said at the time: "Fabian's portraits are lightning silhouettes cut by a master with a very sharp pair of scissors."

Maxim Jakubowski: THE STATE OF MONTANA
1 899344 43 8 half-C-format paperback original £5

Despite the title, as the novels opening line proclaims: 'Montana had never been to Montana". An unusual and erotic portrait of a woman from the "King of the erotic thriller" (Crime Time magazine).

Also available from The Do-Not Press: RECENT TITLES

Miles Gibson: KINGDOM SWANN
1 899344 34 9 – B-format paperback, £6.50

Kingdom Swann, Victorian master of the epic nude painting turns to photography and finds himself recording the erotic fantasies of a generation through the eye of the camera. A disgraceful tale of murky morals and unbridled matrons in a world of Suffragettes, flying machines and the shadow of war.

"Gibson has few equals among his contemporaries" —Time Out

"Gibson writes with a nervous versatility that is often very funny and never lacks a life of its own, speaking the language of our times as convincingly as aerosol graffiti" —The Guardian

Miles Gibson: VINEGAR SOUP
1 899344 33 0 – B-format paperback, £6.50

Gilbert Firestone, fat and fifty, works in the kitchen of the Hercules Café and dreams of travel and adventure. When his wife drowns in a pan of soup he abandons the kitchen and takes his family to start a new life in a jungle hotel in Africa. But rain, pygmies and crazy chickens start to turn his dreams into nightmares. And then the enormous Charlotte arrives with her brothel on wheels. An epic romance of true love, travel and food…

"I was tremendously cheered to find a book as original and refreshing as this one. Required reading…" —The Literary Review

Paul Charles: FOUNTAIN OF SORROW Bloodlines
1 899344 38 1– demy 8vo casebound, £15.00
1 899344 39 X – B-format paperback original, £6.50

Third in the increasingly popular Detective Inspector Christy Kennedy mystery series, set in the fashionable Camden Town and Primrose Hill area of north London. Two men are killed in bizarre circumstances; is there a connection between their deaths and if so, what is it? It's up to DI Kennedy and his team to discover the truth and stop to a dangerous killer. The suspects are many and varied: a traditional jobbing criminal, a successful rock group manager, and the mysterious Miss Black Lipstick, to name but three. As BBC Radio's Talking Music programme avowed: "If you enjoy Morse, you'll enjoy Kennedy."

Ray Lowry: INK
1 899344 21 7 – Metric demy-quarto paperback original, £9

A unique collection of strips, single frame cartoons and word-play from well-known rock 'n' roll cartoonist Lowry, drawn from a career spanning 30 years of contributions to periodicals as diverse as Oz, The Observer, Punch, The Guardian, The Big Issue, The Times, The Face and NME. Each section is introduced by the author, recognised as one of Britain's most original, trenchant and uncompromising satirists, and many contributions are original and unpublished.

Also available from The Do-Not Press

The Hackman Blues by Ken Bruen
ISBN 1899344 22 5 — C-format paperback original, £7
"If Martin Amis was writing crime novels, this is what he would hope to write."
— Books in Ireland
A job of pure simplicity. Find a white girl in Brixton. Piece of cake. What I should have done is doubled my medication and lit a candle to St Jude — maybe a lot of candles."
Add to the mixture a lethal ex-con, an Irish builder obsessed with Gene Hackman, the biggest funeral Brixton has ever seen, and what you get is the Blues like they've never been sung before. Ken Bruen's powerful second novel is a gritty and grainy mix of crime noir and Urban Blues that greets you like a mugger stays with you like a razor-scar.

Smalltime by Jerry Raine
ISBN 1 899344 13 6 — C-format paperback original, £5.99
Smalltime is a taut, psychological crime thriller, set among the seedy world of petty criminals and no-hopers. In this remarkable début, Jerry Raine shows just how easily curiosity can turn into fear amid the horrors, despair and despondency of life lived a little too near the edge.
"The first British contemporary crime novel featuring an underclass which no one wants. Absolutely authentic and quite possibly important."— Philip Oakes, Literary Review.

That Angel Look by Mike Ripley
"The outrageous, rip-roarious Mr Ripley is an abiding delight..." — Colin Dexter
1 899344 23 3 — C-format paperback original, £8
A chance encounter (in a pub, of course) lands street-wise, cab-driving Angel the ideal job as an all-purpose assistant to a trio of young and very sexy fashion designers.
But things are nowhere near as straightforward as they should be and it soon becomes apparent that no-one is telling the truth — least of all Angel!

It's Not A Runner Bean by Mark Steel
ISBN 1 899344 12 8 — C-format paperback original, £5.99
'I've never liked Mark Steel and I thoroughly resent the high quality of this book.' — Jack Dee
The life of a Slightly Successful Comedian can include a night spent on bare floorboards next to a pyromaniac squatter in Newcastle, followed by a day in Chichester with someone so aristocratic, they speak without ever moving their lips.
From his standpoint behind the microphone, Mark Steel is in the perfect position to view all human existence. Which is why this book — like his act, broadcasts and series' — is opinionated, passionate, and extremely funny. It even gets around to explaining the line (screamed at him by an Eighties yuppy): 'It's not a runner bean...' — which is another story.
'A terrific book. I have never read any other book about comedy written by someone with a sense of humour.' — Jeremy Hardy, Socialist Review.

Also available from The Do-Not Press

Charlie's Choice: The First Charlie Muffin Omnibus by Brian Freemantle – Charlie Muffin; Clap Hands, Here Comes Charlie; The Inscrutable Charlie Muffin
ISBN 1 899344 26 8, C-format paperback, £9

Charlie Muffin is not everybody's idea of the ideal espionage agent. Dishevelled, cantankerous and disrespectful, he refuses to play by the Establishment's rules. Charlie's axiom is to screw anyone from anywhere to avoid it happening to him. But it's not long before he finds himself offered up as an unwilling sacrifice by a disgraced Department, desperate to win points in a ruthless Cold War. Now for the first time, the first three Charlie Muffin books are collected together in one volume. 'Charlie is a marvellous creation' – Daily Mail

Song of the Suburbs by Simon Skinner
ISBN 1 899 344 37 3 – B-format paperback original, £5

Born in a suburban English New Town and with a family constantly on the move (Essex to Kent to New York to the South of France to Surrey), who can wonder that Slim Manti feels rootless with a burning desire to take fun where he can find it? His solution is to keep on moving. And move he does: from girl to girl, town to town and country to country. He criss-crosses Europe looking for inspiration, circumnavigates America searching for a girl and drives to Tintagel for Arthur's Stone... Sometimes brutal, often hilarious, Song of the Suburbs is a Road Novel with a difference.

Head Injuries by Conrad Williams
ISBN 1 899 344 36 5 – B-format paperback original, £5

It's winter and the English seaside town of Morecambe is dead. David knows exactly how it feels. Empty for as long as he can remember, he depends too much on a past filled with the excitements of drink, drugs and cold sex. The friends that sustained him then – Helen and Seamus – are here now and together they aim to pinpoint the source of the violence that has suddenly exploded into their lives. Soon to be a major film.

The Long Snake Tattoo by Frank Downes
ISBN 1 899 344 35 7 – B-format paperback original, £5

Ted Hamilton's new job as night porter at the down-at-heel Eagle Hotel propels him into a world of seedy nocturnal goings-on and bizarre characters. These range from the pompous and near-efficient Mr Butterthwaite to bigoted old soldier Harry, via Claudia the harassed chambermaid and Alf Speed, a removals man with a penchant for uninvited naps in strange beds.
But then Ted begins to notice that something sinister is lurking beneath the surface

BLOODLINES the cutting-edge crime and mystery imprint...

Hellbent on Homicide by Gary Lovisi

ISBN 1 899344 18 7 — C-format paperback original, £7

"This isn't a first novel, this is a book written by a craftsman who learned his business from the masters, and in HELLBENT ON HOMICIDE, that education rings loud and long." —Eugene Izzi

1962, a sweet, innocent time in America... after McCarthy, before Vietnam. A time of peace and trust, when girls hitch-hiked without a care. But for an ice-hearted killer, a time of easy pickings. "A wonderful throwback to the glory days of hardboiled American crime fiction. In my considered literary judgement, if you pass up HELLBENT ON HOMICIDE, you're a stone chump." —Andrew Vachss

Brooklyn-based Gary Lovisi's powerhouse début novel is a major contribution to the hardboiled school, a roller-coaster of sex, violence and suspense, evocative of past masters like Jim Thompson, Carroll John Daly and Ross Macdonald.

Fresh Blood II edited by Mike Ripley & Maxim Jakubowski

ISBN 1 899 344 20 9 — C-format paperback original, £8.

Follow-up to the highly-acclaimed original volume (see below), featuring short stories from John Baker, Christopher Brookmyre, Ken Bruen, Carol Anne Davis, Christine Green, Lauren Henderson, Charles Higson, Maxim Jakubowski, Phil Lovesey, Mike Ripley, Iain Sinclair, John Tilsley, John Williams, and RD Wingfield (Inspector Frost)

Fresh Blood edited by Mike Ripley & Maxim Jakubowski

ISBN 1 899344 03 9 — C-format paperback original, £6.99

Featuring the cream of the British New Wave of crime writers including John Harvey, Mark Timlin, Chaz Brenchley, Russell James, Stella Duffy, Ian Rankin, Nicholas Blincoe, Joe Canzius, Denise Danks, John B Spencer, Graeme Gordon, and a previously unpublished extract from the late Derek Raymond. Includes an introduction from each author explaining their views on crime fiction in the '90s and a comprehensive foreword on the genre from Angel-creator, Mike Ripley.

Shrouded by Carol Anne Davis

ISBN 1 899344 17 9 — C-format paperback original, £7

Douglas likes women — quiet women; the kind he deals with at the mortuary where he works. Douglas meets Marjorie, unemployed, gaining weight and losing confidence. She talks and laughs a lot to cover up her shyness, but what Douglas really needs is a lover who'll stay still — deadly still. Driven by lust and fear, Douglas finds a way to make girls remain excitingly silent and inert. But then he is forced to blank out the details of their unplanned deaths.

Perhaps only Marjorie can fulfil his growing sexual hunger. If he could just get her into a state of limbo. Douglas studies his textbooks to find a way...

The Do-Not Press
Fiercely Independent Publishing

Keep in touch with what's happening at the cutting edge of independent British publishing.

Join The Do-Not Press Information Service and receive advance information of all our new titles, as well as news of events and launches in your area, and the occasional free gift and special offer.

Simply send your name and address to:
The Do-Not Press (Dept.DNA)
PO Box 4215
London
SE23 2QD
or email us: thedonotpress@zoo.co.uk

There is no obligation to purchase and no salesman will call.

Visit our regularly-updated web site:

http://www.thedonotpress.co.uk

Mail Order

All our titles are available from good bookshops, or (in case of difficulty) direct from The Do-Not Press at the address above. There is no charge for post and packing.

(NB: A postman may call.)